I watched _____ s, a
birth sack spring _____ ours
and ribbons. Just visible in the g_____ ___ s the
tiny curled spine of a foetal moon.

Will you marry me?

The velvety voice seemed to come from every side
and within all at once. I looked around, startled.
The basketball court was empty.

Up here.

I looked into the sun's glare and the X-ray shadow
of the moon. 'Who are you?'

Don't you know?

'You're the moon.'

Will you marry me?

I laughed a loud syllable.

Can I take that as a yes?

The timbre of the voice, so intimate and real,
pierced my reverie, and I felt a dizzy rush of fear. I
was losing my mind! 'Who are you?'

*You know me. My cold, wet finger stirs your blood.
My fingerprint touches each of your eggs. Marry
me . . .*

About the author

A. A. Attanasio was born in Newark, New Jersey, in 1951. He graduated from the University of Pennsylvania in 1973. He received an MFA in Creative Writing from Columbia University in 1975 and an MA in Linguistics from New York University in 1976. He is the author of such highly acclaimed novels as *Radix*, *Wyvern*, *The Last Legends of Earth* and *Kingdom of the Grail*. He lives in Hawaii.

The Moon's Wife

A Hystery

A. A. Attanasio

NEW ENGLISH LIBRARY

For my mother – and yours,
women who shaped us in darkness
out of the light we are but do not know.

First published in Great Britain in 1994 by Hodder & Stoughton
A Division of Hodder Headline PLC

A New English Library paperback

10 9 8 7 6 5 4 3 2 1

British Library C.I.P.
A CIP catalogue record for this title is available from the British Library

ISBN 0 450 60640 6

Printed and bound in Great Britain by
Cox & Wyman Ltd, Reading, Berkshire

Hodder and Stoughton Ltd
A Division of Hodder Headline PLC
338 Euston Road
London NW1 3BH

Contents

She of Days

I was a single woman and still living with my mother when the moon asked me to marry him. Under less extraordinary circumstances I would have thought myself perfectly crazy to believe such a thing could ever happen. After all, I prided myself on being a practical person, a scrupulous bookkeeper, with a reasonably firm grasp of life's commonplace demands. The one and only weird experience I'd ever had in all my twenty-three years was a bout of déjà vu that came over me briefly during my Cost Accounting finals in business college. So certainly, the moon's proposal was outrageous, except that, in a way, I had been supremely prepared for it. A couple of hours earlier, in the local supermarket, I'd had my first public experience of the moon's erotic power.

It happened while I was picking through potatoes in the produce department. It had been a tedious day at the lading company where I worked, and all I could think of was my dinner. Already that day I'd had to skip lunch when the front office demanded I double-check some figures on the reports the boss would be taking to the stockholders' annual junket in the Caribbean later that week. I was starved, intent only on not forgetting to buy chives, when suddenly, from somewhere nearby, I heard a huge brass door slam. The echoes throbbed like a heartbeat.

I looked up, startled. Oblivious shoppers milled about with their carts, children whined for sweets, and a clerk was hosing down the lettuce. I could feel the thundery beat of the echoes inside my body, making my flesh quiver. Didn't anyone else hear it? The deep, palpable vibrations touched my bones, and I flung quick gazes to either side of where I stood, amazed to see that no one else was feeling what I felt. The echoes diminished, tingling inside me, cool, magnetic, a tickling static that brushed through me again and again, prickling sharply as the beat of the echoes faded.

A spasm of chilled delight shook me, and my eyes widened as I realized what was happening.

I grade my sexual climaxes by how many palpitations precede them. Some of my female friends never feel these initial throbs, being caught up in the momentary onrush of pleasure. But I can be compulsive about counting things most people don't notice—the steps from my work station to the rest room, the squiggly lines on a postage cancellation mark. Before my most spine-stretching crests, the maximum had always been three prickly flutters, tops.

But this one pulsed an unprecedented four times—four slow, icy hot beats that shuddered through me with mounting intensity. Why was this happening to me? Anger volted through me. It lasted only an instant before my sexual convulsion blew it away, but for that first moment of recognition, I was mad as hell, I guess at myself, at my body's betrayal, for subjecting me to this humiliating public display.

You must understand, I'm not particularly repressed or prudish about sex. Okay, it had been two years since I'd last made love to a man, but till then I'd had my quota of lovers and sexual adventures. So, in that flare of angry panic during the hair-trigger eternity of the instant before I climaxed, I could think of no reason on earth why this was happening to me.

My knees buckled. I lurched about and braced myself against

4

the vegetable counter. I'd never experienced ecstatic transport standing up before in public, and in a complete panic, I tensed all my muscles, trying vainly to suppress the seizure. But that only made it worse.

The first wave of ecstasy swept through my body like a mule kick. It would have thrown me into the potato bin if I hadn't grabbed the counter's edge with all my strength. As it was, I jerked and stamped in a fit of furious delight. An electric current coursed through me, so vibrantly pleasurable that tears literally spurted from my eyes.

At the jarring and fiery peak of it, I nearly submitted and lay back shamelessly on the bed of potatoes to let the lubricious power jerk through me—it felt that good—but the shocked expressions of the other shoppers stopped me. The electric current in my body subsided, supplanted by a dizzying humiliation. Rainbows stitched the edges of my sight, and a sudsy music sizzled in my ears. It was the ferment of blood sluicing into my brain and burning hotly in my face.

Through my tears, I saw an elderly couple standing by the broccoli and staring at me aghast. The old woman approached and put a hand on my arm that sent a jagged thrill running along my flesh like an insane laugh. I jerked away, and her concern deepened. "Are you all right, miss?"

I gazed at her in a daze, pinpricks of hot light streaking away like shooting stars. My nerves sparkled. *No!* I wanted to shout; I wasn't all right. Something was terribly wrong. My soggy muscles could barely support me as I backed away, spuds toppling when I clumsily pushed off from the bin. Flinders of sharp, almost painful pleasure sparked from my body. I felt like a frost-tipped matchhead, striking flares of icy fire with every movement.

Bewilderment came later. At that moment, all I felt was acute embarrassment and shock. It wasn't pale-at-the-gills, cold-sweat shock but something considerably weirder—a kind of spell that was part exhaustion, part jangled nervousness. I looked every bit like a drunk, slouched over, with my head lolling back and reeling across my shoulders. My vision belled, as if I was staring through a peephole, seeing the world through a fish-eye lens. Orange and black streamers, jack-o'-lantern banners, and cardboard ghosts strung with black thread from the ceiling's fluorescent panels shone strangely from within.

Had there been anything of "me" left, I'd have succumbed to my panic for sure. But I was gone, at least the equivalent of six daiquiris away from myself, yet without the numbness of alcohol. And paradoxically, as stunned as I was, still I felt uncommonly alert, as if I was seeing the world more intently than I ever had before.

Everything gleamed, the whole store glazed in ice. My gaze skittered across a cornucopia of vegetables and fruits, and the animal gladness from my sexual ecstasy expanded beyond me. The very air shimmered in the first stirrings of a mirage. I touched a potato in its crepe of ice and tasted with my fingertips the moldy darkness carried up out of the earth. The heat crinkles in the air became an angel's flapping robes, infusing radiance into every object they touched.

It felt as if I was awake and dreaming at the same time. And I think I might have just stood there forever, hypnotized by the bright colors and organic shapes, listening to my slamming heartbeat slow down and the wash of Muzak swirl closer, were it not for my embarrassment. I didn't know what the gaping onlookers thought of my seizure, but I cringed as though they could see right into the depths of my wanton heart. Why was this happening to me? My mind could make no sense of the turbulent joy and shame clashing in me. I sidled away and nearly tripped over a heap of pumpkins. Down the aisles a welter of tiny eyes watched me from the faces on boxes, cartons, and jar labels, and I hurried for the exit, still dazed by the sensual voltage bristling inside me.

Past a glass counter stacked with glossy donuts, automatic sliding doors opened on the parking lot. Late-afternoon sunlight ricocheted off windshields and chrome bumpers. The lancing rays cut through my distress, and instantly I felt better, greatly relieved of the self-consciousness that had afflicted me only a moment before. That in itself should have warned me that something in my mind had gone awry. But, as it happened, the shame bleached happily away in the fierce brilliance of the sun, and like a schoolgirl set loose for the summer, I bounded out the door, frisking through the frosty wind and its pouring leaves.

The world seemed huge, the sky an immense tapestry of cloud animals, a cumulus circus above the shabby trees and the glittering snakeskin of the highway. Leaving my confused fright behind, I skipped along with the wind's gold coins. Brains skewered with autumn's woodsmoke, I wandered into the starry field of cars.

Before I knew it, I was in front of my own sad car, a green, rust-trimmed compact faceted with dents. In the state I was in, it looked remarkably like a magic tortoise. For a long while I sat behind the steering wheel, thinking anything, just staring at the dusty shell of the hood and watching the sunlight lose itself in the bird droppings.

Later that would be the scariest moment, remembering how I just sat there, a zombie. I don't deny that it felt good, my insides softly pulsating, shiny. But something was unquestionably missing. The erotic pyrotechnics had blown my will into a million pieces, like silver dust motes falling in the afternoon rays. Slowly the motes began to gather themselves into a dim awareness that something essential had been horribly misplaced.

Apparently, I started the car and went off to find what I had lost, though in truth I have no recollection of actually backing out of the parking space and wending my way through the lot onto the busy road. I recall only the tumbledown clouds and the breezy joy of sailing along the highway into the orange hills.

I exited into the familiar, peak-roofed neighborhood of Arcadia, New York, the drowsy village on the Hudson where I'd lived my whole life. Old, lumpy trees fronted clapboard houses, pumpkins grinned from porches, and battered pickups lined the rut-warped driveways. On the side streets, kids threw footballs or clustered around portable CD players and smoked cigarettes. I recognized them, the sullen boys slick as newts and the spindly girls in miniskirts, exposing their knobby pony legs. A few years earlier I myself had been one of these puckish waifs in denim, with the same extravagant makeup and feigned languor.

But I had worked hard to put that phase behind me. Three years had passed since I had stood on those very street corners talking about boys and clothes. No one waved to me anymore when I drove by. Yet I still suffered pangs of nostalgia when I saw those kids. They made me wonder where everyone I knew from those days had gone, and where, at twenty-three, *I* was going.

God knows, I didn't want to be a bookkeeper forever. I had plans. Truth be told, they were more like pragmatic dreams. I was going to go back to school to become a CPA, and before I was thirty, I would have my own accounting firm. And if I married at all, it wouldn't be until then and only for love, which naturally meant finding someone smart, with an athlete's body. Each day I tailored a different variant of the dream, matching my accounting skills to my husband's medical practice, or software emporium, or skydiving franchise.

But that day, gliding in the magic tortoise, lithe with sexual energy, I was myself a dream, a sleepdriver floating through the neighborhood. I wafted toward the elm-cloistered street where I lived with my mother, and my body flinched. A lonely feeling glowed purplish among those gnarled boughs and buckled sidewalks. Night prowled the narrow yards.

In a gust of fright, I accelerated past the street. I had never been afraid of going home before, even during darkest adolescence, but I simply could not face Willa. When the street sign disappeared in the rearview mirror, my anxiety waned and I slowed down.

Reverie led me up the brighter streets, and I climbed into the radiant hillsides. At the top, a wending road tunneled with walnut trees led to Tappan Down, a rocky park of fern holts and oak groves that overlooks the Hudson. It was still daytime up there.

The park was empty except for an old woman feeding squirrels and birds and two boys shooting hoops on the basketball court. I pulled up to a whitewashed log and parked in a long shaft of red sunlight. The glare mirrored the windshield, and I saw my face there, but didn't recognize myself. My distraught hair splashed out from an impishly lopsided face. I looked crazed. But the rapture that possessed me obscured that. Feeling luminous as the tingling sunbeams, I didn't even bother to fix my hair before getting out.

The air smelled of river mist and leaf rot. Sitting on the shell of the tortoise, feet propped against the painted log, I gazed down at the fiery trees and pitched-roof houses of Arcadia. The vista had every appearance of a storybook village huddled cozily on a bluff above the river's gray swerve. I blinked at the world like an opium smoker.

As a young girl, I had come up here often to play hide-and-seek with my friends among the numerous tree haunts and rock slabs. Later the same hideouts served as love coves for my first clumsy dalliances with boys. From here I could see my whole life—schools, friends' houses, the cemetery where my father was buried—even the brick warehouses and industrial barns on the riverbank where I am paid to balance books. From this distance in the charred light, the dismal docks and quays looked like a glisteny mess of kelp, oar-weed, and devil's apron thrown up on the shore. That's where I lived most of each day, a bug too small to see from here, crawling among the river's detritus. This perception struck me as disgustingly funny, and I laughed coolly till I realized I was laughing at myself.

It sobered me to see literally how small my life was. Every

place I had ever been lay under my gaze, caught between the bright artery of the highway and the dark vein of the Hudson. And all I could do was stare, serene as an iguana. By this point, the dust motes of my will had gathered into a fuzzball, and I distantly sensed something was wrong. I thought about it and remembered shopping and being clouted with an erotic seizure. That very word occurred to me, *seizure*, and for the first time since this craziness began, I winced with real, unmitigated fright. My God, I was crazy! The idea seemed to swoop down out of nowhere, blacken me with its shadow, and soar off. Far away, muted by enormous distances of silky euphoria, it circled. I knew I should have thought more about it than I did. Of far more interest at the moment, however, was the setting sun, with its green transparencies and scarlet jellies. Up there something important was happening. I watched the sun lower itself slowly to the hills, a birth sack spilling its yolk in a slither of oily vapors and ribbons.

Just visible in the glaring caul was the tiny curled spine of a fetal moon.

Will you marry me?

The velvety voice seemed to come from every side and within all at once. I looked around startled. The basketball court was empty, the old woman gone.

Up here.

I looked into the sun's glare and the X-ray shadow of the moon. "Who are you?"

Don't you know?

"You're the moon."

Will you marry me?

I laughed a loud syllable.

Can I take that as a yes?

The timbre of the voice, so intimate and real, pierced my reverie, and I felt a dizzy rush of fear. I was losing my mind! "Who are you?"

10

You know me. My cold, wet finger stirs your blood. My finger-print touches each of your eggs. Marry me.

Panic whirled inside me. But up front, here where the smallness of my life was laid out before me, I felt a bewildered joy. "Why?" My voice came out slow, trepidatious. I was insane—hearing a voice in my head—yet my fear at this was not durable. It faded quickly away, as if I had been drugged into placidity. That inspired more fear, but that, too, numbed away. From a distance I heard myself ask, "Why would you want to marry me? I'm nobody special."

Darkness answered. The sun set and took the moon with it. And all the joy inside me vanished as abruptly as it had started. Blue-black and clotted clouds lingered like a mangled afterbirth, and the first cold stars wobbled in the abyss.

I was named Sigrid, after my mother's Swedish grandmother. I hated the name. It made me feel like I should have braids in my hair and wear Viking horns, even though, as a kid, I was skinny as a seam, and even now I'm hardly a Valkyrie. Like a lot of girls my color, I wanted a darker name—something like Ciara—to distract from my candy-bright bangs and pink eyelashes. At school they called me Siggy, but when I finished business college and got my bookkeeping job at Broughton Lading, I went back to being Sigrid. I wore my hair short, my dresses long, and my shoes flat. That lasted two years, until the night I found myself alone on Tappan Down, disheveled and bewildered, not Sigrid anymore.

Once the moon set, I was myself again. The moon took my erotic rapture with him and left me drained and frightened. Nothing this total had ever happened to me before. The only thing that came close was the death of my father, when I was twelve. That had hurt so bad, I couldn't think straight for months. I had to repeat seventh grade. But this—I was afraid that I was losing my mind, that I would be sent to some asylum and would spend the rest of my life talking to the moon and doing obscene things in front of people. I didn't want to be crazy, and I clutched wildly at alternatives. Like maybe I had eaten some bad food or someone had slipped me a drug. Frantically I reviewed my meals, going back to the hurried grapefruit and toasted bran muffin at breakfast, the coffee that served as lunch. Randy Miezner, the company's resident jokester, had brought me my coffee. Had he spiked it? Maybe I wasn't crazy after all.

But that didn't sit right. What drug would cause such sexual transport, such a violent access to pleasure? If such a chemical existed, it would change the world. And Miezner would no doubt be putting it in his own coffee.

Practicality forced me to face the most likely fact: Something was wrong with me, with my brain maybe. My shock over this thought actually helped me to detach enough to use some common sense. If I hadn't been so stunned, the implications would have reduced me to sobs. At any instant, another seizure could wrack me. I realized I had to get help.

As I drove cautiously to the donut shop at the bottom of the park, I tried vainly to recall some of that animal gladness that had soaked me to the bone just minutes ago. All I felt was shame, though—like it was my fault I had gone insane.

By the neon heartbeat of a giant donut-lady, I used the pay phone to contact the nearest hospital. But as I began to explain to the operator that I'd just suffered a seizure of some sort, I panicked and hung up. My bowels tightened, and I had to go to the rest room and splash cold water on my face before it occurred to me that perhaps I was really okay. I wasn't hearing voices anymore, and my body felt drained of all sexuality. The thought that what had happened was some inexplicable fluke, that it might never recur again, provided immense relief and helped me momentarily deny the situation I was in. In fact, now that I had no actual symptoms, I didn't feel as pressing a need to go. So long as I drove carefully, I told myself, I could afford to wait, set up a proper appointment, and face the glum facts after I had straightened myself up.

I went home slowly, taking the side roads, listening for the first ticklish sign of another episode. When I turned onto my street, I recalled the hallucination I'd had driving past here earlier. The chilling perception of loneliness bruising the air around my house frightened me, because it was true. The people who lived in this house had been lonely a long time.

Our place looked much like the others from the outside, a gaunt white box with a steeply sloping roof of large green shingles. But inside, because of my mother's love for satin, it was the curdled dream of a pasha: satin sofa, thick shiny drapes, skirted tablecloths, braided footstools, bossed fabric lampshades, a TV console cover dripping gilt and tassels, and in the bathroom, slip-ons for the toilet bowl replete with silky twists and corner pleats.

Willa herself looked like one of the enamel figurines she bought at thrift stores and then arranged preciously on her mantels and windowsills: Diminutive and frail, she had a porcelain constitution, with china-pale skin and very broad, flat cheekbones. The cheekbones were the one good thing I'd inherited from her, along with her green eyes. The curly, coppery hair that she liked to wear in a sphere around her head, like a frothy helmet, was her own creation. Her natural hair was brown and lank.

I'd been happy in that cluttered house, and so had my mother, until my father died. After that it became a hollow place, and I spent most of my time with friends and often came home only to sleep. That was fine with Willa, who had gotten a little desperate after losing the only man she'd ever had. She preferred being alone with her beau of the season so long as she knew I was with friends. I never blamed her for this. She's the kind of person who can do only one thing at a time, and anyway, my father left a big absence in our world that we both worked hard to fill.

I still miss my father. Large and quiet, he had taught me to have emotions without them having me. Mostly, he did this by spending a lot of time with us. But there were other ways, too. He was, for instance, amazingly patient with *things:* It didn't matter whether it was hanging valances for Willa or fixing my bicycle, he always seemed to be doing what he wanted. When he succumbed to diabetes, there was much grief and it was really hard for a year, but remembering who he was, and wanting so much to be like him, I stopped crying and the grief found its place.

Not Willa. She'd married too young, at eighteen, and let him do everything for her. His job as a maintenance engineer for the school district exploited his mechanical knack. But he also liked to cook, the tactile feel of cooking, and to talk to people about food. Grocery shopping was a natural way for him to do both, and he consequently wound up doing all the marketing himself. And being fastidious about dust and squaring things away—habits picked up from his two tours of duty as a helicopter mechanic in Vietnam—he ended up doing most of the house chores too.

Willa was thirty when she found him dead in the storm ditch out back. Hypoglycemia had felled him while he was trimming the hedge. She missed a whole winter at the umbrella factory that year, and we almost lost the house. Together we figured out how to balance a checkbook and cook a meal. She never learned how to drive and hated to shop, and so I did those things for her, eventually taking up most of the responsibilities that had been my father's.

That night, when I came back from Tappan Down empty-handed, Willa looked at me annoyed. "I thought you were bringing home dinner," she groused from her bedroom doorway, which looked straight down the stairs at the front door. I could see she was wearing the black bathrobe that had once belonged to the kung fu boyfriend of a year ago. The room behind her flickered with TV light. From those two facts alone, I knew her mood precisely. She was tired and had already prepared for bed, so the workday had been a bitch, or maybe it was that time of month for her. Either way she was grouchy, but only a little, because she had on the soaps she taped while at work, and she only watched them when she was feeling okay about herself.

"Pizza night," I declared, acting rushed. I didn't want to tell her anything about what had happened to me, since she would just get worked up and there was nothing she could do to help me. "I got a presentation tomorrow." That wasn't exactly true. I had worked out a way to save the company some money by having some of the divisions share accounts, and Frank Broughton, the owner, whose habit it was to come down to the docks once a month, would collect his messages in the morning and pick up the manila envelope that had my scheme in it. The idea seemed puny now.

I went to the kitchen, ordered a vegetarian pizza, and gave Willa a moment to return to her TV, then I pranced upstairs, flitted past her door, and slipped into my room. I didn't even bother to sit down on the edge of the bed before I called my best friend, Marti Greere. She and I go back to third grade, when we were the class roughnecks. Her machine was on, and I left no message.

I took a shower, changed into my pajamas, and spent the evening sitting in bed, taming my fear by watching TV. I gave myself my own brain-impairment tests, checking my memory by reciting poems from my childhood and repeating strings of random numbers by rote. When I held my arms out to the sides, I could see my thumbs twitching in my peripheral vision. I even got out a jump rope I hadn't used in eight years and did jumping tricks until Willa knocked on her wall.

Nothing seemed awry. I felt fine, just scared was all, too scared even to eat the pizza when it came. From a public medical-information phone line, I learned the symptoms of a stroke, none of which seemed to apply to me. I wrote down everything that had happened that day from the time I'd woken; it was sobering to see on paper how boring my life was. I kept trying Marti, but apparently she was out for the night. Finally, exhaustion overcame my anxiety, and I fell asleep with the lights and the TV on.

When I awoke, brash sunlight filled the room, birds yakked, and a morning talk-show host was cheerfully flipping omelettes on TV. My stomach rippled with hunger. But my head felt clear and my body rested, and I was glad I had slept dreamlessly.

I knew I should call someone, but who? My family doctor? My gynecologist? Or some neurologist I didn't know? I felt so normal, I couldn't even bring myself to call in sick at the office.

"I thought you had a presentation today," Willa greeted me, a mite sarcastically, in the kitchen. She was wrapping her lunch for work—leftover pizza and a brown banana. She wore her factory clothes—a lumberjack shirt over snug jeans—and she looked so ordinary and familiar, I nearly blurted out everything. But before I could, she added, almost as an afterthought, "The oil bill hasn't been paid yet, baby. It's gonna be a cold winter."

"Geez, Willa, the oil company is just a block from where you work." I opened the refrigerator and found only congealed pizza and an apple. "Why can't *you* take it over there during lunch or after work?"

She looked exasperated. "It's too big a bill. Haven't you looked at it? We have to set up a payment plan."

"So? Our credit's good."

"I don't want to have to deal with those people."

"What people?" I took the apple, closed the fridge and leaned back against it. It was the same old fight we'd had in a hundred different variations. "You just talk to their credit manager and they set up a plan. They get extra points and we get our friggin' heat. It's easy."

"I know," she replied without looking at me, preoccupied with putting the wax paper away. "But you're so much better at these things, baby."

"Because I've had to be." I tried to put as much weariness into my voice as I could. "You know you can do it, Willa. What would you do if I wasn't here?"

Willa gave me a hopeful look. "You're seeing somebody?"

"No. You're changing the subject."

She frowned. "Then why would you leave?"

"I mean, if something *happened* to me."

The flesh between her eyes twitched. "Why are you talking like this?" One thing about my mother, she was no crystal gazer. "You've never been healthier since you gave up cigarettes."

"I'm just saying we've got to be realistic. I'm as vulnerable as anybody else. What would you do without me?"

"If I lost you, baby, I'd go crazy."

"Don't say that," I blurted. "You're a strong woman . . . when you want to be."

Willa made a sour face. "So are you gonna drop me off at the shop on your way to work, or should I be strong and take the bus?"

On the drive to the factory, I wore my sunglasses so she wouldn't see that I wanted to cry. Fortunately, my mother is too self-absorbed most of the time to be very observant, and she happily whiled away the time gossiping about the sexual misadventures of her coworkers. It had been a year since her last boyfriend, and with forty-one already five months behind her, she had become more preoccupied than ever with romance.

After kissing Willa good-bye, I took the time to deal with the oil bill. I guess I was challenging myself to be normal, proving yet again there was nothing wrong with me. The fifteen minutes it took also gave me time to figure out what to do next. I had to see a doctor, no matter how good I felt. I knew that. But I wanted to go to work, just to be sure my money-saving plan got picked up by Mr. Broughton and wasn't misplaced in the frenzy to prep him for the stockholders' junket.

I was, I admit, ambitious. In the two years I'd been with Broughton Lading, I'd made it a point to carefully study not only the business but also the people who ran it. I figured vertical movement was possible, but only if I got out from under the specialists above me. My options were to go to school and become a specialist myself, which eventually I would do—unless I could exercise my other option, which was to do something smart under Broughton's nose.

Yesterday's seizure still frightened me, yet it seemed strangely manageable in its remoteness. Nothing had happened since, and I decided I could well risk going into the office to watch over my plan. In an effort to assuage my fear, I promised myself that at lunchtime, I would call Dr. Pappageotes, our family physician.

As I punched in, Marti waved to me from her work station in the pool, the suite of operators chatting into their headmikes, taking shipping orders. Despite the neon pink fins protruding from the ceiling that were supposed to serve as sound bafflers, there was no muting the white noise of the pool. It was the noise of profit making that laved over me each day at my computer stall, a noise I happened to like because it meant I was right there in the current of currency, in the flow of the economy that carried me and my plans. That noise sometimes actually sustained me during my long hours of number-crunching. None of the other pool operators felt that way, though. To them it was just another boring job, and most of them thought I was aloof and greedy, because I had gone to business college and tried to dress like a real professional instead of a hooker. Marti agreed with them, but she was an old friend and figured I'd eventually get wise and stop acting so stuck-up.

I wanted to stop by Marti's station, but the brass, who were usually on the docks or in the warehouses supervising shipments, were in the glass-walled pool manager's office. Broughton would be here soon. The pool manager, Adele, a gravelly-voiced platinum blonde Willa's age, but a sharp dresser and with a sharper mind, stood sipping coffee with the keg-shaped men in ties and rolled shirtsleeves who ran the docks. When she saw me at my monitor, she waved me into the office and handed me a sheaf of printouts detailing all the buyers and shippers whose accounts had to be balanced before the boss's trip. In the midst of describing what I had to do next, she broke off, and her face went soft and simple. Frank Broughton had just entered and stood, radiant in his blond curls and camel's hair coat, kibbitzing with the pool operators.

Broad-shouldered, with a tiny seahorse cleft in his chin, Broughton was the type that could charm women and men alike with his looks. His chrome-blue eyes shone bright and boylike out of a tan face that had aged handsomely, scratched at the edges with fine, pale sun scars.

A giant brass door slammed.

The shock jerked me to my toetips, and I gave a startled look to the others. Thundery echoes shook the air to quivers, the vibrations humming in my bones and tingling along my flesh. "Oh, no!" I cried out with the first throbbing beat of a mounting climax. "Oh, no!"

I knew from yesterday not to tighten up. That had thrown my body into a convulsion, and I wouldn't be able to go on living if that happened to me here. In the eternal instant before the next jolting palpitation, I stared at the people before me the way someone standing at a crumbly brink peers over a cliff. The operators in the pool, most of whom I had known from high school, could see me through the glass wall. And just a few feet away were the beefy warehouse chiefs and dock bosses, whose occasional winks and playful grins I'd always ignored. They would be sniggering about this all their poker-playing lives! And Adele! She had once confided that she liked me because I was spunky but levelheaded, a no-nonsense player who reminded her of herself twenty years ago. Obviously, not for long.

The second pulsebeat flared through me, and the third, and then the fourth as time gushed forward and Frank Broughton ambled in. I thought that if I just let it happen, if I didn't try to lock it out, it would shudder through me quickly and I could stay on my feet. Instead, a pile driver's impact struck me head to toe, and my knees gave out.

Frank swooped forward and caught me as I fell. In his arms, I shook, the whole length of me rippling with quakes of gusty bliss. A moan escaped, and my teeth chattered with my effort to restrain a wail. Close up, Frank's face shone with withheld sunlight, like amber. His pores were almost invisible and his lips looked pale, windburned, and manly. I saw his blond eyebrows, shiny as silver feathers, rise and then knit with puzzlement and concern. Exquisite waves of ecstasy crisscrossed in me, and then my eyes rolled up into the lightning of my brain.

Mind, there was nothing prurient or even voluntary about this experience—except for my reluctance. Like a sneeze or a muscle spasm or a deep baritone saxophone blast, the sexual undulations shot *through* me. And to the extent that I was self-aware, I was vexed with embarrassment. But my self-awareness was a mere splinter in a maelstrom. I had no self-control. I was utterly passive, acted upon—reduced to the first and final thing all of us are, spastic protoplasm.

But that was precisely what enraged me. I am not a passive person. Even in my most reckless days, I've always held my life firmly in my own hands. What was happening to me in Frank Broughton's arms thwarted every effort I'd ever made to create myself. So I took no joy in that conflagration of bloodfire. I felt possessed. A shriek from the outermost demon powers in the void resounded in my flesh, deafening into radiance.

Perhaps this sounds like ranting. It must, because that was what it was like. I clung with all my might to my shard of self-consciousness. If I had let go, that infernal luminosity refracting into a prismatic frenzy in my body would have broken my mind.

The hammer blows of my heart replaced the brass door's echoing boom. My body bucked, but in Frank's strong embrace I didn't fall or flail. The wild energy in me, so ably contained by the press of his body, whirled from my toes to my brain, with no way out. I thought I would explode, and I clutched Frank as hard as I could. And at that instant the orgasmic force diminished, and I felt it slide out of me—and into his hard body.

When I opened my eyes, Frank was staring at me with a peculiar expression, like he was about to cry but had decided to laugh instead.

Strength returned to my legs, and I stood taller and tried to step back. But he held me, and gazed hard into my face. "Who . . . are you?"

"Sigrid, are you all right?" Adele asked with urgent concern, snapping loose from her shock.

The air sparkled with radiant motes, and Frank's features, outlined in fiery light, shimmered as though their atoms were about to burst apart.

Adele wedged herself between us, and still Frank held on to my hand, staring at me with intense curiosity.

"Sigrid!" Adele shook me gently. "What's the matter?"

The terrible anxiety that had gripped me a moment ago was gone. I no longer feared that I would humiliate myself. On the contrary, I felt poised at the very crest of the moment, as relaxed as an anchorwoman with a ten-second lead time, knowing I had the capacity to pull off anything, say anything, do anything. I could have sunk myself back into Frank's arms and kissed him full on the mouth if I wanted to. He looked bedazzled enough to accept it.

Marti told me later that she didn't recognize me, I seemed at that moment so, well, sultry. When I'd first cried out and then slumped into Frank's arms, she'd jumped up so fast she pulled the cord on her headset. But by the time she rushed across the pool to the office, Frank and I were already gazing into each other with bedroom eyes. It was the weirdest sight she'd ever seen, she said.

"I'm sorry," I heard myself saying, my voice a sticky indigo tremor, dark and bluesy, pitched for Frank's ears. It surprised me that it didn't waver or crack. "I shouldn't be here. I think it's the flu."

"You should be home in bed," Adele admonished.

Frank's hand tightened on mine, moved by the suggestion. "What's your name?"

"Siggy Lindo," I blurted out. I hadn't used that name in years, yet it sounded right.

"Let me take you home, Siggy," Frank offered.

Adele protested: "Frank—the meeting. Everybody's here now. And you've got your afternoon all blocked before your flight to Kingston." She pushed open the glass door. "Marti, see that Sigrid gets home." She arched a penciled eyebrow at me. "Though with shakes like that, maybe you should take her to a doctor."

"Or the Pussycat Lounge," one of the dock bosses stage-whispered, eliciting a few chuckles from the others before Adele's stern glare nailed them.

Marti hurried to my side, and Frank reluctantly let my hand go.

"Be well," he said in a hush that told me he meant it.

Adele seized his arm and ushered him toward the gaggle of baffled dock bosses, and Marti guided me quickly out of the office. My insides shivered with each step.

"Jesus, Sigrid," she whispered close to my ear, "you really singed his eyebrows."

The pool operators watched in snickering amazement as I punched out. Marti didn't bother punching out. This was company business. She snatched her red leather jacket and my tweed coat from the rack and escorted me silently to the parking lot before snorting into riotous laughter.

"What was that all about?" she asked, poking me in the ribs. "I thought Adele was gonna have an infarction!"

The breeze off the river with its freight of odors carried me

22

toward my car. All care had fled, all anxiety blown away, dwindling among goat-tufted clouds into the gutters of the sky.

"I'm sick, Marti."

"Yeah, you look spacey. What's going on? Are you lit?"

"I feel lit. Better than lit." I leaned back against my car and jubilantly opened my arms to the morning. "I feel like dancing with the clouds!"

"Whatever it is, I want some."

A shadow swept in off the river, and a purple gloom descended on us while a hundred yards away the Hudson glared like molten silver. My arms fell, and I squinted into the crackly light. "I'm sick. Seriously, really—I think something's wrong with my brain." I told her what had happened to me in the supermarket the day before, and her jaw dropped.

"You mean, that was a real orgasm in there?"

"A real O."

"That's too bizarre." Her mischievous grin slipped away, and she shook her head ruefully. "I gotta get you to a doctor. Gimme your keys."

"Just take me home," I said. "I wouldn't know what doctor to see."

"Yeah, who handles involuntary orgasms?" she half-joked, though I could see the precarious balance of her smile. Her broad Slavic face gave the impression of imperturbable calm, but I happened to know how to read every shade of smile and hue of her eyes, and I saw she was anxious for me. I knew I should have been worried, too, but I wasn't. Truth be told, I had never felt more serene in my life. As she drove through the October haze of the familiar streets, I studied my friend through the calm of my fish-eyed clarity.

Marti Svoboda-Greere had been wise-looking since she was a kid. Wise-looking, that's what we called it on the street corners when someone was impudent. Marti had a rude-faced flippancy even when she was sleeping. With her black hair and blond eyebrows, she was the one who looked like the janitor's trashy daughter, not me. Actually, she came from a strict Ukrainian family who had reined her in tightly until she was eighteen. I used to sit in the tree outside her bedroom window at midnight giggling with her and making her jealous with accounts of all my lurid sexual explorations.

I'm not proud of that now. In fact, the remorse I felt for introducing Marti to the fast life was so real for me that for a while it became something of a joke between us. She often used to say that I loosened her up and she straightened me out.

For a couple of years after high school, when we both worked at the umbrella factory, we partied hard, completely in stride, picking up and putting down boyfriends in synchronous rhythm. The future didn't concern us. All we wanted was to fool around and have fun—dancing and drinking, working like we slept, when we had to. We never once said it to each other, but we must have known we did it because of our fathers. Hers had held her too tight, mine couldn't hold me at all.

Then Marti found a man who could hold her—Buster Greere, an army technician—and she married him. Partying wasn't so good after that. I got tired of the moves at the clubs and the bars and spent more time alone at Tappan Down or just driving. I became introspective and began wondering where I was going. I couldn't imagine marrying any of the cowboys I sported with and knew I'd never meet anyone at the umbrella factory that I'd want to hold on to. Suddenly I saw myself becoming just like Willa, a factory girl at forty-one, still dating jerks. I grew old overnight. I wanted to get out of Arcadia, but there was Willa, reminding me every day that she needed me. At twelve it had made me feel strong to do things for her like my father did. But that had worn thin by the time I could drive, and she became like a bossy stepsister, only worse because she never got bossy enough for me to hate her: Sometimes she was funny when she was happy and I liked her at those times. I was out of high school and two years into the factory before I started thinking of how I could get away without actually running away. I had saved enough money for a Carneval spree in Rio. Marti and I had been planning it since fifth grade. I used the money instead to enroll in business college. Like my father, I was not very imaginative or creative in an artistic way. But I had a natural ability to work with real things, commonplace things, like columns of numbers and inventory lists and money. A year later, Marti was divorced and I was a bookkeeper.

What is destiny? I mean, I never planned to be a bookkeeper. If Marti hadn't married Buster, who knows what would have happened to me? Maybe we would have gone to Rio after all. Maybe I would have fallen savagely in love with some Latin surfer who could barely speak English, and maybe I'd be living with him now in a houseboat on the Amazon. More likely it would be Marti on the houseboat. She was always sexier than I, with her D-cups and swan legs, and her angelic face of petulant weariness.

"It could be stress, Sigrid," she remarked helpfully, driving with her knees while she took out a cigarette and lit it. "Stress kills people. I've read it in a dozen magazines."

I took the cigarette, though I'd given them up twice already. The menthol frosted my lungs, and I handed it back. "Don't call me that."

"Stressed? Hey, working with Adele-from-Hell, who can blame you?"

"No. Don't call me Sigrid. I don't feel like Sigrid anymore."

Marti bobbed her head with understanding. "You don't look like Sigrid no more, neither. And you know something?"

I declined another drag on the cigarette.

"That's fine with me. I always liked you better as Siggy." She sighed. "We had some good times together, didn't we?"

I nodded and cuffed her affectionately on the arm. Well, I

thought, maybe she was right about the stress. I hadn't had a boyfriend since school. Maybe what was happening to me was as simple and primal as that. Uncontrollable lust.

When we got to my house, I left my shoes in the car, rolled off my pantyhose, and walked barefoot through the embers of autumn around to the back of the house. While Marti smoked another cigarette and watched, I danced across the yard, kicking leaves into the wind so they swirled briefly like elvish specters. The demonic strength of the pulsing energy in me colored everything, and I was not myself. I was horribly and wonderfully more. I danced wildly yet with sure and casual control, doing marvelous moves I could never have done straight. Exhaustion eventually plopped me into a leaf drift under the stark maples, and I piled the debris atop myself like a tattered blanket.

Marti dropped the smoldering butt of her cigarette under her heel and went inside to call doctors. I tried talking to the moon. "Mr. Moon! It's me, Siggy. Do you still want to marry me?"

He didn't answer, though I knew he was up there in the quicksilver glare of the sun. Drunk with ecstasy, I thought it was funny that I had heard the moon's voice in my head last night. I wanted to hear it again. I wanted to be as crazy as I could be, because it felt so good. My mind was evaporating away from me like the ether of my sweat in the chill air.

A scalloped fungus on a tree caught my attention and enraptured me in a silent study. I peered into it as through a peephole to a tiny fairyland, seeing the gray weather there, the miniature ice ferns, the rich and mottled decay of this world flourishing into another. So—stress had reduced me to peering at tree trunks. I laughed at myself, lay back, and closed my eyes.

Behind my lids, a brazen company of elves cavorted in a kind of waking dream—naked, feral kids with glossy, lissome bodies and hair like sunset clouds.

Their frisky antics aroused me. I touched myself at my hottest tip, and the intensity of feeling in my swollen flesh jolted me so hard I kicked off my leaf cover. Gently, my fingers circled back. I stroked myself softly between my legs, nip and tuck, feeling deeper into my luck with each caress. I came cleanly, sobbing with delight, my back pressed hard against the minty earth.

Afterward the elves were gone, and I lay there gasping, smelling my own musk and the spicy leafcrush beneath me. I opened my eyes and saw Marti watching from the window, the phone against her ear. The curtains dropped back into place, and I lost my gaze among the tattered angels aloft in the sky's glass bell.

The strangest thing about all this was the felicity. Everything felt good. Just watching clouds shearing in the wind was a joy. And a normally simple joy like autoeroticism filled me with ecstatic well-being vaster than mortal comprehension. If I had been at all religious, I'd have thought I'd seen God. The world seemed whole, beautiful, and just. I beheld divine radiance shining through trees and rocks. Even a lump of dogshit in the storm ditch below gleamed, bejeweled with flies.

Marti came out of the house and sat on the ground next to me. "You need an admitting doctor," she said, very slowly and seriously, "or the paperwork for the insurance people gets too complicated. I think we should go see Dr. Pop."

Dr. Pappageotes had delivered both Marti and me and had been Willa's family doctor when she was a girl. His office was in his home, not far from where I lived. Sitting in the waiting room with Marti after surrendering urine and blood samples to Bea, the leathery old nurse whose knobby fingers had given me every injection I'd ever had, I floated. My serene attention drifted in and out of my body. I watched the elves caper behind my closed lids until that began arousing me again. To calm myself, I took in the familiar but now faded lithographs on the walls depicting the history of medicine from Hippocrates to Salk, the scratched wooden magazine racks, and the bulky red vinyl furniture that had remained virtually unchanged since my childhood.

Bea called out my name, and I left Marti flipping through magazines among the few red-nosed, rheumy-eyed patients in the waiting room. In the exam room, the pungency of basil clashed with the sharp antiseptic smell of cotton-stoppered bottles. Through a bay window with yellowed lace curtains, I could see Mrs. Pappageotes, the doctor's wife, in her *potager* herb garden, which had grown riotously taller than the windowsill. Pole beans hung in tatters and radicchio squatted in serrated bunches among a tangle of fennel and red chard. For an instant I thought I saw the naked elves from inside my mind peeking out from among the autumn trees.

Dr. Pappageotes entered, his bald head bowed, the sparse hair above the oysters of his ears pure white now. His bespectacled eyes gleamed with the same patriarchal benevolence that had seen me through my childhood illnesses, the two fractured arms of my tomboy days, Willa's emotional collapse after my father died, and a couple years ago, my nicotine withdrawal.

"I told Mrs. Pop you were coming, Siggy, and she has some kale from her garden she wants you to have. Help me out, will you, and take some for Marti and the ladies at your office, too. If Mrs. Pop makes me eat any more, my blood's going to turn green." He winked and leaned against a tall stool beside a counter neatly arrayed with vials and shiny instruments. "So what manner of ill brings you here, young lady?"

I told him about my two spontaneous orgasms, and he listened impassively as I described how blissfully aroused and dreamy I felt. I even told him about the dancing elves and the light I saw around things.

He frowned at that and peeked into my eyes with a penlight, asking me obvious questions.

He told me to close my eyes while he touched a sharp pencil to my toes and fingers. I watched the retinal afterimages behind my lids rearrange into a dumb show of strange creatures I'd seen in art books, in chapters about the Middle Ages—basilisks, griffins, chimeras—all of them phosphorescent and moving, changing into one another, an alchemical cartoon of transformations much stranger than the elves. Watching these rippling gargoyles greased me with erotic feelings. But there was nothing human about these creatures, and the turgid desire they stirred in my body scared me. I tried shifting my focus. In the wild silence of the medieval animation behind my closed lids I saw the hulking, bearlike silhouette of my father standing on a ghostly plain of twilight. My eyes snapped open.

Dr. Pappageotes pocketed his pencil. "No indication of stroke," he said levelly. With a hand under my shoulder, he urged me upright. "How are you feeling now?"

I sat up into a bleaching brightness. Spectral rays of silver luminosity shone from behind the doctor and tickled me with sexy urgency. What I had seen behind my lids I then saw with my eyes open: fey shapes flitting around the room, blurs of electricity breaking free of the glare and mutating into fiery wriggles, like salamanders made of sunlight.

"I'm seeing things, Doc," I confessed. "Weird things. It's scary. But it also feels good, sort of . . . " My voice trailed off, for I had just noticed that the transparent beasts were closing in. Figments of fabulous, tawdry creatures overlay the room—rainbow-hued seahorses and tiny bat-winged vipers sparking in and out of sight.

Impulsively, I snatched at the air and grabbed one. It squirmed in my hand, vibrant as a toad. When I opened my fingers to see what it was, I glimpsed a wee four-legged fish that darted away like a lizard. A visceral laugh shook me.

"What are you seeing, Siggy?"

The incredible loveliness that possessed me at the sight of these astonishing creatures was so palpable it displaced all my fear.

Inexplicably, I felt that if I tried I could even possibly share it. "Let me show you," I said with genuine enthusiasm, and obeying a crazy compulsion from deep inside me, I rubbed my palms together until a pale blue smoke seeped from them. Then, pushing my hands out toward the doctor as if throwing him a beach ball, I embraced the air around him.

Suddenly, the wispy white hairs at the sides of his head stood out as if electrified, and all consternation in his face vanished, displaced by the wide-eyed, wondering stare of a young child at Christmas. "My God—" he muttered, staggering backward. "Wh-what is that?"

I giggled lewdly. "I don't know, Dr. Pop. But it sure feels good, doesn't it?"

He slid closer. With him came the electric mishmash of harlequin creatures from inside my head. Their devilish follies intensified, beastshapes oozing into one another and the lit specters of sprites and elves parading closer with sinister vitality, strutting like drum majors and sparkling show girls, carrying the world with them.

From the midst of these ever-flowing mutations, Dr. Pop stared blinking at me. And I could feel his befuddlement. His mind was telling him that there was something wrong and limited about the way I was looking at him and snatching at unseen things. But I had no doubt his body was somehow experiencing the sensual glory smoking off me.

"What are you doing?" he mumbled loosely.

"You feel it," I said with certainty and grabbed more of the syrupy light out of the air. "It's real, isn't it?" I kneaded the palpable radiation, twisting it like taffy. It looked silver-green between my fingers and arc-welder white where it was most stretched. "You want more?" I asked, and not even waiting for his nod, eager for him to fully partake of it, I grabbed his thumbs. I don't know what I was thinking. Obviously not much, or I would have jumped out of

30

my skin. Before these strange fits came along, I'd never hallucinated in my life, not even in my most drunken flings. Yet there I
was, grinning stupidly at the flitting apparitions and my shining
hands. Crazy joy shivered deep in my muscles, yearning toward a
brighter fulfillment than flesh can hold.

A luxurious smile hoisted Dr. Pop's heavy features upward, as if
they'd been grapple-hooked, and his eyes rolled up into their sock-
ets, showing their soapy whites. Abruptly he jerked free, grimaced
in pain, and clutched at his chest. Before I could even reach to
catch him, he collapsed in a sodden heap before me.

At the sight of his crumpling, I yelped with alarm. Around his
motionless body, the radiance that had been shining through him
remained in the air—and in that smoky luminance, I swear I saw
Dr. Pappageotes still standing, looking at his fallen body with a
befuddled scowl. I was too scared to move. The apparition looked
at me, bemused and helpless.

Bea rushed in, striding right through his phantom shape; she
sized up the situation in a glance and immediately threw herself
over Dr. Pappageotes's fallen body. Heaving him to his back, she
probed for a pulse, listened for breath.

"I killed him!" I heard myself shrilling. "Oh, my God, Dr. Pop,
I'm sorry! Oh, my God—oh, my God!"

Dr. Pappageotes's shadowy form watched Bea clasp her rooty
hands below his sternum in an attempt to massage his heart back
to life. For a moment I dared hope he would come back. But from
behind him a misty glare brightened and spread fanwise. Then,
inside the ghost, a small sun ignited, and the apparition blew away
like a flame, leaving behind a thin thread of ectoplasmic smoke.

"He's gone," I croaked with despair.

But Bea continued laboring furiously over the body. Two
patients, a frail mother and her glossy-faced teenage son, stood
gawking in the doorway. Marti nudged through and took up pumping the corpse's chest while Bea checked for a pulse.

"I killed him!" I cried again and again, wanting only to dispel the enormous peace that began to replace my shock. I knew I was somehow responsible for his death, yet, mysteriously, a great warring contentment rose up in me and conspired to make me feel that, despite everything, all was well. Over and over again I chanted, "I killed him—I killed him—"

I couldn't watch them toiling over his body anymore. I turned and stared out the window at the forlorn garden. Cherubs, gnomes, trolls—the transformed dreamcreatures I had seen earlier around Dr. Pop—watched me slyly from the ragged plot.

A raw wail spun me about, and I saw small, bird-frail Mrs. Pappageotes enter, her fists to her forehead, her eyes shrill. She pranced back and forth before her prone husband, nearly tripping over Marti's legs.

I strode stiffly to her side. "Mrs. Pop—I'm sorry! I didn't mean to! It came through me—I didn't mean to hurt him!" I babbled nonsense. I lost track of what I was saying, or even feeling. With a skewed mix of horror and intractable wonder, I assailed the poor old woman with ranting remorse.

Mrs. Pappageotes regarded me aghast. Then the harpy cry of an ambulance matched my hysteria, and Bea came between me and the shocked widow. A sharp, glittering pain in my arm broke my raving, and I saw the syringe pull away in slow motion. Bea's elderly and melancholy face spoke mutely, and I pushed her aside.

All protest stalled in me with the frosty sensation of the drug lacing my blood. The shine in the air turned ice-green as medics shouldered their way into the room. Out of nowhere a raven materialized in the illusion-light, opened its wings, and enclosed me in its darkness.

Will you marry me?

My eyes peeked out, and I found myself on my back in a hospital bed. A lipstick smear of sunset stained the window facing me, and a crescent moon hung like a smile above the housetops.

Don't let me frighten you.

The first thought in my head was of Dr. Pappageotes. The hopelessness I felt about him overpowered the chill-edged numbness of whatever drug I'd been given. I would have offered anything to find that he wasn't dead after all. I wanted to believe that what was happening to me didn't have anything to do with what had happened to him. Fat chance. In my heart, I knew it did. And besides, the voice in my head kept telling me so.

Choose more carefully whom you touch with my glamour.

I tried to sit up and succeeded only in craning my neck. The ceiling and walls shone with twilight, warm as brandy, and I saw that I was in a private room. Shimmer-beings moved through the air, which I pretended were the effects of the sedative.

Please, Siggy, don't ignore me.

I groped for the call button I knew was somewhere at my side and pressed it.

Wait. Before you alert the others, listen to me. I have only a short time to speak to you.

"What about?" I said testily. "Dr. Pop?"

He lived a long time.

"Yeah, but now he's dead!"

And, obviously, you think I had something to do with it, right?

"I don't know," I replied sourly, sinking back onto the pillow. Jesus, now I'm talking back to a voice inside my head, I thought. Am I that completely unhinged?

Even so, even if I didn't know what the hell was happening to me, one thing I was absolutely certain of was that somehow I had done some terrible, terrible wrong. And now a good man was dead. I pressed the call button again. When the nurse came and flicked on the room light, I told him flatly, "I'm hearing a voice in my head."

He summoned a doctor, and I told her the moon was talking to me again, and I didn't want to talk back. Clearly, it was the moon that had given me some supernatural sexual strength that had killed Dr. Pop, I said, so I just wanted him to go away now and to stay out of my head forever.

For heaven's sake, Siggy, can't you hear yourself? the moon chided. *You sound totally loony.*

The clamor inside my head was driving me crazier than I already was. *Siggy,* the moon was saying in my inner ear, *Siggy, your only mistake resides in wanting to share your gift. Use the glamour on yourself. Then you will see what you will see.* To my outer ears, however, the doctor was softly, rationally explaining that she had some medication that would make the voice go away, but she thought it would be better to wait so I could be observed and tested. When I spotted Willa hovering in the doorway, for a moment my heart actually leaped with gladness; she was such a familiar, caring face.

I gestured her over, but the doctor rose to intercept her, I guess to warn her that I was raving and to ask her not to alarm me further by being upset herself. In the moment they took to whisper, I thought about what I should tell her, whether I should tell her what I suspected, or knew, or even the part about the man-in-the-moon.

"Baby, you've been working too hard," Willa said as she practically crawled into bed beside me. "You're just suffering from exhaustion. You're going to be okay."

If you won't touch yourself with my glamour, the moon suggested, *touch her.*

"No!" I shouted, but with clenched teeth, afraid that my lunar electricity would kill her as it had Dr. Pop.

Willa, misunderstanding me, looked frightened and clutched at my gown. "Don't talk like that, honey! You *are* going to be okay."

The doctor interceded, taking her by the shoulders. "Mrs. Lindo, please! Your daughter should rest."

Heavens! How have you put up with her all these years?

The blanching fear in Willa's face helped me ignore the moon's psychic and somewhat patronizing voice. I took her hand and tried to appear calm. "Maybe it's something I ate. I don't feel so good right now, Willa. But the doctor is going to help me."

"That's right, baby. You'll be home soon."

My concern for her muted my despair, and I attempted a smile. As soon as my face lifted, I felt a surge of well-being course through me to her.

Ah, you've got the idea now. See how light a touch you need? A little glamour goes a long way.

Willa looked palpably relieved. She kissed my cheek, assured me five more times everything was going to be all right, and left smiling.

And look, Siggy, about Dr. Pop—you shouldn't blame yourself. Okay, I take full responsibility. The glamour overloaded him. I should have told you.

I waited for the doctor to leave before I said, "Hey, I know you're just a voice in my head. The doctor has medicine that will put you out like a small-time tension headache. I know you're not real. But, okay, maybe you're an important part of my own mind, my subconscious. I'm open-minded. Ain't that the truth? So, if you know so much, tell me—what's happening to me? Why am I having orgasms? Why am I hearing you? What's wrong with me?"

You have nothing wrong with you, Siggy Lindo. You have a body and mind of excellent health. Don't misconstrue what has happened to you. Sickness has not touched you. I have. I want you for my wife, Siggy Lindo. The pleasure comes to you from me—as a gift. As does the glamour. Try it on yourself and really open your mind. Just don't overexpose others to it. I offer the glamour, and whatever other pleasures I can give you, as part of my wooing— the usual courtship ritual, you understand. If you look, you'll see that they arrive and depart with the rising and setting of the moon—except for the first. It took me all day that first time to break through the modern veneer of your soul.

A twang of dread plucked my heartstrings at the fact that a voice in my head was actually conversing with me.

That constitutes the main problem between us, doesn't it? You think I exist only as a figment, a mental derangement. You refuse to accept—or even to consider—that, in fact, the moon has come to you. Why not?

"It's absurd."

Absurd? The moon's laughter rippled like the shadows of a fire. *My dear, none of my other wives ever thought so.*

"Other wives? What other wives?"

Oh, don't get me wrong—I take only one wife at a time. You needn't concern yourself about them. And I don't do this very often, either, mind you—just every twelve or thirteen generations or so, when my longtime fascination with things terrene—earthly things—overcomes me. Of course, the ocean interests me most of all, which probably should not surprise you. But now and then, I do enjoy a commingle in the open air. I must say, though, I have never encountered a less enthusiastic prospect than you, and I've done this hundreds of times.

The moon's dulcet voice mixed seductively with the effects of the sedative, and I calmed down enough to actually forget my condition and feel curious about who was speaking to me. But before I could ask any more questions, Marti showed up at my bedside. She made a typical Marti crack about knocking 'em dead and then felt obliged to give me a spiel about how old Dr. Pop was and how his demise had nothing to do with me. "So, by the way," she concluded, "how are you feeling?"

I told her that the moon had been talking to me.

"The moon? Geez, Sig. He's talking to you right now?"

Touch her with the glamour. Gently, gently. You can make her see.

"He tells me I should touch you with the glamour."

"Uh-huh. Is that his way of saying I'm ugly?"

"Nah. The glamour's what he calls that sexy energy that's running through me."

"I saw you in the backyard, touching yourself." She smirked like we were kids again. But I could tell she wasn't really buying it.

"You want to feel it?"

"Go ahead," she said kiddingly. "But hey, you should probably save it for Broughton. He's the one who got you this private room and the flowers, you know. You sure did a number on him. He held up the stockholders' charter flight two hours to make sure you were taken care of."

"Really?" I could feel the raw fear in me beginning to scab over with other, more complicated emotions—first, protective feelings of affection for Marti and Willa, and now outright awe that Frank Broughton would go to such unbelievable lengths to help me. Me!

"Yeah, really. He went and made arrangements with some of the best specialists in the country. He's even hired a paramedic team to fly you to a clinic in Manhattan!"

"That's crazy."

"Takes one to know one, I guess. But I really think you ought to do it. I mean, he says the company's picking up the tab. Don't you think we should see if his money can talk louder than, you know, Mr. Moon up there?" She smiled mock-casually, but I saw the brittleness at the corners of her mouth.

Make her feel the glamour, Siggy. It will put her at ease.

I ignored the voice. "I guess it would be good to know exactly what *is* going on with me, huh?"

"That sounds more like you," she said and allowed a nervous laugh to betray her worry. "Willa's out there now putzing with the medical forms. I better go give her a hand."

My eyes hurt, and I asked her to turn off the light on her way out.

She seems a good friend.

"She is." I lay in the dark, staring into the window's purple light, where the moon balanced above the rooftops like a voluptuous shell. My eyes relaxed.

Then why didn't you show her my gift? Why didn't you touch her with the glamour? Must I continually have to prove myself to you before you believe me?

No sooner were these words spoken than I suddenly noticed an odd, aqueous shine radiating through the top sheet of my bedcovers. I threw back the covers and gasped. Electric and strange, a spooky brightness covered my entire body, the same kind of effulgence that appears on ships' masts during storms—soft flames in odd colors: green, blue, iridescent fire running over my flesh in swift, livid patterns, visible right through the hospital gown.

Whatever it was, it was so thick I could gather it up in my hands and shape it. My mind raced. Could others see this? Dr. Pop didn't seem to, though he sure felt it. I molded the pale fire in the air between my palms and sent flares of it shooting across the room.

You like my gift?

"Good Lord, I don't know," I sputtered. I shut my eyes and opened them again. It was a beautiful hallucination, I had to admit, but at the same time it scared me to death to see it all over my body. I felt the sedative I was on blunting my senses to the moodiness of a vaguely troubling dream. Was this a genuine psychedelic experience, like the kids of Willa's generation had? Willa claimed she had smoked marijuana twice and fallen asleep both times—the extent of her hippie past, foregoing free love to marry my father. The kids I knew in school who smoked the weed had all seemed too lethargic and spacey to ever tempt Marti and me to try it during our own boisterous adolescence.

But this was something else. A feeling akin to power ennobled the illusion and made me think I was actually handling tangible energy. "Is this what that sexiness I've been feeling *looks* like?" I asked aloud.

Yes. I've given you the strong eye, that you may see it.

"God—I don't believe this! And—and this is what got into Frank, isn't it? I mean, why he's so crazy about me all of a sudden, going to so much trouble for a gofer he never bothered to notice before."

He happened by at the wrong moment.

"Yeah, well maybe it was the right moment," I mused, wondering just how far this glamour could allow me into his well-heeled world.

No, Siggy. He cannot love you as I can. You've simply touched him with the glamour, and so he has become infatuated with you. But I love you for your soul—and I can give you so much more than he can.

I felt a petulant disappointment. If I was going to have a waking dream, why not enjoy it? "C'mon. Why can't I have him? Why not? He's beautiful. And he's rich."

I want you for myself.

"I've already told you—that's absurd. You can't have me. You're a rock."

There was a slight pause. When the voice in my head spoke again, it sounded quieter, yet resonant with the soft anger of hurt pride. *Oh, yes, I do have a body of rock, don't I? Eighty-one quadrillion tons of rock, in fact, spinning around you at two thousand miles an hour. Sure, you might think a quarter-million miles away seems a little distant, but only because my size makes me big enough to wear the oceans like a beard, strong enough to lift tides in the crust of the earth, and yet subtle enough to touch the iron in your veins and feel into your deepest cells. Not that you've ever noticed, or even looked up. To you, I remain just a rock. Why look up to that?*

You would appear insane to think I could have anything to say—to you or to anyone. Not for nothing does the word lunatic *mean crazy as the moon. I have a reputation as a crazy astronomical body, swelling and ebbing, appearing and disappearing, sometimes almost invisible in broad daylight and other times blazing for all to see at the darkest hour of night. I can seem truly wild. My phases darken and brighten, like lunacy. People call me a rock, all right, but what rock reflects light that makes people insane, or turns them into wolves? I have a thing about wolves, you know. They pay attention to me. As do moonstruck lovers and poets. My beauty awes them.*

Sure, I have the form of a rock. But believe me, I exist as no ordinary rock does. Fancy as gourmet cheese, and with a weekday named after me. Throughout the ages, men have revered me, but women have paid me particular homage. In fact, some think of me as a woman. But to that I say "nonsense." Why the epithet "the man-in-the-moon," if you question my gender? Each month you bleed for me. Your menses makes a blood sacrifice in my name. Even your idea of a month comes from me, the word itself named after me, this huge rock floating in the sky.

What you need, my dear, you'll find in a little moonshine, something to loosen your rational limits, so you can see my true nature—a rock with a hot heart. Energies pass between us every day, so why not words? If this rock can tickle the earth a thousand miles below your feet, why not your brain? If I could reach into your brain, Siggy, I'd tell you that I exist as more than just a rock, in the same way that you exist as more than just skin and bones. Here in the paste of your brain, we meet each other as tiny lightnings. Where I live, life has the same electrical shape: lightning moving in patterns—only with bigger amplitudes. And if I could get you to believe this, if you could see that I live here with you, in your most real part, then you could give my offer an honest consideration. I really want you to marry me.

My eyes fluttered as I listened to this, and I rocked to the rhythms of his sweet speech. He had an eloquence that I can't begin to imitate. I can convey only what he said, but not his music, for his song was beautiful beyond the mere words. In truth, the more I listened, the more helpless I felt in the presence of his charm, though I knew nothing could come of it. It was just a voice inside my head, I kept telling myself—although, admittedly, a voice with an angel's timbre.

"Why?" I asked in a feeble, frustrated whine. I tried to make myself snap out of my reverie. "Why me? And don't say 'why not.'"

That has the heft of a fateful question.

"I'm just a bookkeeper, Mr. Moon. A lot of people can fill my shoes. There's nothing fateful about that."

You appear in the world as just a bookkeeper and I just a rock. But appearances manifest only as a doorway, Siggy.

"Oh, yeah? And what do we find inside?"

We find our true identities. Oak-king and clove-queen in each other's arms.

"I don't understand."

You don't have to understand to believe.

Indeed, in the grip of the moon's glamour, I did truly believe for that instant that my life was—could be—far bigger than I had dared suppose. After all, hadn't my magic stopped one man's heart and captured another's? I was desirable after all, a man-eater, lusted after by the moon.

But wait. "Even if I believed you, why would I want to marry *you?*"

Ah-hah. For the usual reason, I suppose. As my wife, you will have undreamed-of power, for yourself and for others.

"Power to do what?" So here was the catch. Here was the deal with the devil: I would turn into one of Charlie Manson's minions, and for what? "What do you get from me?" I asked skeptically.

I half-expected a smartass reply but heard nothing more. The moon's horns disappeared behind the houses that crammed the horizon. A hollow, amorphous silence filled the room, a silence of bloodhush and heartthump and dim street static. The moonmagic was gone. One moment I could see God's blueprint in the air around me, fiery and breezy in an unfelt wind, and the next it slid away and I lost it.

Frightened, I stared blankly at the sooty shadows of the small room. I had never been in a hospital before except to visit my father once and some friends. Now here I was—headsick—talking to the moon like a raving madwoman. A hot wave of shame moved through me, and I wept.

The night seemed huge, cold, and treacherous, and its heart beat to the sobs of the widow Pappageotes. My secretive hope that Dr. Pop's soul was still alive, that he somehow persisted in the same heaven I wanted for my father, did not work. He was dead. A veritable doorknob.

I heaved a wet sigh and made myself stop crying. It was insane to think I had killed him. Yet I knew I had. I also knew about people who heard voices, people whose brains were addled with drugs or disease. The thought of Mrs. Pop alone in her house, her husband's well-handled instruments glinting in the night shadows, saddened me. But I had only been a witness to what had happened— to him and to myself.

The real shame I felt as I lay there in the tepid dusk was over how incredibly stupid I had been just moments ago, believing I was unique, an object of beauty desired by the moon and any man I touched. The only redemption available after that was to admit that my condition was purely physical, beyond my control—that something had gone haywire in my brain. That excuse was all I could manage in the darkening hour. That, and a plaintive gratitude to Frank for helping me. Without him, I would have woken up in some noisy ward among the other damned.

I didn't want to be crazy. But the alternative was unthinkable. Marry the moon? Impossible! When Marti came back in the room to announce that all the paperwork had been taken care of and a helicopter was waiting on the roof for me, I clutched her hand so fiercely, so desperately, that she grimaced for a second, then knelt at the side of my bed.

"Don't sweat it, honey," she tried to reassure me. "Hey, Broughton's sweet on you, you tramp. You're gonna get the best medical care there is, and you'll be back in no time and probably with a ring on your finger, I bet. And don't worry about Willa. I'll stop by every day and make sure she's all right."

"Marti, listen—what if I'm not crazy?" I tried to keep my voice level so she wouldn't think I was raving. "What if, you know, the moon is *not* just a rock? What if something wonderful is happening to me?"

The cracked smile on Marti's face silenced me, and I began to weep. "Hey, why are you crying? This isn't so bad. You got a couple big-time O's out of this, not to mention Frank's hot attention and a few days off with pay, right? Any woman in the pool would trade places with you in a shot. Believe it. They're chartreuse with envy."

I mustered an amused laugh.

From around her neck Marti removed a silver medallion black with tarnish. "It's the Virgin Mother," she said, slipping the delicate chain around my throat. "I know you don't believe in God and all, so I guess I'm really doing this for me, but I think she'll help you. If it gets bad, pray to her."

The only time I'd been in any kind of holy place since my father's funeral was to accompany Marti when she popped into church to get sprinkled with ashes or have her throat blessed with crossed candles. I thanked my friend and clutched the medal still warm from her flesh. It seemed the perfect antidote to my lascivious fits—a divine virgin.

Willa fluttered in, turned on the light, and began promising I'd be better in no time. I almost wished I could still hear the moon's sage voice simply so I wouldn't have to lie there and listen to her fret anymore—not about me but about how hard it would be for her to survive without me around. "You be strong, now, and do what the doctors say," she instructed sternly, not bothering to mask her percolating anger at me for leaving her to fend for herself.

If I made any indication at all that I wanted her to be with me, she would come. But I was grateful that the doctor had already told her there was no need for her presence. A battery of special brain-imaging tests were being arranged by phone to be conducted the next day. The results would be ready when they were ready, and she might as well await them at home as in the wards of a mental clinic, not able to see me anyway because I would probably be sedated and sleeping.

I hoped for her sake there was nothing so seriously wrong with me that it couldn't be fixed. But the sinister likelihood that I was losing my mind persisted, creating a slur of acid in my stomach. And though I tried not to, I wound up weeping on Willa's shoulder.

A few minutes later, after I'd let Marti convince me that it was better to know exactly what was wrong with me before I got too bent out of shape, two men in flight jackets arrived. They put me in a wheelchair, carried the airline bag Willa had packed for me, and took me up the elevator to the rooftop and the waiting helicopter.

Willa and Marti snatched at me in the whirlwind, and we parted, smiling through our tears. On the upward climb I peered through the porthole at my mother and best friend dwindling into the spangled night, and a chilled, vacuous sensation gripped me. At that moment I'd have given anything to hear it again—the soft, reassuring voice of the moon.

Manhattan shone brightly beneath the soft stars. At the hospital on whose roof we landed, I would only be tested, not treated. I filled out endless forms, routine blood and urine samples were taken, and eventually I was inserted in a huge metal donut, where I spent forty minutes on my back not moving.

That was the beginning of many long waits to come throughout the day. I listened attentively for the moon's voice, anticipated hallucinations, and fell asleep in a hospital bed experiencing nothing but restless dreams of wandering through endless corridors searching for a door and finding none.

Early the next morning I dressed in black slacks, a tangerine pullover, and my down jacket. An ambulance whisked me to the psychiatric clinic where I would be treated, according to Frank's arrangements. It was a mustard brick monolith in the upper Twenties off Madison, tucked between a rambling apartment complex and an office building fronted by some sort of Scandinavian furniture store. For the next couple of hours I waited anxiously in my room, a cubicle the color of egg yolk and very sparse, without a sharp corner or object anywhere in sight. The handles of the windows had been removed, and the corners on the bureau and writing desk had been beveled smooth and round. The overhead light, locked in a wire cage like a sallow bird, cast a wan glow.

On the way over, I had seen some of the patients wandering in the halls, hollow-eyed and muttering. It was a loony bin, all right, the kind of place nightmares are made of, or at least take place in. The urge to bolt was so strong, I became convinced that the longer I waited here, the more certain it would be that I would never leave.

The first physician to check me out was a neurologist with a beard right off a Smith Brothers cough-drop box. He tapped my knees with his rubber hammer, poked my back with a sharp stylus, and said he couldn't answer any of my questions until he gathered more data. I spent another ninety minutes waiting in the TV room across the hall from my cubicle, whittling time with old magazines, morning talk shows, and worry. The next doctor who arrived, a physiopathologist, was even worse. Bald as a bullet and just as to the point, he quizzed me about my family's history of disease, lingering a few seconds over my father's diabetes and Willa's grandmother's epilepsy, before he disappeared into the maze like the first.

I ate breakfast with the desultory air of a death-row inmate tasting food for the last time. It occurred to me to look in the morning paper for when moonrise was due. If the voice in my head was right, I'd have another erotic seizure—another gift from my lunar suitor—sometime in midmorning, I figured. Until that day, I'd never paid any heed to the moon, and it was only after I'd checked several of the old newspapers that I realized the moon rises fifty minutes later each day, which did seem to jive with the time of yesterday's spontaneous orgasm.

By the time an attendant arrived with a wheelchair to take me to my next doctor, I'd finally figured out that the phases of the moon were directly related to the sun. Science had never been my strong suit in school. The full moon rose only as the sun set and then went down as the sun came up. The quarter-moon was when the sun and the moon were at right angles to the earth. Did everybody know that? It seemed so clear; obviously I hadn't paid close attention in class. And certainly, I had never bothered with the moon's position in the sky before, except for a few picturesque full moons I remember making out under in Tappan Down. Regretfully, I realized how small a part the natural world played in my life.

The attendant wheeled me to a cozy, book-lined office where a short Asian woman wearing a long white coat and with a rope of black hair the length of her spine introduced herself as Dr. Chen, my psychiatrist. I glanced about for a couch and saw none. Her smile showed small pearls for teeth.

She had me sit in one of the big leather chairs, and then she sat down in the other, quite close to me. I was nervous, afraid of what she would find; I decided to force her hand: "So, Doctor, what's wrong with me?"

"Why do you think something is wrong with you?" she asked, and began writing on her clipboard. Naturally, I told her everything—Mr. Moon, the overwhelming sexual convulsions, Dr. Pop's death, which I still felt responsible for, everything.

When I was done, she leaned closer, and I could see myself in the ink of her eyes. "It's the moon we should talk about."

"But I've told you everything."

"Yes, I know. You told me what happened and what you felt. But I think we should talk about what it means."

"It means I'm nuts."

"'Being nuts' is a condition, Siggy. But meaning is something else altogether. What might the real significance of these episodes be for your psyche, apart from any possible physiological causes? Perhaps the love of the moon is symbolic. After all, each of us is like a solitary planet, aren't we?"

"I don't follow," I said with an edge, tired of waiting, of not knowing, of getting poked and probed and being scared and alone. "Just tell me straight up. What do the tests show?"

"The tests are inconclusive," Dr. Chen allowed. "There may be something wrong with your brain. What I am trying to do here is assure you, from what I perceive in this one preliminary talk, that there is nothing wrong with your mind."

"What's wrong with my brain? Is it a tumor?"

"No. It's not a tumor. It's—" she paused for a split-second eternity to consider her words—"it's an anomaly."

She showed me a blue photograph of my head cut in half, top to bottom—a magnetic resonance image that, she said, revealed a congenital defect the size of a lentil. Located at a busy intersection in the front of the brain called the interventricular foramen, the defect touched both a higher cortical center, where my sense of "I" resided, and one of the most primitive neural remnants, a usually dormant cell cluster practically nonexistent in humans but well developed in crocodiles and snakes, called the uncus.

"I have a defective brain?" I asked, my voice sounding far away. I *knew* it, another part of me was saying.

"Oh, I wouldn't put it that way. Apart from these acute aberrations, your behavior has been quite normal. And even during these upsetting episodes, your brain displays the very healthy tendency to make sense out of what it is experiencing. It's very much like dreaming, where random firings of neurons from deep in the brain are translated in the higher centers to experiences that, while absurd, have a vivid sense of realism. You yourself have called your hallucinations waking dreams. You know the moon is not *really* talking to you, even when he seems as real as me sitting here. That leads me to suspect the problem may not be global, as in schizophrenics, who wholly participate in their delusions. You seem to have real detachment, so your condition is workable."

"How? I can't keep having orgasms in the supermarket."

"We have to know exactly what we're dealing with first. I would like you to stay here for a few days while we observe you."

My heart sank, but not as deep as I had prepared myself for. I didn't have cancer. That was good. Until now I'd been too afraid to even consider I might be dying. Maybe this was fixable. Yet the prospect of staying in this hotel of horrors for several days depressed me. I decided to jump into the deep end right away. "Is surgery an option?"

"Of course, but our last option. If therapy is ineffective and your condition remains unresponsive to the battery of drugs at our disposal, then, yes, psychosurgery is indicated. But you've lived your whole life with this anomaly. If we can determine what has activated it, maybe we can turn it off without surgery."

"I really don't want to stay here any longer than I have to."

"I understand. And it looks like luck may cooperate with you. Normally, there's a two-week wait for the scanning devices I need to observe what's happening in your brain. But a cancellation quite by chance has given you a slot this morning, and serendipitously at the hour of moonrise—which you think may coincide with the onset of your next event. The opportunity seems too good to pass up, so I'll reserve that time for you with the SQUID."

The very name made me nervous—Superconducting Quantum Interference Device. Dr. Chen tried to allay my fears, but I couldn't listen anymore. I felt battered, dismally confused, and everything seemed to be happening so fast. I felt obliged to call up Willa and tell her the news; I just didn't have the strength for that task. Straightaway, Dr. Chen got me on my feet. She said the morning air and a brief turn about the clinic's manicured courtyard would clear my head, especially after hearing all that medical jargon. She offered to push me in my wheelchair, but I insisted on walking.

The clinic enclosed an open-air circle of mossy cobbles, stone benches graven with rococo sprites, and in the middle, a small fountain with spitting lion heads. All around, a dolorous assortment of patients in street clothes and hospital gowns stood, sat, or lay sprawled about on the benches, some looking more kempt than others. A few seemed to be holding conversations with some potted ficus trees nearby, but most of the others gazed into space with the fabled vacancy of lost souls. One emaciated woman, her thin smock unable to hide the razor-edges of her pelvis, was standing up on tiptoes, grasping fervently at the mild light of the clear autumn sky. Another, a long-haired man with a matted beard, sat in stony abduction from reality, staring sadly into space with Christ's eyes.

We walked once around the courtyard, and as we walked, I got the creepy feeling that I was reviewing variants of myself, not just what I had become at the supermarket two days ago but, more to the point, what I could become in the future. A stringy lady squatting against the red ivy, chewing silence, almost could have been

49

me, I swear. Maybe she, too, saw life's blue fire and heard the moon's burnished whisper in her ear.

By the time we went back inside and got into the medical van that would take us across town to the university imaging center, my orgasmic displays and the waking dreams from the tiny, fixable flaw in my brain seemed almost a blessing. It was physiological, that little lentil. That, I supposed, had been Dr. Chen's objective, to get me to see that and put my troubles in perspective. In any case, she had won my confidence in her skills as a physician. On the ride over, I felt relieved enough to confide in her how ashamed I was about the whole situation.

"I'd always thought it was just me inside my head. And now look what I did. I feel so responsible for what happened in the supermarket and to Dr. Pop and all. What a friggin' mess." I think I actually moaned. After years of putting up with Willa's self-pity, it felt good for a change to wallow in some of my own.

Dr. Chen nodded kindly. "Each of us is many. In fact, every mind is actually a conglomerate of many different selves, some more civilized than others. In your case, Siggy, the chairman of the board, was simply usurped by some raving party animal in the mail room." She shot me a small smile, amused at herself.

The SQUID looked like a couple of telescopes with the lens covers on. The crew-cut technicians who operated it wore aloha shirts and chewed gum. I reclined in a dental chair, and the telescopes peered into my skull. With a cricketing hum, the machine projected a grid shaped like my head onto a video screen. Areas inside the grid lit up in colorful overlapping pond ripples revealing the activity in my brain.

One of the gum poppers was explaining something about magnetic fields in my head when, sure enough, I heard the giant door slam, and its brassy thunder, an eight on the Richter scale, shook the small room.

I cried out, the voltage of a massive orgasm writhing through me, a viper of lightning. My cry caught in my squeezed throat, and I watched gusty colors on the video screen flash in synchrony with the garish pleasure blowing through me. I thrashed.

When the spasms stopped, I relaxed into the smoke of my body. The smoke had no voice. It was a cloud sliding off the sun. Wherever I looked, the windowless room brightened, and I realized that the sun was blazing through me, shining out of the smoke of my body.

Out of nowhere Dr. Chen hovered into view, her black hair unbraided, flaring like a cobra's hood. Beaded lizard eyes stared deeply into me, and painted spectra brushed the air between us. She asked questions, but my body had become smoke and couldn't speak.

Somehow, I knew that if I did speak, I would speak fire. Something would happen. I looked about for the medieval cartoons I had seen the last time. If I closed my eyes, they would be there, the imps and cacodemons. But they weren't anywhere in the room.

Dr. Chen's face pressed closer, this time her hair braided, her cumin complexion luminous, human, caring, and efficient. She asked more questions, but I wouldn't speak. I fixed my attention on the spluttering colors of the video display and noticed that they had slowed almost to normal. But inside the rotating image of my head, in the middle of my brow, an ember blinked like an eerie third eye.

A surf of voices washed around me. I ignored it and stayed focused on the serene aftermath of my climax, a bliss limpid as water. In its flow, no harm could come to me.

This was the first spontaneous orgasm I'd had during which I felt relatively safe. The gum-snapping technicians coolly attended to their consoles. Dr. Chen placed a comforting arm on my shoulder while she observed the monitor, studying the shadow games in my brain. This was the place of evaluation, the theater of science. Here we could learn what had really happened to Dr. Pop.

I rubbed my palms together until blue vapors seeped between my fingers. When I held my hands up, rays slashed in every direction. The sacred feeling of wholeness and perfection, so slippery and elusive when I was normal, was strong in me at that moment, muting all my anxiety about what was happening. Nothing seemed odd to me. The blue fire I'd summoned up appeared perfectly natural, and I looked proudly to Dr. Chen for her reaction. Her eyes reflected the computer's phosphor scrawl, and when I gestured to her, she gave me a calm, benevolent look. It was then that my whole body flinched to realize that she couldn't see the conjured flames that I held in my hands. She couldn't see any of it!

I turned to the others; they were busy monitoring their instruments. One gave me an encouraging thumbs-up sign. Clearly, he too saw nothing of the arc of fire between my hands. Another technician came over and asked me to lower my arms, afraid I'd upset the device. No one could see what I saw, what I was doing.

Desperately, I wondered if the machine's electric eye could see what I saw. Without thinking, I packed the astral fire like a snowball and tossed it at the monitor. With a high-pitched whine, the screen showed static, then blanked out. The technicians moaned. Obscenities flew, and someone muttered something about the supercoolant pump cutting out.

Dr. Chen helped me to sit up. "A glitch," she said tersely. "But no matter. We got what we came for. The anomaly in your brain is hot. It's definitely the responsible agent in your episodes."

"Doctor," I blurted, and the sound of my voice lit up the smoke of my body. "You don't understand. *I* did that." Inside, I felt my fire brightening. No one could see my blue energy, but I knew for sure it was as real as my fingers and toes. "I threw my power at the machine, and it stopped. I—I *swear* I'm not making this up. I think that's what must have happened to Dr. Pop."

"Well, then, we're going to have to study this power more carefully," she said seriously, though I could tell she was humoring me.

"You don't believe I did it, do you?" I glanced about at the perplexed technicians.

"Can you turn the machine back on, then?" she asked me indulgingly.

Her sarcasm masquerading as scientific detachment irked me, but I tossed another dollop of fire at the monitor anyway. Nothing. I shrugged and smiled meekly. "I know this sounds nuts, Dr. Chen, but this is real. No shit. Would you like to feel it?" I grabbed a handful of the azure light frothing in the air.

Dr. Chen shook her head dismissively and helped me off the table. "Come on, Siggy. Let's get you, and the data disc of this session, back to the clinic before we experiment any more."

She insisted I ride in the wheelchair to the medical van, but I balked. I felt myself surging with phenomenal strength and clarity. Confidence boomed in me. I believed with certainty that I could touch the world and actually be felt. This was indeed the glamour the moon had talked about. But he too had warned me to be careful. Whatever I touched with this power was libidinally changed.

Outside, the sun's feathers overlay the city. White fire saturated me, and I raised my arms, feeling I could fly. Two attendants took me by the shoulders and hoisted me into the van.

On the ride back to the clinic, I experienced a mischievous urge to touch Dr. Chen with my blue fire, purely to see her amazement, to validate me. But of course, I had reservations. Hadn't Dr. Pop and the computer stopped, literally dead in their tracks, like they'd been lightning-zapped? Frank had been strong enough to accept the glamour, but it wasn't as if he came out exactly unscathed, either. What would it do to her? I decided I didn't want to find out, not in such close confines.

I gazed out the window at the skyscrapers flashing sunfire, the gleaming crowns of man's pride. No woman would have erected these phallic monoliths, I thought to myself. Our energy did not go up and out, but down and in. I cupped my breasts, which contradicted me, for they pointed up and out as assertively as any phallus. They shivered in my hands: soft, white miniature rabbits. I could almost hear them mewling for their milk and their babies. Their desire had the same erotic reach of the skyscrapers.

So the breast is the female phallus, I thought, struck for the first time by their similarities. Their firmness, their readiness to give milk comes from the same iron in the blood that men use to erect their penises and their buildings.

As we wove through the traffic, I shared this observation with Dr. Chen, who listened with benign interest.

"If you think you can manage it, you should write these thoughts down."

The pleasure pervading me shimmied with the vibrations of the taxi, blooming and dimming like watery light. "Why do I feel this way only when the moon is up?"

Dr. Chen shrugged. "The lunar connection could well be an ancient biological clock run amok. But that's pure speculation. I need to know what you're experiencing. How are you feeling now?"

I told her about how inexplicably aroused I felt. Sex had always seemed little more than a recreation to me as a teen. Sure, I fell in love a few times, until I got the hang of it and saw that it was nothing more than something people did by rote—fall in love, get married, have babies. Which is why I was opting for a career, hoping to become something more than my biology.

"That sounds like you take your beauty, your sexuality, for granted," Dr. Chen remarked.

But of course I didn't. Like all girls, I used to think, when I was fifteen, that I was ugly. The impossible red hair, the freckles, the bony body—I had all but resigned myself to life as an old maid. Then my scrawny frame filled out, and I discovered that boys didn't give a hoot about hair color or freckles, at least when the other body parts were forthcoming.

Now that I was jangling with lusty impulses, I felt I understood the urgency men made of sex. I queried Dr. Chen about what her observations revealed of me and if she still thought that this muscular possession was a workable problem.

She took advantage of our arrival at the clinic to put off my questions and hopped from the van. But when she offered her hand to help me out, I found I couldn't move. Peering out the door, I could see the tiered windows of the clinic's brick facade flapping with ghosts, specters, vaporous beings, literal swarms of them. That's what they looked like—misty mannequins, ragged silks of no color, membraneous jellyfish with scallop-edged tissues, rippling gills of ectoplasmic fungus thriving off the debris of rotted lives.

I was so startled that the smoke of my body thinned out, and I teetered for a moment on the threshold between this world and the world within this world. Out of nowhere, my father's bearish profile cast its shadow through the windshield. At the sight of him I jumped up so quickly I whacked my head on the roof and sat down in a drizzle of tiny stars.

My father's ghost turned out to be the van's beefy driver coming around to take me out. I groped forward before he could put his hands on me and looked appealingly to Dr. Chen. "I don't want to go inside," I said in a cracked voice. "I'm scared."

Even the flavor of sunlight seemed colder here. A blast of wind sucked the heat from me. With a quick snap of my head, I caught a fleeting glimpse of a luminous sprite dodging and veering through the crowd, a blurry, frost-tressed girl laughing as she tousled people's hair and clothes. Another look, and she was thin air.

The ghostly shapes in the asylum windows, too, were gone. The windows stared blackly, portholes to the land of the blind.

The van driver took my arm firmly, and we followed Dr. Chen into the clinic. Fear kept slamming in my chest. Something distinctly evil and oppressive forged itself out of nothing and made a mockery of the fern plants, the cheerful wood decor. I resisted and was bodily hoisted off my feet by the hulking man, rushed kicking and screaming past a bronze bust of the clinic's founder to a steel door at the back.

Once inside, where the other doleful patients watched, I knew I had to shut up or they'd sedate me. I chewed a knuckle and fought back tears. I counted things—doorknobs, linoleum squares. Dr. Chen patted my shoulder and led me to the courtyard, rewarding me for my self-control. My eyes darted, watching for the ghosts.

She sat me down on the stone lip of the lion-head fountain and spoke firmly: "Siggy, we actually know what's wrong with you. You're one of the lucky ones we can help. Now I know you can understand, so listen to me. What you're feeling is strange and disorienting, I know. But you only have to endure it for a short while. With the information we have now, we can begin to make you better. If you want some medication to help you, I can give it to you. But it will make you groggy. I don't think you need it, do you?"

I peered at the patients in the courtyard, who were up to their usual antics. I saw what I suppose would be called their auras, though they were more like translucent forms, cubist angles and crystal facets that distorted the air around their lost souls and broken minds and warped brains gathered together in forfeiture. Lord, I knew I was not like them! It was a fact insisted upon from within me, from the rapture that had shrunk into the whisper of my blood. No, I was not like them. I may have looked totally crazy, even acted it, but I knew with magnificent certitude that I was whole. Dr. Chen herself kept telling me so. And I knew that if I listened deep enough, long enough, I would find again that joyful life force in me that was as flawless as water.

I closed my eyes, and instantly I was transported to a red river's edge in a night world. Capillaries looped like lianas, and arterial integuments laced the banks. Carried by the scarlet flow, a corpse rolled with the current. It was me, drowned in blood.

56

Strangely, the sight didn't frighten me, though it was ghastly and eerily detailed, with clots in my hair and the red wind crawling over the surface. It was another waking dream. I could almost hear inside the dream's contours Chen describing its symbolism, its visual truth that I was mortal. The glamour through its rapture carried my mind like my blood carried my body.

With prescient certainty I knew also that this particular truth was granted me at that moment because of the presence of so many damaged people around me. Witnessing their suffering, I could not help but partake of their horror as well. Not the terrible dread of their minds, most of which had been drugged numb, but the palpable anguish in their flesh, where the distortion remained no matter the drugs. In that watchful instant, I felt I had truly joined them. All souls are one, you see, and all souls are suffering.

So, I thought to myself, my body filled with their pain, I was like them, after all. And with that boisterous thought, the gory vision suddenly burst into clear blue radiance. The sky above the courtyard stared down into me, and its blue power poured through my eyes. Startled, I lowered my gaze and faced my fellow sufferers.

What I saw next was a most curious sight. Those who had been muttering to themselves or conversing with the trees now sat quietly, watching me with almost vehement attentiveness. And the long-haired man, the one with the matted beard and Christ's eyes, stood up slowly, achingly, holding his hands toward me like a cold man befriending fire.

Over the next several days Dr. Chen, with her usual brisk efficiency, tried teaching me coping mechanisms so that she could leave me alone long enough to attend to her other work. She showed me how to take slow, deep, serial breaths to stay calm in the face of my hallucinations, and she instructed me to visualize a

tropical beach or a forest morning, some happy memory that
would steady my nerves.

I remembered fishing with my father in the summer of my
eleventh year, in late August, the week after I had toppled out of a
tree and fractured the ulna of my left arm. Trawling a forest brook,
my lure got tangled because my bad arm had botched the casting.
My line snagged on the upturned crown of an oak that had fallen
in the water. I waded in after it and was stooping toward the root
cluster when I saw the snake. It was large and the color of dead
leaves, lying among the black roots, the gold wedge of its head only
inches from my face. Reflex would have whipped my head back,
but I forced myself to freeze. I had learned somewhere that snakes
attacked only movement, and this frog-fattened serpent was
already tensed to strike. Any move could trigger it, an eye blink, a
tremor, a running sweatdrop, or, I imagined, the scent of my fear. I
held myself still, focusing tightly on the tiny tar-bubble eyes and
the tattooed head. The cobbles under my feet became star-distant,
and I seemed to be floating in a strangely serene world of glassy
light and the heady, soporific fragrance of honeysuckle. Gently I
floated away, wading backward until I was sure the lethally nerved
spine could not reach me. Only then did I relax enough to breathe.
A ripple pulsed through the snake, then faded into the watery
shadows.

That was the same disturbing memory that kept recurring
whenever I tried Dr. Chen's visualization technique. I suppose it
was an accurate image of how I felt there in the clinic, surrounded
by all of its phantoms with viper faces and flanged jawhinges.
Quite truthfully, I was scared witless. Once I tried staying perfectly
still, as I had done before with the water snake, and the vaporous
illusions closed in, a squalid troupe of hellish beings, grotesque,
skull-headed clowns, fanged trolls, and thumb-sized worms with
shrieking fetus faces by the hundreds.

I panicked. Dr. Chen found me screaming and batting the air, running through the corridors desperate for an exit. So much for her coping mechanisms.

The drugs the doctor gave me—first by injection and later in a rainbow assortment of pills and tablets—did not make the demons go away, but they numbed my fear. I sat for hours watching the monstrous legion of half-world things floating around me in a wavery submarine light, flashing their angry piranha teeth at me. None of them ever touched me, unless I closed my eyes to them. Then the horribles bit me. My body broke out in welts of pin-prick toothmarks that Dr. Chen called "a hysterical urticarial reaction."

When the sun set, I could hear the voice of the moon, now muted by the effects of the drugs on me, calling me from his cold and remote empyrean. *Siggy, you must get away—get away—away.*

But there was no getting away. Frank kept sending me flowers; Willa and Marti visited, and I saw them watching me from the far end of a funhouse corridor. I knew I was pretty messed up by then. Two days had passed since the drug therapy had begun. My orgasms had mysteriously stopped, all rapture had vanished, and time seemed bleared. Dr. Chen was trying different drug combinations to see what worked. I had become a wood bole carved into the shape of a woman. I couldn't speak much and kept repeating "Take me home." And all Willa kept saying through her tears was "Poor dear, poor dear." A halo of snaky shadows writhed about her, and every touch of her grasping fingers was a spider's kiss.

Later, Marti's broad, beautiful face leaned over me. "If I thought it would do you any good, kid, I'd steal you out of here. But the doctors say they can truly help you if you stay long enough. Willa's gone ahead and signed you up for a three-month treatment program."

I tried to protest, but words came so slowly that by the time I could find my voice, Marti was gone, and the ghostly freaks skulking around my bed smiled sickly, needle-toothed smiles at her parting.

If you'd listened to me in the first place, you wouldn't have fallen into this pit.

"Help me. Please. Don't scold me. Help me."

So now you think you might see me as more than just a rock?

"Help me, Mr. Moon."

Say you will marry me, Siggy Lindo, and I will get you out. Say you will marry me.

"I will marry you, Mr. Moon. Whatever that means, Mr. Moon. Whatever you want me to do, Mr. Moon. Just get me out of here, Mr. Moon—Mr. Moon—Mr. Moon—"

Hold on, Siggy. I can't help you from up here. I'll have to come down. Hang in there. I'll find my way to you. Stay calm, and I'll come back for you soon.

His voice came and went in my head with the confounded tides of my medicated state. Even sleep allowed no refuge. Whenever I passed out, a freaky dream recurred. I sat up in bed, but it wasn't my bed. Frank Broughton lay next to me, his handsome profile shining ardently, sun dust suffusing around him into the dark. I put my hand out to stroke him, and moonlight running in from a window above gave me a queer pallor, fish-silver skin, and black fingernails. As I touched Frank, his body misted away with an acid hiss, leaving only brittle, amber bones. I hugged the bones, a necrophilic succubus, a true man-eater, and they turned to dust.

Dr. Chen wrote all of this down but explained none of it. Every day by the lion-head fountain, she interviewed me for an hour. Spider-sized devils with stingray wings, tar-clotted heads, and blister eyes wallowed like sewage inside the clinic. So I spent as much time as I could in the courtyard where the blue wind thinned out the gang of chittering devils. Dr. Chen made me repeat my story endlessly, like an incantation. And I did. I thought that if I was a

good girl about that, I'd get out sooner. I would have done anything to be healed. I didn't want to wind up here forever with the
others, drifting about that courtyard like fumes, staring into their
isolation with empty eyes.

In my room at the clinic, I pressed my body against the window
slot, my cheek a moist slug on the pane. I peered down at the
street, where people's lives crisscrossed. Destinies mingled. All far
below me, bodies moved freely through the world.

The body means everything, I started thinking, angry at the
treasonous behavior of my flesh. Maudlin mutterings occupied me
as I gazed down for hours on the small, headlong lives following
their invisible paths, streaming past one another.

On days when the mix of drugs filled me with nervous energy, I
walked it off on the rooftop among the somnolent potted trees.
Autumn leaves spun in the wind like lees in a cup, and I almost
believed I could read prophecy in them. My future was as dark as
the ruined light in the dead leaves, as frail as the dim warmth in
the pale October sun.

Doomful feelings shrouded me, and I knelt beside the claw of
a leafless tree, bowed my head into the mysterious weather of my
hair, and prayed. I clutched the medallion Marti had given me and
appealed to the Virgin Mother as I would to an older sister: "Can
you help me? I've never prayed before—but then, I've never bothered you or God before, either. Can you heal me?"

The moment continued to fill with traffic noise from below.
My prayer withered. All my life I had relied on myself. Why should
God help me now? Was I more worthy than any of the others on
this rooftop wandering through their illnesses? I stared at them
through my hair and saw their haggard faces filled with the years of
their suffering.

I released the medallion and stood up. Clinging to the storm fence, watching the dry leaves spinning downwind over the rooftops of Manhattan, I stared at the city as though I had never seen it before. A thousand towers of silver glass stood, each in its solitude, like erect statues of saints rigid with their excess of love.

The wingbeat of my heart fluttered harder to behold what the accomplished God of silence had made of the world. Where hills and trees had loomed for thousands of years, a miracle stood—a dream made of steel tresses and tiered concrete. My head buzzed to look at it. It was the answer to a million years of people praying never again to fear the dark. Even in broad daylight it seemed to shine with its own power, the caught breath of God bright with inconsolable desire, reaching back to heaven in spires and ramparts, the very heights of our depths, uplifted with our prayers and moral as stone, never again to fear anything.

I wanted to be healed just so I could wander this holy city and participate in its frenzy and bravery. *Freedom is nothing until it's gone,* I muttered in my head, remembering how free I had been before I'd lost my mind and had come here to find it. I had used my freedom to work for a living and to take care of my mother. Watching time slide through the streets below, carrying the traffic, I wished I could walk against the flow and go back up the avenue of days to seize my life. I'd quit my job. I'd tell Willa to grow up. And I'd leave her once and for all and come to this place where lives are cut out of dreams so that all the pieces fit. And my broken mind would be the last piece of the puzzle to find its place before night's black angel rose from the asphalt pathways and called for me to walk with her in this garden of loneliness.

Such was my condition when I met my fateful guides—the two seemingly harmless old ladies who would change the whole meaning of my life and suffering. At first they appeared as hospice workers in official yellow jackets: well-meaning, if slightly bumbling, volunteers whom I saw every day serving fruit juice, reading stories aloud to the bedridden, strolling and talking with the other patients. It happened on an afternoon when the chemical cocktail of the day had left me literally seething with panic and crouched on the floor. Nothing seemed holy and God-given that day, my primitive heart drumming with fear at the shapes of black fire crackling around me.

Then the two old women came into my room. In the honeyed light slanting through the narrow windows, they did indeed seem suffused with a sacred glow, and the char of fiends in the air parted for them. I think it was, in fact, Halloween day.

"How do you do? I am Drusille Farrior." The larger of the two swelled before me. I squinted to make sure she wasn't a hallucination. Big-boned and Teutonic, she looked strong, her gray hair pulled severely back into a bun that accentuated the block of her forehead and the marble of her chiseled features.

The other old lady, short and scrawny, had fleecy white locks and a jutting face as starved as a sheep's. "And I am Glendil Braidwood," she said with a deprecatory little smile. Both wore dowdy, old-fashioned clothes with lots of buttons and black knob-heeled shoes. I could not respond to either of them; my mouth worked mechanically but made no sound.

"Tsk. Rest now. We already know who you are, child," Drusille said, offering me a thick, spatulate hand. "Tsk-tsk. You shouldn't be on the floor." She stood me upright and wiped the drool from my shivering chin with a soft cloth.

Glendil fingered the black medallion of the Virgin Mother dangling from my neck. "The Woman God," she said reverently. "So, you know about Her, dearie?"

"Now, now, there will be time for that later, Glendil," Drusille shushed her when she saw my perplexity. "Look at her. She's in a miserable state."

"It's the drugs."

"Let me tell you something about Dr. Chen," Drusille said confidentially, gazing levelly into my eyes. The strength of her stare alone kept me standing on my feet. "Never mind her reputation as one of the nation's top neuroscientists. The truth is, she's merely a researcher, not the healer she pretends to be. To her, you're simply a collection of data, something she can write up in a journal and share with other scientists. Bluntly put, she's less interested in you than in what she can learn from your case—for the general benefit of all humanity, of course."

"Yes, that's all you are to her," Glendil agreed, shaking her head soberly. "A psychiatric case. One case among the hundreds she's already catalogued to feed her career."

"She doesn't know the slightest thing about what's wrong with you," Drusille continued, her pale eyes hot. "She doesn't even know who you are. To her, you're just a twenty-three-year-old bookkeeper with a funny brain. She's experimenting with you, you know."

My panic tightened. "How do you know about me? Who are you?"

"Why, we're volunteers, dearie," Glendil answered. "The office gives us a small biography of all the patients so we can better relate to them."

"But we know more about you than that," the other crone acknowledged.

They looked at each other, seeking a mutual agreement, then Glendil leaned closer, giving me a conspiratorial look. "We are wicce."

"Vulgarly known as 'witches,'" Drusille added with some disdain.

"We worship the Woman God—the Creator who mothers all things."

"The moon asked us to help you."

At the mere mention of the moon my heart stopped, and I felt the air seep out of my lungs. Drusille hoisted me up by the shoulders, sat me on the edge of the bed, and fanned my face. "Sigrid! Don't act so shocked. The moon told you he was coming down for you, didn't he? We're here to prepare you."

"Consider us something like your bridesmaids," Glendil offered brightly.

I frowned, not entirely sure if this was real or one hell of a hallucination. "I don't understand. Have I . . . been talking about the moon in my sleep . . . or something?"

"Quite possibly, dearie," Glendil said merrily, patting my hand. "It's just the drugs that are confusing you. Drusille, give her the amulet."

From the pocket of her hospice-worker jacket, Drusille removed a small God's eye, like the kind I used to make as a kid from yarn and sticks, only this one was woven from grass, feathers, and bird bones. "It'll keep the bottom feeders away. They are disgusting, aren't they? Shoo now!" She flapped her arms vigorously.

They placed the amulet in my hand, and instantly the hideous, accordion-winged aberrations that had been harrying me pulled far into the corners of the room.

"There, now, that's better," Drusille said, reading the relief on my face. "Those filthy beasts have been thriving on your glamour. What a feast it's been for them!"

"You . . . you know?"

"Of course, dearie," Glendil chirped. "We don't see them as well as you do, of course. We haven't your gift. But we know about them. All the wicce do."

"What *are* they?" I asked with revulsion, watching the bat-snouted imps shivering blackly in the corners.

"Astral parasites," Drusille answered with obvious contempt. "They feed off broken minds."

"Leaky auras," Glendil chimed in knowingly. "Broken minds have the leakiest auras, you know, and these entities thrive on that prodigal energy. That's why there are so many in this sanctuary of unfortunates."

"And that's why we are here," Drusille explained. "We offer the damned what comfort we can. The doctors certainly aren't going to protect them from the bottom feeders."

"It's one of the community services we try to provide as caring wicce," Glendil submitted proudly.

I clutched the amulet to my breast and tried hard to shear through the muddle of fear and muzziness induced by the drugs. The faces staring down at me—one big and raw-boned, the other sunken and wizened—studied me like the fates deciding my span of fortune.

I found the voice to ask, "Excuse me, did you say the moon is coming?"

"Oh, yes," Glendil responded fervently. "How wonderful that he wants you for his wife."

At that point, I swear, I was no longer sure if I was breathing in or out, and I took a big gulp of air.

"Steady, now," Glendil said, sitting next to me and taking my hand. "Granted, it is a great responsibility, but you can handle it, or he would not have chosen you."

"Handle what?" Confusion stymied my every effort to think clearly. This was too much for my overloaded brain. Distantly, I was aware that either something enormously wonderful was happening to me or my brain had finally given out.

"There, there. Glendil, look what you've done to her. Now is not the time to be talking about responsibilities." Drusille took Glendil's arm and stood her up. "The poor girl's simply drugged out of her mind."

Glendil peered into my slack face. "But you understand us, don't you? You've noticed that your glamour comes and goes with the moon, though in here reception tends to get quite obstructed, unfortunately. Nevertheless, Siggy, the moon is waxing. Your glamour grows. Soon you will become all that you really are."

"Enough, Glendil. You sound like you're recruiting her for the army."

I asked, almost voiceless, dreading the answer, "What do you mean? What am I?"

Drusille rolled her eyes impatiently. "Shush, child. We'll talk again later, when you're less sedated."

Without taking her merry eyes off me, Glendil hushed Drusille with an impatient wave. "You know who you are. You just don't know the many names there are to describe you. And that's exactly why we're here, to help you understand, to help you find the words. It must be terribly confusing to be chosen by a god and then wind up here in this sad, and terrible place. But don't be afraid. We're here now—and soon your consort will be with you."

"This all seems so—" I almost said crazy. "Strange."

"Oh, it is. Wondrous strange. But it is not unknowable or unpredictable. You'll see. And we'll help you, because we are wicce, and if there's one thing we know, it is the ways of the moon. We know it like the tides. We know how to handle him. And you as well—in all your guises and forms. For you are but an innocent daughter of the Woman God, not the clove-queen vixen these astral demons would like. The moon prefers his women that way, you know: naive—a sleeping beauty fallen among men. It's his male pride, a bit old-fashioned, perhaps, but I doubt he'll change now. He likes to be the one who confers the glamour, the one who transforms his bride into the enchantress, a sorceress, she of spells, queen of horns, sister of the nethermost, consort of night, mistress of the lunar hours, dusklover of the waxing and waning powers that he alone can bestow on she of days."

I blinked with confusion.

"Don't let these titles and dominions befuddle you, child." The big woman, Drusille, smiled kindly. "Simply remember that you are Siggy Lindo. And for the world of men, whose lives are but sparks adrift in a nameless night, that is enough. But to the wise, for whom each spark is all sparks, one light made of every color, we see you as you really are, child—not a child at all, but of an age to the iron old earth and strong enough each year to carry summer up out of the ground. We know the truth of you." She arched her brow, and the cold orbs of her eyes looked lidless. "We know you are the moon's wife."

Where the Moon Lives in Us

The witches swore me to silence by making me hold a finger sheathed in blue flames to my lips as I repeated aloud: "By the silence of my destination beyond death, I will speak of this only to the Lady of the Wild Things." Then, with stern admonitions to let not a drop of medication pass my lips, they left in a cloud of lavender air.

After the door closed behind them, my drugged stupor persisted, but unbelievably, the demons kept their distance and their numbers decreased. I realized with some amazement that my fears also had abated. Still uncertain of my bearings, however, I paced my cubicle absentmindedly, holding the witches' amulet before me and making the scorpion shadows retreat into their surly corners. For the first time in days, I think, I managed a small smile.

Could I have been wrong all these years about the truth of things? Was it possible reality was not as I had thought—not the matter-of-fact world of good and bad deeds, of money and blood, of cause and effect? What if, instead, this energy I was feeling was *real* and all its forms—its sexual transports, its seething panics, its ambitious ideas, its striving, and yes, even its glamour and blue fire and demons fit into some extraordinary system I had never dreamed existed? Could it be that maybe this energy had laws of its own, which we, for lack of a better word, called *luck?* Could it be that maybe these odd old ladies, these witches, were privy to those laws?

In the face of such reckless possibilities, my mind went blank, as absolutely blank as a blown monitor. It was too much even to imagine.

Not much later, the sun set and the moon floated at the top of the window, high in the sky, a silver cipher staring across the glittering city. I heard no voice. "Mr. Moon—" I entreated but received no reply.

That night I slept dreamlessly, and when I woke in the morning, for the first time in days I wasn't absolutely wrung with sexual desire. Those witches—for, I'd decided, why not call them that?—those witches had changed something wordless in me. I examined their amulet, but it seemed nothing more than plaited grass and feathers binding thin chalks of bone. Only after I stared at it a long while did I think I perceived a faint quartz glow around it. But the moon was down, my glamour weak.

The nurse brought my breakfast and my medication, along with that day's bouquet of white long-stem roses from Frank. The card read simply, "Dreaming of you."

In the old days, I thought to myself with bitter irony, before this calamity, I would have *killed* for long-stem roses and the attentions of a Frank Broughton. Now I just looked at them and shivered at the thought that he was seeing me in *his* dreams the way I looked in mine—a silver-skinned ogress crushing his bones with deathly passion. Thank God I had slept dreamlessly that night.

The nurse waited for me to swallow the pills. Except for the witches' visit, my memory of yesterday was smudged, and I knew that at the very least the drugs would obliterate me again. With dutiful submissiveness, I swallowed the pills for the nurse, then went to the bathroom and brought them up again.

My gorge burned less with stomach acid than with anger at Willa for locking me in here and letting them drug me. All I had wanted was to be admitted and healed, not treated like a prisoner; and I was equally enraged at Dr. Chen for subjecting me to her alleged experiments. I mean, if the old ladies were right, who knows what stupid drugs she was foisting on me? But when I faced Chen later that morning at the lion fountain, I could say nothing to her about my anger. The words stuck in my craw.

"You look much better today," Dr. Chen noted. "I think we're closing in on the right combination and dosage of medication."

Gradually, I told her about yesterday's panic attack, but I still couldn't bring myself to say anything about the witches.

"Moonrise this afternoon is at five-seventeen," Dr. Chen informed me. "We'll see then if this medication is as good as the others at suppressing your climax response. If so, I think we'll have the chemical key to your problem."

"I can go home then?"

"Well, I want you to stay for a while, another week at least," Dr. Chen counseled. "Just so I can keep an eye on you for side effects. Not that I expect any. But these drugs are so new, it's best not to take chances."

As Dr. Chen talked, I saw out of the corner of my eye the two old witches in their lemony hospice jackets, tending to the other patients in the courtyard. They pretended not to notice me, even when they escorted their wards to the lion fountain and stood beside us. And it occurred to me then how easy it might have been for them to eavesdrop on my drugged and rambling confessions each day to Dr. Chen. The realization actually made me feel disappointed: So maybe, I realized, there was nothing remarkable, nothing psychic, about their knowledge of my relationship with the moon after all.

I wanted to ask Dr. Chen if the crones were really hospice workers or in fact outpatients play-acting some therapeutic role, but my voice, through some fierce inner reticence, refused to shape the question. And later, when I approached the old ladies directly, they told me with furtive shakes of their heads to go away.

For most of that day I watched TV without concentrating. All I could do was wonder what the hell was going on and who those hospice workers really were. I was still pretty muzzy-headed from the drugs in my system, but enough clarity had returned to make me question everything the old ladies had told me—and everything Chen had told me as well. I mulled over the hypnotic hold the crones had used to keep me from speaking about them to Dr. Chen. Still, I could not believe the old ladies were really witches, I mean, like the kind in fairy tales. But what *were* real witches? Anyway, I had seen the photograph of that lentil in my brain. I knew I was crazy. But crazy enough to believe in witches?

At five-seventeen I sat in Dr. Chen's office, ready to be smacked by another orgasm. But none came. A few mica flashes in the air alerted me to the glamour, and the doctor's ocher complexion shone from within, like a lampshade. I told her that, and she wrote something in her log, and said, "A dosage adjustment might help."

For the third time I tried to tell her about the old ladies, but I simply couldn't, which began to scare and frustrate me. The amulet they had given me was in my sweater pocket. I took it out and placed it on the table.

"What is this?" Dr. Chen asked with interest, picking it up.

Hard as I tried, I couldn't say anything about it, and I became more frightened.

"What's the matter, Siggy?"

"Nothing." I reached to take the amulet back, but as Dr. Chen handed it over, it fell to pieces, the grass twine springing apart, sending feathers drifting and a bone stem spinning across the polished desktop. A cloud shadow darkened the windowlight, and gloom coagulated around us.

"Oh, I am sorry." Dr. Chen gathered up the mess and handed it to me. "Is this something you made?"

I shook my head and saw a billowy paisley in the air, those tiny malefic visages with leathery, misshapen heads, hordes of them, swarming between us again like a cloud of gnats. I put the pieces back in my pocket and adopted a relaxed posture. "It's nothing. I just thought it was pretty. I think I can fix it. I'm going to sit outside for a while, if that's okay."

She watched me diligently as we parted, the haze of ten thousand sharp-toothed mummy faces arrowing behind me like a wake. I hurried to the TV room, swiped aside the tattered magazines from the reading table, and frantically began piecing together the amulet. All around me the menacing little heads burned against my skin like frenzied mosquitoes. They were growing before my eyes, sprouting clawed limbs.

Batting the devils away, I struggled desperately with the amulet. As I fitted the feathers and the bone shards into place and wove the grass braids into a knot, the demons mercifully retreated. A nurse entered and berated me, "Look here! What have you done to yourself?"

My ears and cheeks were nicked and bleeding—either from the demons, or maybe from my fingernails as I had frantically struck at them, I didn't know. I barely had time to pocket the fixed amulet as the nurse bustled me to the infirmary.

My scratches were cleaned, my fingernails trimmed, and I was lectured on my behavior as if I were an unruly child. I didn't care, because at that moment, seeing the Dracula shadow of massed gnomes cringing from me, I was convinced I had a power unguessed by my keepers. As soon as I was released from the infirmary, I decided I had to seek out the witches once more. There had been too many coincidences in one day to let things lie, and besides, I needed to learn more about who they thought *I* was. But they had already gone home for the day.

I had dinner in the dining hall and tried to convince myself that, okay, I was crazy. But maybe the witches were crazy too, and that being the case, maybe I should submit myself wholly to Dr. Chen. I compared myself to everyone else at the long tables being served by the working patients. No one here was actually insane. Those people, the real lost souls, who thought they could fly out windows or believed they were trees and didn't need human food, were fed in isolation in their rooms, sometimes with tubes. Among the people in the dining hall with me, I distinguished four types: the mad, who thought they were Jesus or CIA spies; the weird, who muttered rapidly and erratically while enacting private rituals with their food; the sick, who exposed themselves and masturbated in public; and the crazy, who appeared normal but were haunted by some error in their brains. I myself belonged to the latter, as did, I suspected, the bearded longhair with Christ's eyes who sat opposite me at table, eating silently and staring furtively at me.

By meal's end, I had convinced myself I needed surgery, not more drugs, otherwise I would go mad and start believing I was a witch myself and then maybe I'd go even more insane and turn myself into an animal or a rock and never come out. Already I'd crossed the line by my dependency on the witches' amulet, and that saddened and alarmed me by turns.

That night I dreamt I was a black leaf on a huge, storm-bent tree in a green dusk. The wind screamed across a rimland of smashed rocks and tugged at me. The cold cut. I couldn't hold on anymore. When I let go, I flew off, higher and higher, whirling and spinning madly, away from the whipped blur of the world and into the omnipotent darkness.

I woke with a jolt and sat up into a too-dark room. A hulking shadow shape slouched closer, and my skin prickled with the warm magnetism of an animal presence. Swiftly, I jumped to my knees in the bed and slapped on the wall switch. Overhead the caged bulb burned black as a ruby, and by that bloody light I saw my father standing at the foot of my bed, his features possessed of a crazed tenderness, like *I* was the corpse to be pitied. Then, with a hissing pop, the light flared out, plummeting us into darkness.

"Daddy?"

I stumbled around the small room, feeling with the amulet into every corner before I was sure I was alone. Then, believing the apparition had been a dream I'd carried into the waking world, I sagged to the floor and wept, sick with years-old grief at my father's death and so unbelievably angry at what had become of me and how that would have saddened him.

A sliver of aluminum light settled on the windowsill and began to grow. I watched till it stepped into the room; then I took my gown off and lay down naked before it so that it crept its slow silver inches over my feet and up my legs. My painted fingernails looked black, my pubic hair a goat tuft, and my fish-silver skin shiny. I was molting. At the instant the heatless moonfire touched my eyes and I gazed into the bright face of my lover with his shadowy beard, I changed into mist.

I rose and wisped through the window glass into a faultless night of star clusters and a mute moon in the glare of the prismatic streets. Like a vesperal breeze, I lofted above the city rooftops and could see below me drifting corpuscles of car lights and planet smoke steaming phosphorescently from sewer lids. Accelerating down the black river to the broad expanse of the sea, I saw moon-dented waters fly under me in a speed blur that left a platinum shine trailing behind, frosting away like a comet's tail.

Black as a piece of the night, I shot south through darkness to deeper darkness until my flight ended abruptly on a moon-soaked beach. A couple lay naked atop a blanket, asleep in each other's arms beneath the star-blown night. It was Frank with a woman I didn't know. At the sight of him, some ancient, dream-bound impulse drove me forward, and the lightning glow of my body roused him. He squinted up at me, gagged with fright, and belted out a mighty scream.

The woman beside him jumped awake, and I grabbed her face in a splayed grip of black nails and chrome fingers and shoved her to the sand. Her eyes rolled up, and she lay still.

As Frank scrambled away, I obeyed a savage impulse, leaped onto his back, and rode him hard into the surf. As soon as we hit the water, his flesh dissolved in a sparkling flash-powder gust, and I tumbled in the waves with his slippery, steaming bones, howling shapeless cries at the moon.

The next morning, the nurse found me sprawled naked on the floor and woke me by dropping the breakfast tray loudly onto the small table. "Medicine time, Sigrid."

I roused groggily, staggered into my gown, and swallowed the bright pills I was given. My body ached from my strenuous dream assault on Frank that night, and once the nurse left, I shuffled wearily into the bathroom, barren of emotion, and expelled the pills.

Willa and Marti visited shortly after my prebreakfast purge. They told me how good I looked, with a lilt in their voices usually reserved for small children and dogs. Without much gusto, I fixed my hair as plausibly as I could, dressed, and ate my breakfast while they plied me with stories about the various tiffs and love affairs going on at work. I shared with them my observations of the four types of derangement I'd observed, and I lied about how bored I was. Both seemed uncomfortable with just about anything I chose to discuss.

Though I wanted to, I couldn't say a thing about the witches, and I didn't bother showing them the amulet. Nor did I ask Willa about signing me out, because I knew that was hopeless, and I didn't want to make her any more stressed than she already was. Even without the glamour, I could see the fine cracks in the fragile bone china of her face, ready to break into tears at the slightest provocation. To my surprise, she held herself together through the whole hour-long visit, though I could too well imagine the emotional turmoil Marti had to deal with on the drive home.

I felt tired, but I didn't dare sleep. I didn't want any more of those obscene dreams, and I swore that if I didn't find the witches that day, I would take my medicine again, just so I could rest. During my morning session with Dr. Chen in the chill air of the courtyard, I saw the old ladies helping the longhair, the one who had Christ's eyes, back to his room. He had woken from some daydream shouting starkly at space, at nothing in particular.

"How very remarkable," Dr. Chen observed with keen interest. "First sound he's made in seven years." She marked the time in her notebook before getting back to questioning me further about my father and last night's nightmare.

When Chen was done with me, I set off to find the witches. But again they were gone. Angrily, I went to the front office wanting answers to a few questions. But, as had happened before, I found my voice unable to ask anything about the old ladies, and once more I shuffled away frustrated.

The rest of that day I spent playing a few listless hands of gin with a woman who kept consulting an invisible tally sheet. She was winning. I returned to the TV room after dinner to stand by one of the narrow windows that faced an alley running east into the night. I wanted to see the full moon rise. But it was coming up behind the buildings, and all I saw in the alley's ribbon of agate sky was its chrome glow.

Far away, a huge metallic door boomed ominously shut, and steely thunder rolled a long way out from an inner sky. But this time it brought no orgasm, only a dull fanfare of desire piping from a depth as distant as loneliness.

The sky brightened, silvering the glass and reflecting me looking careworn and rumpled in my torn jeans and sweater. A square-headed figure loomed up behind me and cast the broad-jowled, bristle-topped reflection of my father. I jumped nervously. No one was there but the usual residents, with their customary vacuous stares and skittish gestures.

From across the room, the woman I had played gin with earlier called out to me, "You know him? He never talks to nobody. You know him or what?" Her voice echoed down the hallway.

Pounding excitement nearly deafened me. Where my father had been, only his shadow remained, his precise profile standing as erect as a stark black cutout, a shadow cast by a nuclear glare. And weirdest of all, as I approached him, he got smaller. "Daddy?" I rushed at the shadow-cut image of my father, and he dwindled to a sootspeck, retreating into the distance of a skewed dimension where I couldn't follow.

I dropped to my knees, perplexed and hurt. Other sootspecks gathered in the air around him, clumping together and bristling like iron filings magnetizing to a new shape. A spidery form as big as a man and as writhing as the underbelly of a horseshoe crab shivered into reality, and fear blew me backward to my feet.

I yanked the amulet out of my pocket, but it snagged on my sweater and fell apart in my hands. I yelped and retreated three paces before the arachnoid thing was on me, its mouthparts biting one thrashing arm while numerous pincer claws snatched my other limbs and stabbed at my body. Screams of pain tore through me, and I collapsed to my back under the chitinous bulk. Deftly, it secured both my arms in its talons, and the abstract puzzle pieces of its face opened, exposing rows of tiny razor-sharp teeth and a gullet of countless rippling centipede legs. I wailed in terror and pain.

Hush, now, Siggy—hush—this behavior will only make mat-

ters worse. Calm yourself down. Relax. Remember me? Yes. I've come, like I said I would. I've come to help you. No trouble can touch you now. Relax.

I strained toward the moon's voice and saw the east window glaucous with moonlight. A man's rangy silhouette eclipsed the glare and bowed over me. Miraculously, the abhorrent monster-thing vanished and took with it my pain, leaving only the startled aftershock of a woken dreamer.

"Come on," the stranger said in the moon's suede voice. "Hurry. Get up before one of the staff sees you."

I sat up, my hands feeling for wounds that should have been there.

"You still think staying in this place makes sense?" the silhouette asked, squatting beside me on the heels of his crushed leather shoes. Lambent moonlight played on his face. I could barely make it out, but I could see that he had very soft eyes. "You should have listened to me instead."

Raven wings of hair loosely parted down the middle swept back from a broad, open face. My eyes adjusted some more, and I could discern further a straight nose and the small enigmatic smile of a Greek statue.

"From the way you've acted, you'd think I'd mistreated you," the figure admonished. "Haven't I made you feel good? Treated you like a bona fide *queen?*"

Even after he helped me to my feet, I just stood there gawking numbly at him. Was this, too, part of the waking dream? He wore pressed gray slacks with a plaited belt, a night-blue blazer, and a cranberry shirt, collar open, thin silvery tie knotted loosely. He could have been one of the shrinks, only he looked far too hip.

"Don't you know me?" he asked in that startlingly familiar voice.

The stranger's eyes widened beseechingly. And then I recognized him. Without the matted beard or the long hair, he appeared strikingly different than he had in the courtyard or the dining hall where he had watched me with Christ's sad eyes.

"You?" I exhaled with such force I practically choked. He gave me a chipped-toothed smile, and I stammered uneasily: "I thought . . . I mean, Dr. Chen told me you haven't spoken in seven years. And now—your voice—"

His smile fell off. "Ah. Well, I trust this won't offend you, but you've got it all wrong. The one who hasn't spoken in seven years serves only to *ex*carnate me, but in fact, *I* remain intrinsically myself—the man-in-the-moon, currently appearing before you as . . . the moon-in-the-man!" He grinned and opened his arms to show himself off. "Not a bad body. What do you think? Can you go for this?"

I shook my head, already stunned and wobbly from the harrowing hallucinations—and now *this* weird act. Were it not for his voice, I'd have run away. Having identified the man as the forlorn longhair in the courtyard, I figured he too, like the witches, must have learned of my lunar obsession from eavesdropping during all those outdoor sessions with Dr. Chen. I backed away slowly, but his exact mimicry of the moon's voice stopped me.

"Aw, come on, Siggy. Wake up already." His shoulders sagged, and he swung his head dejectedly. He appeared totally sincere. "What do I have to do to convince you?"

I glanced around for demons and saw them diminished to tiny black insects packed in the corners like grime. Several of the patients caged their eyes from the clean-shaven man, and the gin player slipped out quietly.

I turned back to the man, and I gasped to see an effulgent glow bathing him all over. At that moment a fissure opened inside me. Part of me, the part already made susceptible by the glamour, was somehow absolutely convinced that the moon had indeed come for me, "excarnated" into this unlikely soul. After all, those demon things *had* fled from him, hadn't they? And what was even more astonishing was that he had the exact same voice as the moon's.

Still, I clung to the last remaining shred of rationality in me, not allowing myself to believe that anything this strange could happen in real life. It could all be a hallucination. I felt simultaneously supported and mocked by science. And in the fissure between two such contrary feelings, there I stood, in this big, impenetrable knot of numbness and inertia—as if I had been plopped into the exact center of nothingness, suspended between what I imagined was real and what must really be real—I honestly could no longer tell which was which.

If this man was not the moon, I reasoned, then how come he sounded just like him, spoke with the precise inflections I had heard in my head when the moon spoke with me? Because, I responded to myself schizoidally, I was really hallucinating now and only imagining the similarity. But in the grip of my glamour—with the air all gelatinous with psychic energy and my heart still thumping—my reasons sounded flimsy indeed.

He stepped closer, and I edged away. "Okay, look," he said with some exasperation. "I understand how difficult this must seem for you, so I'll come down still farther. I will put all pride and distaste aside and hang around this hellhole until you wake up to the fact that I have actually come down here for you. But as you well know, better places exist to spend one's time on earth, and I'd like to get to one of them before too long, if you don't mind. I haven't got forever."

With that, he turned around and walked out of the TV room.

Within an instant of his leaving, the soot in the corners clouded into the air, singeing my flesh and burning my lungs. I rushed from the room. There, in the man's wake, the tiny demons seemed to break into even finer dust particles, and as I came up behind him, I was astounded and quite relieved to see no stain left in the air at all.

"You've reconsidered already?" he asked in that congenial voice of his, stopping and turning to face me with a look of mild amusement.

I pursed my lips. "Whoever you are, stop playing with my head."

His pale, boyish face contracted. "Oh, no, " he replied, wearily annoyed. "You won't let it go, will you? This whole rational act you picked up from your father—"

I began spluttering, and he raised both hands to stop me.

"Cut it out—please. You can't expect me to justify my existence to you. You don't even ask that of yourself. You should feel satisfied that I bothered coming for you at all."

"Wait a minute, Jack," I found my voice. "Are you really telling me that you're the moon?"

"No." He jerked a thumb to the ceiling. "The moon floats around up there. I consider myself the moon-in-the-man. I told you, I've excarnated. I've taken this body for my own. And I don't want to play with your mind. For your information, I want to play with your body."

I stepped back.

"Wait. I apologize. That came out wrong. I didn't mean to sound so crude. I haven't excarnated in over three hundred years, so I find myself a little off-balance. My bodily feelings seem so strong. I find you very attractive. I think I've gotten earthstruck."

The authority of his delivery, his total conviction in playing the part, blew my disbelief away, and I reeled back from him a few more steps. Instantly the demon vapors nipped at my ears. I found myself edging back to him, despite myself. "I don't even know your name," I managed to say.

He thought about this. "How about Lou, for lunar?"

I looked at his beaming face, and a little wedge of my former clarity made me face suddenly how far-gone this man was. In the neural dark, a neon shapeshow of diatoms and spirochetes closed in around me. "You're teasing me," I said, feeling suddenly at the brink of tears.

"Oh, please, don't cry," the moon said anxiously. "Forgive me. I apologize if I've acted flippant. Like I said, I feel earthstruck, giddy—excited that I actually made it and we can see and touch each other. But I've got to get a grip. Okay. You have a point: I should at least know my name. Yes, that would help me recognize my mortal limits, now that I have them." He grinned euphorically and slapped his chest. "You know, a lot of time has passed, and these appearances simply take some getting used to. Nonetheless, I agree with you. I have to act responsibly, like a down-to-earth human being. After all, I've come for you as a person—as this *particular* person. So let's see." He crossed his arms, closed his eyes, and put a finger to his temple. "Daniel Schel—a significant name, I think, given he does seem pretty much a shell. No resistance filling him up. He appears glad not to have to decide anything anymore. Died to the world in all but the flesh some seven years ago, poor guy. Tragic. Yeah—the Buddha got it right: Living leads to suffering. But let's work with what we've got. And what have we here? Some kind of academic, apparently—ha!—sort of the absent-minded-professor type. So absent, it seems, I find practically no mind at all. Rather Zen, except the wattage has gone way down. His mind has almost completely atrophied—wasted away from grief."

Daniel Schel—or the moon in him—seemed quite at ease and, I suspect, would have rattled on chattily if a nurse hadn't interrupted us to check on my vital signs, for it had reached the hour of moonrise. We had been sitting in the nearby lounge, the TV blaring Loony Tunes before a moribund presence of several patients. As the nurse was finishing, Daniel watched with a bemused expression and peeked over her shoulder.

"'Distraught,'" he read off the clipboard.

The nurse passed him a harsh look and strode off. It made me smile, despite myself.

"You do look distraught, you know," he admonished, crossing the room and turning the volume down on the cartoons, which elicited no protest from the other patients. When he sat down opposite me at the card table, he frowned worriedly. "Perhaps I should have presented myself more carefully. Maybe written first. What do you think?"

"What can I think?" I asked, genuinely confused.

"You know I've never had such a hard time convincing anyone of my true identity before—in times past, I mean." He smiled ruefully. "How different all of you seem this time. Always before, you know, women literally threw themselves at my feet. I hardly remember any of them ever looking me in the eye. And here you sit, boldly staring me in the face, demanding me to prove that I *exist!*"

"You realize you sound mad," I stated flatly. "Totally lunatic."

He reared back as if I'd slapped him, and for a moment I thought I saw a flicker of anger. But the next instant, his sad smile returned, and he laughed quietly at himself. "I think you've got my number, kid. The whole world has fallen asleep. To you and everyone you know, I can exist only as a dream—or else as madness. And so you just simply *can't* see me in the real world." He sighed. "How can I blame you? Your age placed men on the moon, and they found only rocks. Yet I have so much more than mere atoms in my life—just as you do. You have more to yourself than what the doctors can touch with their chemicals. I must find a way to reach you, to wake you up, to get you to recognize the real me."

"But why?" I searched his pale, honest face. "Why me?"

"Because you carry a piece of me in your head. How else could I talk with you from inside?"

"What do you mean?" I gaped. "You're saying this, this thing in my head, is a piece of the *moon?*"

He gave a warm, wholesome laugh. "No, no, not technically. Let's just say that this extraordinary piece of your brain that the doctors call an anomaly enables you to call the moon down. And here I sit. Without you, I wouldn't have had the ballast to come this far into the animal world. But now that I've arrived, I wonder if I belong. Existence down here has much more gravity. Everything seems far more weighty and serious than things do where I come from."

"That does it," I yammered. "I'm going to have to call the nurse if—if you keep bothering me. I mean, why *me?* Why are you *doing* this to me?"

He offered a thin, apologetic smile. "Every dozen generations or so," he explained patiently, "the piece of your brain that receives me recurs in some woman somewhere in the world, and I come to her. Because I want to. It offers me a different kind of experience. Usually, I have fun. But this time, it looks like I may not." He jammed his hands in his pockets and hung his head. "You happen to carry a piece of me in you this time. I'd hoped to honor you by taking you for my wife."

"Some honor," I mumbled, frowning. "It sounds to me like a marriage of convenience for you."

"I'll have you know, this tradition has an ancient and honorable history."

"Have you ever been rejected, Mr. Moon?"

"You want to reject me? Already? I just got here."

"Has anyone ever?"

"No. Of course not. I have the power—the glamour—it works for me every time."

"Well, what about this time—will you let me go?"

"Go?" His perplexity creased the bridge of his nose. "Why? Siggy, I don't think you realize how much I have to give you. You have no idea."

"Daniel—may I call you Daniel?" I asked solicitously. I ignored the wild plausibility that this man could genuinely be who he claimed to be, and decided to try connecting with his human self, his sympathy, the part of him that could relate to me. "Look, I don't know what you're in here for, but confidentially, I have to tell you, this really frightens me. It sort of reminds me of . . . John Hinckley and Jodie Foster, you know?" I sighed haplessly. "I guess I never realized how good I had it until this sickness happened to me. I was actually feeling sorry for myself a while back, working my ass off, no time even for a boyfriend. All I had were my skimpy plans for the future—and, of course, my mother, who, believe me, is not an easy woman to live with. But compared to this—" I just shook my head and looked for his reaction.

"You don't like my gifts?"

"Would it offend you if I said no?"

"I don't believe this," he said weakly, frowning and shaking his head.

He rubbed the back of his neck and stared at me with a forlorn yearning, tears glinting at the rims of his eyes. For an instant the balance of decision swung heavily in the moon's favor, and I felt a wave of sympathy, perhaps even desire, for this oddly endearing, vivacious man, with his unbearable sincerity. He wasn't, after all, bad to look at. But I caught myself. It had to be the glamour—or transference, Dr. Chen would have said—that was making me feel so receptive. I got to my feet, afraid to linger.

"Don't go," he called out.

"I can't stay. Please, don't take it personally. It's just that . . . I'm not myself. I haven't been myself since this whole thing began."

"But the full moon rises, carrying our powers to their peak. From here, we diminish—until the next new moon. Let's not waste this time."

"I'll tell you what. We'll talk in the morning," I promised, "when I'm a little bit more myself."

"More yourself?" He ran long fingers through his dense, black hair and exhaled with frustrated, wistful force. "You've never come closer to waking up. Don't let your practicality dupe you, Siggy. The universe has more to it than what you can grasp with reason alone."

"I'm sure," I humored him. I turned to go and was stopped in my tracks by the sight of more tiny devils blighting the corridor outside the TV room. "Oh, shit," I muttered.

"Come on," he said, getting up. "I'll walk you to your room."

The gangrenous revenants crowding the corridor parted before us, and we were able to proceed unmolested. We walked in silence, but strangely, it didn't feel at all awkward. Despite my resolve to have no more words with him, stray curious thoughts finally got the better of me. "What kind of professor are you—or were you—anyway?" I found myself asking.

"A failed poet," he answered lugubriously. "Does any other kind exist in this age? Poetry only comes out of failure, which means it comes from the soul, the part of ourselves made from all our failures."

I smiled. "I didn't realize the moon was such a philosophical fellow."

"Oh, you know, I enjoy reflecting when I can." He laughed at his little joke, and again I had to suppress an upsurge of sympathy for him, he seemed all at once so charming and eccentric, so utterly lacking in self-consciousness and yet so familiar. "But in fact these thoughts belong to the professor—well, I suppose that does sound like split personality disorder, doesn't it?"

"You see my problem?" I pressed, touching him with my elbow. "What am I supposed to believe? Are you Mr. Moon or Daniel the poet?"

He gave a ragged laugh. "Daniel and I have, let's say, enjambed. I really *have* excarnated as the moon-in-the-man."

"What does that mean—excarnated?"

"Incarnation implies coming into creation from somewhere outside. That didn't happen to me." His fathomless dark eyes glittered earnestly. "I exist inside all creation, like the other gods. We live on the inside, you know, eternal and changeless. And when we excarnate, we exist, for a time, *in* a time, here on the outside, here where everything grows, changes, and decays."

"If you're here," I asked, "who's up there?"

"You mean, who operates the tides while I excarnate?" His laugh clanged like a dropped tray of silverware. "You might as well ask who grows your hair while you do your bookkeeping. The moon as a rock takes care of itself. The moon-in-the-man does likewise."

His funny lucidity and the comforting timbre of his voice worked me over pretty good. How tempted I was to believe that this bright and curious man, with his beautiful eyes and classic features, was the moon! I had to make myself look at the piranha-mouthed apparitions hovering nearby to remind myself I was crazy.

"And did you fail as a poet?" I asked softly.

"Might as well ask if a surfer gets wet," he replied sullenly. I noticed that he alternated frequently between the positively funereal and the blithe. "This society demeans failure, you know? We recognize only success. Yet the whole universe fails all the time, Siggy. Yes, that remains the truth even in this modern age. Science calls it entropy. But we ignore that for the most part and identify with entropy's opposite. Call it progress, if you want, or evolution. Whatever you call it, our failures bind us. The weight of the sea constricts us to our blood, with its tiny cathedrals, each filled with the musical breath of—what? Life? What about life? It defies entropy. And its defiance stands alone and burns in a universe that can only grow colder. Life alone does not fail."

We came to my room, and he opened the door for me. "I'll stay up tonight and keep the beasties from your room so you can get some sleep, if you like."

"What about those old ladies?" I asked, watching his reaction carefully. "Do you know the ones? They made an amulet for me that actually worked."

"Nah," he said derisively. "You don't need their amulets, Siggy. You have the power to protect yourself—you just have to learn to use it." He seized my hand. "Come away with me," he added impulsively.

I withdrew my hand and backed into my room. "Not tonight." I tried to smile apologetically; inside, I felt limp. But there was no way I was going to let him know how much the glamour was prickling me with sexual desire or how much I wanted to pull this dream man into my bed. If he was really the moon, he would know anyway. But I knew, despite my desire, that if I embraced him, it would be for me tantamount to throwing in the towel, a wholesale embrace of my madness.

"From here, as you know, the moon wanes," he said tristfully. "Our power dims after tonight. Soon we will become too weak to fend off all these bottom feeders. This pit has too many of them. If we don't get out soon, they'll devour us for sure."

I nodded as if I understood and closed my door.

He blocked it with his foot. "Wait. Something you said bothers me." He glanced down at his shoes and chewed his lower lip. "You said I wanted a marriage of convenience. But I don't believe that. I mean, of course, without you, without the anomaly in your brain that brings me in, I couldn't know any of this." He gestured airily, then faced me with his boylike clarity. "So maybe in the past, I have taken slight advantage of my priestesses, my wives. But they all fully agreed to the deal. I always tried to recompense them in my fashion. Even the most moonstruck of them found it rewarding, to some degree. And I never abused any of them. Occasionally, of course, life on earth, in the changeable rush of things, superceded my interest in some of those women. But this time I feel different—something about you—and I say this with utmost sincerity—moves me. Perhaps only my fascination with this particular time in history astonishes me so. Maybe I've lost perspective. I don't know. But I want to think you feel what I do. Siggy, I—" his eyebrows lifted with amazement and ardor—"I think I love you!"

A snow job from the moon. I had to close the door quickly or the yearning in his dreamy face would have pulled me into his arms. For a long while I stood with my back to the door, breathing slowly and deeply, trying to steady the wayward venturing of my heart.

Over the next few days, with the moon rising well after sunset, my waking hours were free of the glamour or, as Dr. Chen called it, prodromes. I felt wholly normal now that my body was cleansed of drugs, and I kept purging what I was given. Sooner or later, I figured, Dr. Chen would realize what I was doing. After all, the nurses took samples of my blood practically every other day. I don't know what values they were looking for, but eventually, I assumed, someone would notice that the medication was not showing up in those samples. I didn't care. That would just be another opportunity for me to remind Dr. Chen that I was being held against my will and that I wasn't going to be an unwilling part of her "altruism."

Most of my time I spent in the small library reading romance novels. Postcards and flowers arrived every day, like clockwork, from Frank, who was coming back from his Caribbean junket in a week and was eager to see me. The salacious nightmares about him began again and persisted, night after night: always the same, with me causing him to shrivel to his bones and caressing his skeleton.

When the witches finally sought me out a second time, I had just awoken from a miserable night, and that was my first question: "Tell me," I begged, "why am I having these horrible nightmares?"

"*You* know," Drusille asserted abstrusely.

We were alone in the little library, except for a vapid youth to whom Glendil was reading Greek myths in a dusty shaft of afternoon light.

"Because I touched Frank with my glamour? But—it was an accident," I protested.

"Doesn't matter. He's hooked on you now and will stay hooked his whole life long unless you call back your glamour."

"Call it back? How do I do that?" I asked, alarmed.

Drusille cocked her large head. "You want to? I understand he is quite rich, and handsome to boot."

I sighed. "I know, I know. But the truth is, I guess, I don't love him," I said slowly, with admitted reluctance. I'd had plenty of time to consider the matter of becoming Mrs. Broughton, and the idea didn't appeal to me any longer. Not only because Frank was twenty years older than me, but also because, well, I felt unclean about how I had won his affection. And those dreams. . . .

"We can show you how to use your glamour," Drusille claimed slyly, "and how to stop the demons from feeding off it, too, which is what they do when you're asleep. That's why you have the nightmares. But learning to control your power will take some time, child. We must get you away from here first."

"You can't do that," I said frankly. "My mother committed me. And anyway, I'm not sure I'd even want to go with you. For days you two have ignored me, you know. I don't know who you really are. In fact, I'm cuckoo for even talking to you like this. It's delusional, you realize. We're *all* delusional. And isn't that ducky—we're all feeding off one another's delusions!"

Drusille scowled sternly. "We are wicce—as we have told you from the first."

"I don't understand any of that. I'm crazy enough as it is. And yesterday one of the patients tried to convince me he was the moon. Did you two put him up to that?"

The old women shared a luminous look. "He's accepted the vehicle," Drusille said, looking at me through a glow of awe.

Glendil rubbed her hands together excitedly. "Yes," she admitted proudly. "We thought that boy Daniel would be an ideal instrument for the moon. I mean, the young man wasn't using his body anyway, was he?"

"What did you do?" I asked with a twang of disquiet.

"Don't sound so nervous," Drusille said. "We didn't steal away his soul or anything as gruesome as that. We simply cast a spell that would make him receptive to the moon."

"There really wasn't much to it," Glendil agreed cheerfully, "because there wasn't much to him to begin with. The poor fellow didn't want to live anymore. I'm sure he's much happier now that someone else is doing the living for him."

I put my hands to my head. "Please, stop. I don't want to hear any more about any of this. I'm crazy enough as it is."

"Are you? We told you about the drugs, and you stopped taking them. Don't you feel better for that?"

I hesitated. "Yes, I do. Maybe Dr. Chen will release me soon."

Her mouth opened as roundly as a mousehole, and her eyebrows flared upward in a silent chuckle. "Aah! Dr. Chen will keep you here as long as she can. Haven't you read Thomas Mann's *The Magic Mountain?* You are unique, believe me, dearie. Don't let her abuse you anymore. Come away with us. Bring Daniel with you. We have a home in Brooklyn where you and your moon-king will be treated as the royalty that you are."

I declined—as politely as I could—though it was impossible to hide my uneasiness with these crones. As days passed, they increasingly left me alone. But Daniel sought me out every day—as I had hoped he would. We met each morning in the chilly courtyard. Mostly we talked about being crazy.

"We exist," he said one radiant day, always in that strikingly beautiful voice that made me feel so careless and wanton inside, even when I most resisted it. "So why can't existence alone satisfy us? Why must we also conform to some *idea* of reality? I mean, as materialistic as our culture seems, our society actually embodies the opposite—a landscape of glossy, mentalized surfaces—ideologies, politics, images to live up to, ideas, ideals, identities. Look, for example, at how our society embraces numbers. We *love* the idea that mathematics so closely fits the physical world! All our conventions and conversations, all our *thoughts* about each other and ourselves, cover over the actual world, the vertiginous depths of our physicality, our organic corruptibility, that terrible breaking down of the dead into the living."

As flattering as it was to be spoken to as if I had a *real* mind for a change, I tried to cut through his intellectual rambling, which, charmingly, he kept claiming was merely the frequency he had picked up with this particular soul. Between Daniel's story and the moon's, it was easy to get confused; their identities kept crossing, and I kept trying to separate the strands. It was Daniel's story, ultimately, that broke my heart. Personal history was hard to extract from him, because he tended not to think of his past as his own. But over several days' time, I learned that he was thirty-five, older than he looked; that he had been married to a woman named Jeanette, a political scientist who worked for the state; that their marriage had fallen apart when their only child, a little three-year-old girl named Chloë, died suddenly. And that it was Chloë's death that had plummeted Daniel into his relentless depression. Shortly afterward, he had "submitted to psychic entropy, to the soul's death wish"—that's how he put it when he explained how he wound up in the asylum. He had made a determined suicide attempt, very nearly successful, by slitting the veins in both wrists lengthwise.

"When the doctors brought him back," Daniel told me, lapsing in and out of the third person, "he refused to come out of his body, or as he began to think of it, to get back in. The horror had made two of him—his solid flesh, which still had to suffer the indignities of feeling, and his mind, which didn't want to feel anything ever again. He saw and heard everything but without paying attention. He stepped outside of his body a mere half inch—you know, to that blurred edge where you can hear without listening, look without seeing, exist without feeling. I found him that way. Here but not present. He doesn't mind my using him, and I'd even say he has cooperated. I feel good and comfortable in here."

When he got too serious, explaining himself to the point of delirium, I'd cut off our conversations and retreat to my room or the library. Yet even when we were apart and the glamour was far from me, I couldn't put him out of my mind. I missed his voice. He could have recited the phone book for all I cared. I wanted the massage of his chamois words touching me inside the way it did. I guess because that's where I had first heard his voice, deep in the raw dark of myself.

At night we would sit together in the atrium, with its geodesic glass roof and hanging plants. It was easier there for him, he said, than having to patrol outside my door to keep the demons at bay. As the moon waned and the nights grew darker, the demons kept coming, stronger each night, tar bubbles at first, with thistle-burr teeth, then bulging larger to vicious pug faces, hissing and clicking their pale red teeth. When I asked Dr. Chen about them, she talked dosages. And gradually it dawned on me—or was it that the witches had planted the seed in my mind?—that she had no concept of what I was actually experiencing. To her, I was just an imbalanced chemistry set, and what I needed was a proper neurochemical tune-up.

Even so, her precise rationality, her clever explanations of what my fractured reality was, seemed at times as compelling to me as what the moon had to offer. Sometimes I found myself praying to Marti's Virgin. I wanted a medical miracle. I wanted Chen to save me, for I felt as if I were slipping away from everything I knew, as if I had fallen into quicksand and she was the only overhanging branch within reach, my only link to my past.

Daniel and I began talking through the night. The nurses left us alone, and we stretched out on the lounge chairs under the tarnished stars and by turn dozed and chatted. Near him, I slept dreamlessly, and when I woke, the psychedelic patterns glossing the air close to us didn't look as menacing.

A few times I saw my father's ghost standing among the rubber plants, a clairvoyant smile on his beefy face as he nodded to me and gazed amiably at Daniel. I began to understand that, during those times I had seen him, he had not been there to warn me of danger, as I had first supposed. With growing certainty I came to believe that the opposite was true; at Dr. Pop's office, and then in the clinic—maybe he was there to encourage me, to urge me on. He was unmenacing, a benign, accepting presence, and I stopped being alarmed at the sight of him. He would look at me with such watchful eyes, his big hands gesturing calmly, as he had in life whenever I had to attempt something new and unfamiliar.

At first, when I saw him nodding to me from the spongy shadows, I thought he was telling me it was Daniel I could trust. But as I got to know the moon-king and saw what a gentle, truly guileless soul he was, I realized one morning that it was *me* that my father was assuring me I could trust. That thought was something I had to spend a lot of time pondering in my room. So it went, days and nights passing in an endless stream. I became anesthetized to time—so soulfully weary of hoping I'd ever get out, or that Willa would ever have the balls to take me away—until one day, in the space of a heartbeat, everything changed irrevocably.

That pivotal morning, I was, as was my custom, on my knees in the bathroom, jamming my fingers down my throat for the umpteenth time. I was so tired of it, and the absurdity of my situation hit me hard between the ears. What was I *doing* here gagging up my medication? I twisted angrily with frustration. Wasn't I clear about anything anymore, or was I just screwing around, wasting everyone's time? And who *did* I believe in? Dr. Chen? Those two wacky hags? Daniel, maybe. Certainly, the one I trusted *least* of all was myself. Since my fits began, I had felt betrayed. My own brain was screwing me over.

Lifting my head out of the bowl, I decided then and there I was going to throw my lot in with Daniel. What did I have to lose, anyway? I didn't care what the decision would cost me, or even if it was all a stupid reverie. All I knew was that Daniel felt good to me. The same rapture that I had initially experienced before coming to the clinic I felt whenever I was with him, and I didn't ever want to stop feeling it. It was better than drugs. Desire tattered my insides with its small lightnings, and each night with him had been like a smoldering orgasm that never reached climax.

That morning my torment ended, and perhaps began again on another level. But at least I had made my choice. I belonged with Daniel, whether to share our vision or our madness—it didn't matter which. Only our faith in ourselves and in each other mattered, whatever the price.

It was as I sat there on the floor thinking this to myself, right there in front of the toilet, that I heard the door to my room click open. I hurriedly flushed and left the bathroom.

Dr. Chen stood in the doorway, her dark face impassive, a green vein ticking at the side of her throat. "How long have you been flushing your medicine down the toilet?"

In my rapturous state, I thought she looked cat-eyed, her pupils narrowing to slits.

"Does it matter?" I countered.

She didn't say it, but I figured she was pretty damn upset— more because I'd trashed her data than because I might have endangered myself. I might as well have roamed mumbling through the wards of Bellevue instead of wasting Broughton's money and her time. "I thought you wanted to help yourself," she said tensely, the words glinting before me like broken glass. "I'm sorry it's come to this."

"I want to leave," I said.

"You can't. You're mentally impaired. Your care has been assigned to me and this clinic. And we are going to do everything in our power to help you—whether you cooperate or not."

She ordered me back to bed. As soon as she left, I waded to the closet, through leprous blooms of shadow, and threw everything I owned into my airline bag. I stripped off my nightgown and scrambled into a pair of black slacks, a brown knit pullover, and sneakers. But when I tried to open the door, it was locked. For an hour I stood by the window, watching the wind tear into scraps the steam from the street gratings. I was afraid to look back into the room, for the drumbeat of my heart announced demonic presences. The past few mornings that the moon had been up, the bat-faced devils had left me alone even after Daniel departed. The glad feelings left over from our hours together had seemed strong enough to protect me. But now I felt vulnerable, and I knew that cankerous tar-blisters ulcerated the air behind me. With gritted teeth, I fixed my attention as firmly as I could on the morning's jade light.

I expected burly orderlies to intrude at any minute and jab me with a syringe, and I fumed at myself for having taken so long to take my life back into my own hands. What galled me the most was that I had genuinely believed I was being more sane by staying in the asylum—like some animal happily led to the slaughterhouse.

The lock clicked, the door opened, and I hung my head, too angry to face them, afraid I would lash out.

"Let's go," a familiar voice whispered. Daniel stood in the doorway and waved me to him. "We've got to move fast now. Or do you think it still makes sense to stay here?"

My surprise cut through the last shreds of resistance, and I rushed to him and threw my arms around him. "Please," I mumbled through a sudden upwelling of hapless tears. "Take me with you. I want to get out of here."

I saw Drusille and Glendil pacing nervously in the corridor. Drusille signaled me to hurry.

"How did you find out?" I asked.

"The witches heard Chen calling your mother," Daniel said quickly. "Come on. I know a way out."

"Leave the key in the lock," Drusille said. "No one must suspect we are involved."

Daniel retrieved my airline bag from the room, and I followed him to the heavy door that led to the concrete stairwell. "Aren't they coming with us?"

"No, no. They'll help us more by staying secret."

Apprehension—mixed with a certain giddiness, I admit—fluttered in me as we spiraled down the stairs and opened the steel door that delivered us to the ground floor. The orderlies and patients we encountered paid us no heed, and grinning mischievously, Daniel took my hand, as if we were high schoolers off on a prom date.

With a buoyant stride, he led me past conference rooms and the dining commons to the kitchen. Breakfast cleanup had concluded, and the automatic dishwashers thrashed and hummed. The cooking staff in their white paper hats and hair nets toiled busily, chopping vegetables and stirring stewpots that wreathed the air with steam and the earthen smell of potatoes. We exited through a fire door into the renal stink of an alley and wended our way among massive trash bins stenciled in red paint, MEDICAL WASTE.

Daniel gazed up at the ribbon of sky with a big grin and outstretched arms. "You've returned me to the world," he said without a hint of sarcasm. "You brought me back from hell."

"Daniel, how can you say that? It's you who saved me."

"Equal footing," he said smiling. "A good way to start off."

He took me under his arm, and being close to him felt so natural and right that we practically jogged through the alley. At the street corner I stopped and looked back at the urine-colored brick of the clinic. Ghost rags flapped from the narrow tinted windows, just as I had seen them that first day. There was no doubt then that they were real, though I had trouble believing at that time that *I* was.

"Those poor devils in there," I muttered. "That place is just what you said—a hellhole. It's where they put us when we have only ourselves left. Even in prison there are comrades. But in there we were really and truly alone."

"One does not travel to the House of Hades lightly," Daniel murmured. "We trespass hell whenever we go into ourselves, either through depression, as with me, or by being snatched out of life like you, like Persephone. We go to hell whenever we seek our souls or they claim us for the home of their failures. What Joyce calls the monomyth, the sacrifice of the hero, appears as the great work of all who journey into themselves—into hell. Not that I see myself as a hero, except that the hero exists in all of us, for we all stand alone. This has been understood by every western culture since writing began with the epic of Gilgamesh. The solitary hero persists as a dream that dreams us whether we will it or not, that rises with us when we lie down, that enters when we leave."

I didn't know what the hell Daniel was talking about, but I knew he and I were saying the same thing. A simple truth, really— no different from what my father had told me a thousand times in his own way: that each of us comes and goes alone in this world, so we should at least have the balls to stand alone when it really matters. My father knew it, all right. He had faith in his own destiny. Me, I had made the mistake of wanting to be him instead of just being myself.

Arm in arm, Daniel and I marched briskly through the strong sunlight to Fifth Avenue and on up to Central Park so we could see trees in the real ground again. There was a snapping wind, and my teeth chattered—with cold or excitement, I couldn't tell which.

Along the way, the moon set. I felt the rapture fade away, but not my happiness at being with Daniel. It had been so long since I'd been held, I was enthralled just to be moving as one with him, hip-locked and loose.

Awash in radiance, Daniel looked beautiful. I don't normally think of men as beautiful, but in the sunlight, with his pale complexion, sable hair, and youthful features, he looked like a veritable angel, one of the beautiful fallen ones, graceful, clever, ambiguous, vulnerable.

Daniel talked about going straightaway to the witches' house in Brooklyn and having their coven, known as the Coven of the Shining Face, marry us with great hoopla. "These people live to worship me. They'll provide for us and protect us," he insisted. But I resisted.

"Weren't we just talking about, you know, standing alone?" I asked.

He tousled my hair and we stopped among a crowd of passersby outside Saint Patrick's. "In the dream of the hero, we stand alone. We'll all come back to that sooner or later. You can bet on that. Even so, I feel other dreams yearning as much—some even more—to live in this world among us. But all right. I don't want to argue with you on our first day of freedom. Let's live the dream of the solitary lovers for a while."

He leaned forward slowly, and I lifted my face to receive his kiss. Typical New Yorkers, the pedestrians barely noticed. But I felt myself floating upward in his embrace. It was a small kiss—dry-lipped, almost awkward. Its very innocence made me swoon. He tasted like sassafras, and the acrid sweetness of him lit me up like moonrise. The glamour set a corolla of prism streaks around us, and I came away from him with butyl-blue fire linking our breaths.

Daniel smiled at my astonishment. "The moon's down, and I'm—" I almost said "hallucinating"—"I'm seeing things—beautiful things," I told him.

102

"You carry the glamour with you all the time," Daniel chided softly, "but you only let yourself see it when the moon is up."

Jaywalking giddily through the fitful traffic on Fifty-ninth, we entered the park holding hands. Hurrying past the sun-dimpled water on the pond and along a gravel path, we reached the grassy slopes and climbed among black boulders. From leaf drifts, elf eyes watched us avidly. Sounds of laughter and dogs barking, like the lyric chimes of a dream, rang from the knolls below, where puppies and children ran with winking gaits among the rocks. Atop a stony bluff fringed with spindly trees, we found a secluded spot with just a couple of smashed beer cans and a nest of cigarette butts in the tufted grass.

For what seemed like hours, we sat there, looking at the clouds, laughing, talking. Eventually and inevitably, we made love. What was it like to make love with the moon? The whole while, he talked to me. He spoke in that music that was more intimate than any physical touch. I don't remember what he said—something about needing my receptivity and the darkness in me that held his frail light and other lovely nonsense. His thin, almost weightless body filled me with the most delicate happiness I've ever known. Sex had always before been such sinewy effort. But with him it was almost ethereal, the two of us joined in an electric current, a river-rush of life on the bed of the earth flowing with placid animal energy farther and farther away from the hopelessness where we had found each other.

When we were done, we crawled wearily into our clothes and lay in each other's arms staring about at the old, weary world. Gem-points of astral radiance sparkled briefly like midges among the tree branches and faded away. Directly above, blue space embraced us, looking as washed out as we were.

I could tell Daniel was confounded, stunned to be feeling sound and having tasted happiness after so long alone in the sky, in the wide emptiness enclosing his realm. That gave me a sense of fulfillment. The greedy desire that had possessed me days ago in the supermarket, the ache that had brought me here, was finally satisfied, but with a gentleness more powerful than any passionate paroxysm of my wild days. I saw the world at ten magnifications, every pastel in the bulbous clouds and every wing and leaf in the arterial trees jumping out at me. The elf eyes and retinal flares were gone for now. The world was furiously clear.

Striding down the grassy slope in the fluid flow of our joined bodies, I felt supremely connected with my own fatefulness, as if I had dreamed this as a child, even the knock of his hip and the thistle-points of light riding the wind. There was no doubt any longer that in my innermost heart, I had taken him for my husband.

Daniel and I spent the day in the park and then at the Met, easygoing as tourists, if a bit more furtive. I had, after all, not forgotten that we were fugitives of a sort. With one act, I had abandoned my past and with it, my mother. The future seemed entirely up for grabs. "Unguessable," Daniel remarked buoyantly. Yet I wasn't scared about that. For the first time in a long time, I was inexplicably happy. And happy was enough, for as long as it lasted.

Was it magic or madness that united us? As magic, our coming together meant our destinies were preordered ages ago, perhaps as far back as the first trespass of light in the blackness of space. As madness, we shared a delusion, but it was a wonderful delusion, a castle built of dreamstuff.

"Why not have both?" Daniel asked, his face serene and imperturbable. "Why not have it as a magical delusion? Magic and madness—they have an equality every anthropologist recognizes."

Either way, I knew I could lose Daniel in a flash if he ever wearied of being human, or sane. That was the only thing that scared me. Such as it was, the joy I felt being around him seemed all the more hard-earned and precious to me. I wanted to keep him for-ever.

"Will we stay together?" I asked.

"As the moon, I will stay with you forever."

"But—as Daniel, too?" I pressed, aware that I was asking questions I shouldn't be asking.

An expression of vague disconsolation troubled his features. "Who can speak for Daniel? Daniel submitted to his helplessness completely. He would have sat another seven years, an emptied husk, doing nothing, if we hadn't come along. For that alone, I admire the guy immeasurably. He rejected the tyranny of adjustment. He rebelled. Do you know what fortitude that takes? Rebellion alone makes authenticity possible."

"But you won't do that, will you—rebel against what we have now and . . . and go back into that black space?" I flapped my hands confusedly. "Even though—" I paused. "He *is* you, isn't he?"

"I prefer to think not," he answered slowly. He looked up and must have seen the crestfallen look on my face, for he added quickly, patting my hand reassuringly, "On the other hand, to live authentically, one must accept oneself however one finds oneself, right? So I suppose that the moon-king notwithstanding, I must embrace this excarnation wholly, as if this returns me to myself. From here out, I'll act accountably for it! Daniel and I as one."

I squeezed his hand gratefully. "Thank heaven," I murmured, resting my head on his shoulder. "To tell you the truth, trying to figure out who was Daniel and who was the moon was driving me crazy. I didn't know *who* was talking to me! And, I mean, I think I'm crazy enough. So this makes me feel a lot saner."

"Of course it does," Daniel said soothingly, stroking my hair. Then he lifted my face and looked straight into my eyes. "But watch out for the chimera of rationality. You know what I mean, Siggy? The insanity of sanity. Don't make what you call reality a hiding place from the unknown, a place to keep psychic pain at bay. For Daniel, for me, insanity, the terrors of loneliness, the unexpected, the unwanted became a place to live."

I lay my head back on Daniel's shoulder, grateful enough for his willingness to accept himself as a mere mortal. Mortal, I figured, was something I knew about. Mortal I could handle. It assuaged my fear of the mysterious powers that had brought us together.

At dusk, under a buttery tiger-striped sky, we met the witches. They were waiting for us behind the Met at the ancient obelisk called Cleopatra's Needle.

"Merciful Maud, everyone's in such a tizzy at the clinic," Glendil blurted. "Dr. Chen's notified the police. She told them the two of you fled as lovers." Her old face flushed with excitement. "Isn't this thrilling?"

"Reason enough to get off the street," Drusille advised.

We hailed a cab south to Brooklyn, the old ladies wedging me between them and Daniel sitting in the front, twisting to face us. The witches didn't smell pungently floral the way old ladies oftentimes do, but of something purple and dry, like desert driftwood, and I didn't mind being physically close to them.

The whole ride down, Glendil could not sit still. She squirmed and fidgeted in her seat, her hands aflutter. After a while she broke the silence with a quavery voice: "Your Highness, I think I speak for both of us when I say what a great honor it is to have you here among us."

"Please," Daniel replied with a laugh. "Don't think of it as a special honor at all. You see, I've come to live as a man. Just call me Daniel. And as Daniel, I say that you do *us* the honor of your hospitality. Where would we go without you?"

Drusille scowled. "You must recognize, Your Highness, that you have a responsibility to the coven and to your votaries to convey something of your godhood into this miserable world. I hope you're not serious about living as a man."

"Absolutely serious." Daniel shot me a smile. "This time, no votaries. No rituals and no rites. Let's try an existential slant this time, ladies. Something more modern, more twentieth century—okay?"

Glendil clucked disapprovingly and wagged one finger. "Oh, dear, no. I must agree with Drusille here. Without traditions, we'll be in the abyss before you can say heterodoxical thaumaturgy. No, no, no. You are the moon-king. To our ancestors, you have been the oak-king since the beginning of time. Siggy may call you anything she likes, of course. But we shall call you Your Highness."

"Whatever floats your boat, ladies." Daniel smiled beneficently.

They bowed before him, and he laid a hand on each of their heads. "You honor me, daughters of the Woman God," he said with mock solemnity. He winked surreptitiously at me. "Without you," he intoned, "I would have no earthly home or fare."

"That will never happen so long as our people thrive in your light," Drusille replied soberly and sat up straighter. "The Coven of the Shining Face has been your home since the times of the long hunt."

"And the Coven of the Shining Face will remain your home till time and tide carry the people out of this world," Glendil added with emotion, lifting her head, misty-eyed from the moon's benediction.

Watching this little show, I myself wasn't sure if I should also bow my head. I looked at Daniel, who was smiling like the Buddha and gazing out the window at Manhattan bleeding by in neon streaks.

"Yeah, the world has never looked more beautiful, or imaginary, or ever so deadly," he murmured.

"It is artlessy so," Drusille said, shaking her head. She turned her withered face from the window and looked straight at me.

"You must know, of course, my dear girl," she began, "what a great privilege and responsibility it is to serve as the moon's wife. There is much preparation, much to teach you. Are you even aware, for instance, that in the same manner that you are empowered to call down the moon to walk among us, you are also empowered to call other magicks to your service—astounding magicks that have the strength to change the world?"

"But I don't feel I have any powers at my service," I shrugged. "Whatever this glamour is, it just *happens* to me."

"So it seems at first," Glendil concurred. "Because you haven't learned the craft of it, haven't yet learned that the glamour can be used."

"Your chalice overflows, Siggy," Drusille remarked drily, laying a heavy hand on my belly. "Heavens. I can feel the glamour spilling out all over the place, quite willy-nilly."

"My chalice?"

"Also known as your sacrum, dearie," Glendil said. "The holy bone, the last bone of the spine."

"It's actually five fused vertebrae at the bottom of the spine," Drusille explained in her husky voice. "They connect with the pelvis and together make up the sacred chalice that carries the womb. The glamour is the flow of energy in your body, your life force. Right now, it feels to be blocked a bit in your pelvis, which is probably why it's discharging all those spontaneous climaxes and hallucinations."

"But don't you worry, my dear," Glendil smiled at me reassuringly. "We can teach you how to raise the glamour up out of the chalice and along the lance of the spine. And when the flux reaches the hilt of the skull, you will have the power to summon spirits."

"My God—do I *want* that power?" I asked, shooting an anxious glance at Daniel. "I'd be happy if you'd just teach me how to, well, keep those evil monster-things away."

Daniel, who was watching the dazzle of the city jog past, said nothing.

"If we are to help you, Siggy," Drusille interjected, "you must begin with a spell."

"How do you mean?" I asked innocently. Of course, privately, I was thinking, *Witches, spells, magicks—Jesus, they really mean it!*

"Here, now, think how we call you Siggy," Glendil said brightly. "But you once called yourself Sigrid, yes? You may think they're the same person, but they're not at all the same flow of energy, are they? Because your life moves differently around each name. Do you see? Do you see that what you name yourself changes who you are?"

"So, to prepare yourself, you must spell out who you are." Drusille's eyes, silver as an arctic wolf's, narrowed importantly. "During your sojourn with us, we shall ask that you write your hystery."

"My life history?" I hesitated.

"No, no, your hystery," Glendil corrected. "With a *Y*, dearie. Hystery is the psychic womb, where we go to be reborn. A witch is born not in the body but in the mind. You must spell it out so that we can see how you create yourself, otherwise we cannot really help you."

"Only remake you in our own image," Drusille sneered. "Little good comes from idolatry. We want you as you are, friend or enemy, not some statue of ourselves."

"After all," Glendil continued with a gentle smile, "it is not we who must marry the moon. It is you. And as it *is* you who will work your magicks with his glamour, you must define yourself first. Tell us how you think you came to this moment. Tell us as you believe it happened, not as you think Daniel, or even we, would want to hear it."

"I'm not sure I'm getting all this," I replied. "Drusille, you said 'friend or enemy?' I have no cause to be your enemy."

"Of course not, child," Glendil said with an encouraging squeeze of my hand. "In any case, that will be obvious later. You just concentrate now on your hystery. Everything will flow beautifully from that."

The two old ladies folded their hands upon their laps. And then, as quickly as they had begun their chattering at me, they stopped talking. For the rest of the ride to Brooklyn, there was no more mention of hystery or glamour or spirits, which made me feel even more uneasy. What had I walked into?

I kept looking at Daniel, but he seemed lost in a contemplative dreaminess, staring out the window at the night clouds and the sparse grains of stars.

Drusille began to give the cab driver a series of precise directions, and finally we pulled up to a pleasant, if poorly lit, tree-lined lane somewhere in lower Brooklyn, with rows of brick duplexes on either side of the cobbled street.

"It's a charming neighborhood," I remarked. "Which one is your house?"

"The Hause," snapped Drusille, handing the driver money. "With an A."

I glanced around, not knowing what she meant.

"Why such an interesting way of spelling it?" Daniel asked. He stepped out and offered a hand to Drusille.

"The name has come down through generations to us that way," the large woman said with evident pride. It was the first time I'd seen her brow unfurrowed. "The original owner of the site was a Dutch pirate."

"Jaki Gefjon," Glendil said in hushed tones. "Drusille's direct ancestor. He was a man-snake, you know, a headhunter from Borneo. Only half Dutch. It's his aboriginal blood that makes Drusille seem somewhat remote and pitiless sometimes." She winked and laughed into her hand.

Because of the trees, the Hause wasn't visible from the place where our cab had pulled up. A dense stand of yew, oak, and elm crowded the space between two ordinary Brooklyn structures—a two-family duplex made of brick and an old weatherboard colonial with gables and shutters. Across the street was a park, and the swatch of wolvish forest that fronted the Hause seemed an outgrowth from there.

Daniel touched my shoulder and pointed up. Bats jittered in the dark vault overhead, and an owl's query met us on the flagstone walk.

The witches waited for the cab to pull away before leading us through the trees. Around a bend of cedar and myrtle, a structure loomed in a colossal black crenellated hulk, like some great Gothic movie mansion. In the dim orange light of a distant streetlamp, and with no lights shining from within, it looked formidable indeed, mammoth and rambling. At other times, in the brisk light of day, it would seem much friendlier: an archaic blackstone building with brick cornices, huge bay windows, a gray slate gambrel roof with yellow clay chimney pots, and a widow's walk enclosing a glassed-in cupola and its half-eagle, half-viper weather vane, which later I learned was the wooden image of a fabulous beast called a wyvern. A greenhouse jammed with palms and boisterous blossoms connected the hulking stone front of the Hause to a smaller wooden cottage with a peaked roof and a turret. And behind that was a gardener's bungalow and a hedge maze. That first night, however, it was less a building than a chunk of black sky fallen grotesquely to earth.

The witches led us through the unlocked front door into a darkness that smelled of May blossoms.

"The greenhouse," Glendil informed us, lighting a glass oil lamp. "Its fragrance fills the whole Hause."

Daniel paused on the threshold and inspected the black wood elephant's head in the middle of the door, moving its proboscis knocker up and down.

As one might have expected, sandalwood and camphor resin flavored the air, dark odors to go with the carved chocolate furniture and the exotic clutter that appeared everywhere as the old women's oil lamps illuminated the foyer and the large front rooms. Persian rugs, boulle cabinets, porcelain flatware, red Venetian goblets, a white jade dragon, foxed mirrors, a seigneurial fireplace with a stuffed white owl on a black marble mantelpiece resided together in a jumbled resplendence, and filling half a room, a gamelan—a small Indonesian orchestra replete with bamboo chimes and snakeskin drums.

"Apart from the sacred brass of the gamelan's cymbals, no metal anywhere on the property," Drusille proudly announced.

"Disrupts the etheric fields," Glendil confided brightly. "Even the plumbing is ceramic."

Daniel, who had been peeking into the lacquered boxes and blown glass vials that crowded all the sills and niches, flicked his eyebrows and gave a small whistle. Even the moon-king was impressed.

A brick stove and its fired clay pipes dominated the center of the kitchen. Curtains of dried herbs hung in the window bays, and a white cat lay curled under the table. We followed Drusille to the sitting room where the primitive pieces of the gamelan stood atop a tiger's pelt, waiting for their turbaned musicians to return.

There, in a ritual silence, we were served tea in lacquered cups and nutcakes on delicate porcelain plates. Nothing was said. The two crones sat and watched us drink and eat with almost unnerving intensity.

When we finished our tea, the old ladies led us again, oil lamps in hand, first through a humid little greenhouse with miniature African idols gawking at us through the fronds. Then we exited through a glass door into the crisp night and followed a luminous quartz-gravel path that wound past a turreted cottage. "What do you have in there?" Daniel asked.

"The coven house," Glendil said. "It belongs to the other workers, our fellow coveners, who come here to help when the glamour is stronger than we can shape."

Walking slowly through the night shadows of stately trees, we came to the gardener's bungalow, its stucco walls scrawled with leafless vines. The front door had a round window and a latch and opened soundlessly to an odor of spring loam and old wood. The flickering lamps illuminated a square paneled room shiny red with varnish. Stools, sawhorses, and a venerable workbench, stained mocha from use, ran the length of one wall under a long mullioned window. From the rafters, assorted wickerware and splint baskets hung amid braids of dried herbs and bulbs. Along the other walls and beside a small stone hearth, neat racks of garden tools stood at alert—wooden spades, rakes, and hoes propped next to scythes and shears with razorlike edges of black glass.

"Here is where you will sleep," Drusille informed us brusquely, lighting a glass lamp on the workbench. "And where you will write your hystery as well, Siggy. There are futons and bedding in the closet, and Glendil and I, of course, will see to your meals. The bath is in the back."

The bath was a tiny hothouse of frosted glass containing a black ceramic toilet and a wooden tub with fired clay fixtures.

"The accommodations are humble," Glendil apologized, "but, we trust, adequate for His Highness on such short notice."

"And," Drusille said, turning sharply to me, "just remember— you are but a handmaiden now. When you complete your hystery, then we'll see to it that you get a place worthy of your new station."

"A place truly befitting the oak-king and clove-queen," Glendil promised.

Daniel acknowledged the witches' hospitality with a courteous bow, and the two women looked quite pleased. "There are writing implements in one of the workbench drawers," Glendil remembered. "And I'll see about getting you some decent clothes. The coven house has all manner of garments."

She stepped through the doorway cheerily and disappeared from sight. Drusille, however, gave me one last level stare, not unkindly, before closing the door behind her.

As soon as she left, I slumped into the nearest chair. "God, what a day! This is positively unreal." I spoke in semiwhispers, afraid the two old ladies were still lurking about.

"Does it bother you, staying here?" Daniel asked obligingly.

"Nope," I said with only the slightest taint of forced enthusiasm. "I'd be happy anywhere in the world with you."

He gave me a happy, lopsided smile. "Okay, then. I had to make sure. Those two ducks out there seem pretty queer—capable of anything. I just wonder what they made that tea out of! Tomorrow we might find ourselves in some huge compost heap, ripening to fertilizer."

"Don't say that! Haven't we been through enough already? Say you're teasing."

"Okay, okay, I teased you," he capitulated at once and hugged me. We put out the oil lamp and lay huddled together in our blankets on the futon, exhausted but too wound up to sleep or make love. After all we had been through, I could only feel, not fatigue, but a stone-calm watchfulness, as if whatever illusions once haunted me could return in an instant if I summoned them.

"The voice I used to hear in my head," I said aloud, tucking myself against Daniel, "he's not up there anymore."

His smile was a curl of incense in the dark.

"What is it like up there?" I asked softly.

In the quarter-light of the moon, Daniel looked surprised. "For the first time, you've spoken as if you actually believe me."

"Shouldn't I believe you?"

He paused and after a moment of silence said, "You know, down here, believing really depends on what we tell ourselves. I feel a lot happier as the moon-in-the-man than as mere and powerless Daniel Schel. No, the word *happier* doesn't even convey what

I feel. Secure. I feel secure somehow when I think of life as the moon. The moon creates me. It takes away all the emptiness of the last seven years, all the absurdity of what happened to me, and it makes it something new again, something wholly unexpected. Life before you came went nowhere, Siggy. Now it goes everywhere, out into the wide world, as far as the moon."

"And for the first time," I said, brushing his hair from his eyes, "you've spoken as if you might actually be someone other than the moon."

He breathed a thoughtful sigh. "You know, life as a mortal looked so interesting from up there where everything stays the same—but down here, in this world of freedom, we live in a world of pain. Simple and sad. In past ages, you know, the people worshiped and protected me from that pain. But in the asylum, God knows, I suffered. No one believed me. No one *could* believe me. And now, the love I feel for you goes hand-in-hand with my fear."

"What are you afraid of?"

"Losing you."

"You won't lose me," I said, as if I knew what I was talking about.

"You'd think the man-in-the-moon would have a heart of stone, having seen it all. And over and over, too." I felt him shivering in the cold. "But I don't feel like stone. I feel everything I didn't feel when I lived up there. I feel *everything*."

"So, welcome to Earth," I said with a laugh. "That's why you came down, isn't it?"

"Yes." He gave a self-deprecating little snort. "The moon has a heart of stone, but clearly, when he wants to, he can turn on his pewter smile and let down his famous silver hair." His face floated above me, pallid as foxfire. "I feel happy with you, Siggy. I've never felt happier—in any excarnation."

He hugged me exuberantly, almost with desperation. Deep into the night he held me and caressed me with his svelte voice, whispering about our life together. To him, we were a light crossing the vast continents of darkness between the stars, a love like the great rivers of sleep that carry us through the night. He spoke as if we would live and love forever. But beneath his words I could feel his heart pumping heavily, wary of that place where the moon lives in us.

The next day, in a morning that sparkled like wine, we found breakfast waiting for us outside, on an old stone table whose edges had worn thin like soap. Crisp green apples, hard cheese, currant muffins, and prickly-pear jelly were handsomely arranged on a cherry-wood plate and covered with a glass bell.

We ate as we walked about the yard, discovering exhausted flower beds, rose arbors, trellised grapevines, and rock gardens tucked among the hidden alcoves of the tall hedges that crowded the perimeter. The witches were nowhere to be found. I peered through the panes of the greenhouse, saw no one, and went around to the front door. The heavy booming of the ebony elephant's trunk brought no reply.

"Maybe they come out only at dusk," Daniel suggested in an accent from an old vampire movie.

"Silly," I admonished him. "They work at the clinic, remember?"

From the sidewalk we saw that the Hause was not visible at all. Trees and shrubbery easily hid the structure from passersby, for it sat squarely in the middle of a city block with no part of it fronting the street. It was as secret a place as could be found in the heart of Brooklyn, gained by a single stone path barely visible between the other enclosing and nondescript houses.

We meandered through the old neighborhood, inquiring among the people raking leaves and puttering in their tiny front yards about the two witches. Most of them knew nothing about the old women, and those few who were vaguely aware of the Hause thought it was a private sanatorium, or some kind of religious retreat.

At the corner we found a small grocery, and after pooling our pocket change, Daniel went in to buy a bag of disposable razors. I took a deep breath, found a nearby pay phone, and contacted the clinic. I was quickly connected with Dr. Chen, who informed me in the frostiest of tones that Willa had become so distraught at the news of my disappearance that she had had to be sedated.

"Just tell Willa I'm fine," I replied, with as much composure as I could. "And Dr. Chen? You've got to release me officially from the clinic, because I won't be returning there ever, ever again."

There. Done. I was about to hang up when I heard her urgent voice calling, "Siggy, wait! Are you with Daniel Schel?"

"No," I lied.

"Siggy, you're in very grave danger," she said, disregarding my reply. "You should know that the police are looking everywhere for him."

"Why?" My surprise made my voice sound like a quack.

"Because he was committed to the clinic by court order. He was supposed to be kept confined, but his depressed condition appeared to make constraint unnecessary—that is, until yesterday. He's a convicted killer, Siggy. Seven years ago he murdered his own child and tried to kill his wife."

My ear went numb. Dr. Chen's voice retreated to a faraway piping: "Please, I beg you, stay where you are and call the police immediately—" I hung up the phone but had to hold on to the receiver to steady myself.

Daniel emerged from the store marveling at the variety of disposable razors he'd found inside. But when he saw my pallor, he went silent. "What happened?" he demanded.

At first I didn't want to say, but he wouldn't let it go, so I ended up confessing everything. He listened impassively, without saying a word, then walked to the street curb and sat down.

I sat beside him. "So—is it true?"

The wounded look he gave me punched my heart. "What does your second sight say?" he asked bitterly, almost sneering.

"I—I don't see anything—" I stammered.

"Then look harder," he spat back. His whole face had darkened and looked cloudy and bruised.

Shock reverberated painfully in my chest, and I exhaled sharply. "It's true, isn't it?"

He nodded and hung his head between his knees. I thought he was going to throw up. "Yeah, you heard the truth. I killed Chloë," he whispered. And then louder, "I killed her."

"I can't believe that."

"Believe it. A jury did," he said sourly.

My stomach winced. When I tried to look into him, I saw a ripping fire. Through the veil of flames a face appeared, a smashed, hypoplastic baby-doll head and bits of brain and skull flaring like sparks. I snapped my stare away.

"Why?" I asked hotly. "For God's sake, why did you do it?"

He hugged himself and rocked. "You don't think I haven't asked myself that for seven years? I still don't know."

Sickness hurled up in me. I locked my jaw and waited for the nausea to pass.

Daniel watched me mournfully, with Christ's tristful eyes.

"Okay, you want to know what happened?" he finally managed to say, almost mumbling. It was the closest I'd seen him get to the old Daniel, except that now his pale skin was blotching red. "You want to know? Fine. I'll tell you. Yes! I killed her! But by accident, okay?" He sagged and sat down again, looking bleary. "Yeah, but why should you believe me?"

I reached out and touched him on the shoulder. Reflexively, he began to yank away, but he stopped himself and let my hand stay where it was. After a while he spoke again, his voice softer, again as silver-toned as the moon's.

"We had a thing, my kid and I, where I would call her name—Chloë—and she'd come running to me and I'd hoist her onto my shoulders and whirl her around till we got so dizzy we couldn't stand up straight. She . . . loved it. So, one day we met in a restaurant, and we did it, like we had a hundred times before. Only this ceiling fan whirled above me. I hoisted her up—"

He stopped, his face closing like a vault.

"I believe you, Daniel," I finally heard myself say. "It was an accident."

I thought perhaps he hadn't heard me, for he didn't move except to close his eyes. "Don't, Siggy—just . . . don't say anything till I've told you all of it." He pushed his hair back and pressed his fingers against his temples. "Jeanette—my wife—she saw the accident happen. She'd brought Chloë and her new boyfriend to the restaurant—and then I came in. After years of pretty vicious arguments, we'd separated the month before." He bit his lower lip, and his dark eyes squinted. "She went crazy with anger, thinking I killed our kid just to spite her. She came at me wildly with her fists. Somehow, I don't know how, I knocked her down. She hit her head on the side of a table and didn't come around for two days. The police charged me with the negligent homicide of my daughter and the attempted murder of my wife."

Daniel's words floated like iridescent smoke in the air, and everything around him seemed to pop out in weird relief, the pocked curbstone, the clown-tatters of garbage in the gutter, and the high, crazy cirrus clouds overhead. The world isn't a fair place, I thought to myself. It deceives us into thinking we have some control over our lives. What a fraud. "Come on," I said with a sigh, picking Daniel up and helping him walk slowly back to the Hause. After that there was no stopping him. He talked maniacally, relating all the incriminating details of his crime. Apparently, he and Jeanette were notorious on campus for their mutual infidelities and their boisterous fights. Chloë had been frightened by their arguments. When he met her and Jeanette by chance in the restaurant, it was to reassure his daughter that he had called her to run to him.

Jeanette and the prosecutor claimed Daniel had killed the child in an act of grotesque spite disguised as an accident. Several faculty members summoned at the trial witnessed that he had, during drunken bouts, questioned Chloë's paternity publicly. And it didn't help that a year earlier he had set up an investment to pay for Chloë's college expenses by taking out a hundred-thousand-dollar insurance policy for her.

Daniel had adamantly refused to plead down to manslaughter. It wasn't until the jury found him guilty of murder that the demons started tearing him apart. He began to doubt himself. Who, after all, *had* lifted the child into the whirling blades? Hadn't he seen the low ceilings when he walked in, and the blades whirling? What about the blur of the blades at the edge of his sight, the peripheral movement? Was he *blind*? The questions tormented him.

Of course he was blind, he realized. In his petty fury at his wife, he could see nothing. Who had thrust Chloë into the spinning shadow? Who had stood there with the ruby splash of her blood across his face, and then held the thrashing child's body as her soul fought its way free? Whoever that being was later tried to open his veins. And when that failed, that part of him died slowly nonetheless, in a way so deliciously acrimonious that it left his atheist heart burning with fear and rage and ardor before the evil intelligence of the universe.

Maybe he had wanted to kill her, Daniel began to believe. Maybe, in some primitively unconscious way, she had to die because she was not his. Blood fury had killed her and then had turned on him, wanting to bleed him dead. His survival struck him as the final stamp of disapproval from God. "Yes, God," Daniel declared bitterly, spitting out the word like a curse. "If such a wicked intelligence exists to damn us, then there just has to exist some context, something holding it all together, the good and the bad, the living and the dead. There must prevail a God for whom time equals space, a God who contains not only the evil intelligence but also the grief, the brutal indignation, and the forgiveness that the existence of evil necessitates. Doesn't that make sense?"

Through his rambling monologues, I learned that Daniel's father had been a welder, his mother a homemaker and charity worker. Both had been killed in a rear-end collision braking for a dog when Daniel was seventeen. They had been Quakers—Friends, they called themselves—who believed each individual had a personal relationship with the maker of worlds. Their silent, contemplative worship had seemed to Daniel unadorned, dull, and empty calls to witness—until he found himself on the floor of the pit.

While the stitches were still in his veins, like blue centipedes on the insides of his arms, he surrendered to the silence that had given his parents strength. It carried him away from those who wanted to judge and punish him, and it delivered him to the only one who could, the one who passes greater judgment on the living and the dead. In a court of emptiness, before a jury of silence, he met his maker, not in a power, a presence, or some cause from his inmost heart, but in an absence, a void big enough to carry all continuing existence and precise enough to fill every vacuole of memory, each particularity of smile and gesture that he remembered of Chloë.

That was how he talked about it, becoming more professorial as he calmed down, until he was quoting Keats, "'Call the world the vale of Soul-making. Then you will find out the use of the world.' Suffering—that constitutes the truth of our being and our perishing. The Buddha's first noble truth again: Life means suffering. Hah! Quite an ignoble revelation, don't you think? To go on, we must take that evil inside and transform ourselves literally into the hero with the eyes of the dragon. Someone capable of good *and* evil. Only then can necessity and desire come together."

Sometimes he began to rant, and there was nothing I could say or do to help, except to remind him that he was the moon—cool and serene in his remote station. The day all this was revealed to me, however, that day on the curb, we made a pact that nobody else would know his past, and certainly not the witches. Consequently, after several days of private distraction, of talking furtively of Daniel's past, the witches were visibly upset that I hadn't started my hystery yet. Glendil managed to siphon off some of Drusille's ire with comments about how well I looked and how excited the other coven workers were to hear of our arrival.

To appease them, I promised that I would begin writing at once, and the old ladies left us alone.

Hemmed in by the police on one side and the witches on the other, Daniel and I grew into a special, secret sharing, plotting our freedom and our destinies together with quiet fervor.

"What will the police do to you if they find us?" I asked him one day.

"Lock me away, I suppose—after the usual stupid psychological evaluations." We sat together among the leaf litter beside a stone sundial. "Darkness and unrelatedness occupied me for so long, Siggy, I got to believing I had no future. I saw many truths in that darkness. But I didn't think to preserve them, and like dreams, they disappeared. I lived just to live, inside my own prison—until you came. Now, trying to justify my happiness, I can't. I've seen deeper into my life than I thought my life went."

He crouched like a fugitive, his boyish, perfect face looking austere and baleful. "Beyond crime and illness, beyond pathology, exists a deeply buried unconscious power. It got hold of me, Siggy—and it killed me inside. And then it made me alive again. But as someone new, someone really new, and in a completely unexpected way. I can't figure it, even though I have words for what I think happened. Sin without guilt just took over my life. Simple and frightening as that. I got evil. Or it got me. That power held me for seven years. God stared me in the face and wouldn't blink and wouldn't let me blink until I finally understood the claim of my sin. I had killed Chloë."

He squinted at me to see if I was following him, and though his face caught the sun full on, he looked vexed with shadows. "Evil persists as a tangible and real substance, I want to say that, if nothing else. It killed my Chloë—and I acted complicitly, I helped it." He leaned closer, urgently wanting me to understand. "Evil surrounds us not just as an absence of light, Siggy. I learned the cruel way that evil remains tangled up somehow in the light, a dark side which we've got to extract from the light of our lives, from our happy moods, our good intentions, our hopes, and especially from all that we love. And so I learned Buddha's second noble truth. One can love too much."

I remembered Willa and her craziness after my father died. "Yeah, but you can't always help whom you love, or how much."

"No, I guess not." His dark eyes seemed to collect illumination, and he blinked back tears. "Look at me. Have you got a tissue?" He shook his head apologetically. "I get lost too easily in the largeness of the heart."

As Daniel and I grew closer, my tutelage as a witch began in earnest. Every night, Drusille and Glendil would sit me down and lecture me on the fine points of the spirit world and of the healing powers in the female chalice.

"Perhaps the moon should tell Siggy about the first sorcerers," Glendil said to us one evening, after she and Drusille returned from their work at the clinic. Drusille joined us at the workbench, nibbling at the steamed fish and the beets and radish salad they had presented to us, while Glendil crouched at the hearth, making tea. "Your Highness, would you?"

Daniel demurred with a mild shake of his head. "I'd prefer she hear it from you. As the moon, I never had much interest in those stories."

Glendil straightened up and gave a slight curtsey. "The first sorcerers—a wonderful story. Siggy, dear, you come from a noble lineage. Do you know why there are twenty-four hours in a day?"

I gave Daniel a perplexed look, and he nodded for me to listen.

"The same reason there are sixty seconds in a minute and as many minutes in an hour," Glendil answered. "Time, as we measure it, is a Chaldean conceit. You do know who the Chaldeans were?"

I shrugged.

"The Semitic people who ruled Babylonia about three thousand years ago," Daniel replied for me. "Great people. They had a real sense of pomp. Made a god feel at home."

Drusille's heavy face nodded. "They were the first magicians— the first really powerful ones, you know. The spells they cast then are still working today. Numbers. Time. Money. The alphabet itself. Those are just four of their spells, spells so fundamental you don't even think of them as magicks, do you?"

"Money? Time? You mean, they're magic?" I asked. "I always supposed they were inventions. You know, the fundaments of civilization."

"Oh, indeed, child. Oh, indeed."

"Civilization *is* Chaldean magicks," Glendil said, turning from the hearth with a tray of fiery blue teacups, which she placed on the worktable. "They conjured up the whole thing, and it's been running ever since."

"Gosh," I said, making an effort to convey how impressed I was even though I wasn't sure I understood.

"Ladies, you should tell Siggy what you mean when you say they conjured it up," Daniel remarked nonchalantly.

"Quite so," Drusille answered as Glendil returned to the hearth for the kettle and the biscuits. "You see, Siggy, they summoned these powerful ideas from on high, grounded them in human terms they could easily manipulate, and created the basis for what we now call civilization."

"Summoned from on high?" Daniel inquired with a skeptical flinch of an eyebrow. "I know what you mean, having lived up there, but I really think you should spell it out for her."

"Forgive me, Your Highness, I will try," Drusille said humbly. "From on high, Siggy, means from the celestial sphere." She pointed a knurled finger to the raftered ceiling. "You see, we don't really create anything with this mush we call a brain. The brain is only a receiver, like a radio or a TV. All the original ideas come from up there, from the vast sea of electricity that is the universe." She looked for approval from Daniel.

"Still sounds a little farfetched," he said gently. "Can you clarify that?"

Drusille turned and loosed her stentorian tones at me again. "We realize to most people nowadays it sounds implausible, because most of our age's greatest minds believe the universe is shaped by gravity. But sad to say, from Newton to Einstein, they've gotten it wrong. All wrong! Gravity is far too weak to have shaped the galaxies in the short time that the universe has been around. Electricity is many times stronger than gravity, ten to the thirty-ninth power stronger. You know about exponents, of course?"

I nodded vaguely, trying to visualize a number with thirty-nine zeroes after it. I noticed my palms were sweating; I felt like I was in school again and wasn't sure I'd done my homework well enough.

"Forgive Drusille's condescension," Glendil said, pouring from a devil-red kettle a tea as yellow as Chablis. "It's simply that she's figured it all out. No more mysteries for her."

"And you?" Daniel asked Glendil.

"For Glendil there is only mystery," Drusille answered crabbily. "Isn't that right, darling?"

"Yes, quite right, Drusille, dear." She sipped from her cup using both hands like a geisha. "My feeling is, what can we possibly know about anything, skullbound as we are? We think we know about electricity, or the glamour. But our senses detect shadows only. Far more of the real world exists than we sense or will ever encompass with our knowledge. Just think of the neutrinos, for instance. Billions of those ghostly little things whooshing right through us each second. And who even heard of a neutrino when we were children?"

"Ah, but existence has order," Drusille countered heatedly and leaned her large frame forward to pass us each a cup of tea as fragrant as laurel flowers. "The creative order is exquisite, and in any part we may see the whole."

"A fevered dream, Drusille," Glendil reproved. "A chimera of an analogue with precious little precedent."

Drusille sighed laboriously and regarded us with obvious exasperation. "You mustn't think we brought you here to witness our lifelong debate. In fact, we shouldn't be having this tedious discussion at all in the presence of deity. Forgive us, Your Highness. We thought it might help, you know, with the hystery."

"No harm in her knowing there is no preferred philosophy in the Hause," Glendil chirped. "We have our opinions, but we are not dogmatic. And I dare say, with the strength of your glamour, you'll be teaching us a thing or two before very long."

Another night was spent lecturing me on the three worlds. We were in the kitchen of the Hause, baking that day's loaf of bread.

"Most mythologies know about the Storm Tree," Drusille began, kneading a lump of black dough beneath her crooked fingers. "It has three stations: its celestial branches, its hellbound roots, and its trunk, which braces us here in Middle Earth."

"Tell her who lives in the branches and the roots," Glendil suggested.

"Very well, then." Drusille loosened the collar of her blouse as the warmth from the lit oven fluffed around us. "As you now know, Siggy, we are living inside a five-thousand-year-old spell cast by magicians who knew how to call angels down from the sky and learn their secrets. The spell that they cast is called civilization. What concerns us here is this: Will the moon's wife use her power to preserve this spell or to break it?"

"To *break* it?" I interrupted, unable to see myself wanting to destroy civilization, but Drusille hushed me with a raised, gnarled hand.

"The question is entirely rhetorical, my dear young lady," she said. "You actually have no choice, Siggy, because your body has already decided for you."

"It's an antenna that's tuned to the spirit worlds," Glendil said fervidly. "It receives signals—but only from *one* of the worlds, either from the chthonic powers that have borne life out of the earth or from the celestial beings whose ideas rain down from above."

"Classical dichotomy," Daniel noted with a distracted, pedantic air. "A zoetic flow from below and a psychic one from above."

"Now, wait a minute." I looked at them incredulously. "What you're saying is that . . . is that the two of you are antennas?"

"Everyone is," Glendil replied matter-of-factly.

"Though few know it," Drusille said. "Far fewer still have the receptivity you do."

"You are gifted, Siggy," Glendil smiled kindly at me.

"Or you are cursed," Drusille added, looking at me sharply. "It is entirely a matter of perspective. You see, child, either your receptivity will help civilization or it will help to destroy it."

"And that depends entirely on which of the two spirit worlds your body is tuned in to," Glendil continued with her back to us as she opened jars of tea and lined up glazed blue mugs. "The sky spirits are electrical beings who live in the ocean of electricity above our heads."

"You mean the ionosphere?" Daniel contributed, playing with a lump of Drusille's dough with his fingers. "The solar wind creates it by knocking loose electrons from the atoms of air up there and generating a charged plasma."

"Bigger than the oceans," Glendil said, turning about and opening her scrawny arms to encompass a great magnitude. "And possessing tides, currents, and eddies, just like our oceans. Only this ocean is made of electricity, and creatures have evolved in it, just as we evolved in our primordial seas."

"Up there," Drusille glanced at the ceiling's groined vault, "at the edge of the void, where the stars never set, there is an ocean of light that connects all the worlds."

"Up there the universe is a vast living entity," Glendil affirmed. "Electricity binds it all together. Including us, because we, too, are electrical beings—"

"Muffled by our flesh," Drusille ammended, opening the oven door and shoveling in the raw loaf. "Our consciousness is mere microvolts in the paste of our brain."

"But voltage nonetheless," Glendil piped in. "We hear the electrical beings in the seas of lightning above us. Our forebears called them angels. We prefer to call them seraphs."

"After the seraphim," Daniel told me, "the highest rank in the celestial hierarchy."

Glendil nodded in gracious agreement. "They speak to us as ideas. We think the ideas are our own. But they are, in fact, received out of the air by the complex antenna we call a nervous system."

"Of course!" Daniel erupted excitedly. "That explains all the famous simultaneous discoveries in science, like Leibniz and Newton, who got the idea for calculus at the same time."

"The Chaldeans were the first to grasp this truth that we are antennae," Glendil noted. "Initially, they used the seraphs for religious purposes, abstractly—you know, astrology, numerology—divination. But eventually, under the seraphs' influence, they invented geometry and mathematics. In time they applied what they were learning from the seraphs to architecture, agriculture, metallurgy—"

"Or why there are sixty seconds in a minute and as many minutes in an hour, as we have already explained to you, Siggy," Drusille said, her large face aquiver with passion. "The sky spirits made it clear to the Chaldeans that their magicks work in twelves. And their magicks are still working to this day. We can see their twelves all around us if we but look. We break time the way they did. We cut the circle, the sky, and the year into the same multiples of twelve they did."

"The spirit powers occupy us," Glendil added. "We are but caught in the middle, dear Siggy."

Daniel nodded. "This doesn't sound any stranger to me than some of the stories science feeds us—like, say, the Big Bang, or that we evolved from fish. You know, the answers the ancients searched for, science has answered—but nobody remembers the questions."

"What about the underground spirits?" I inquired. "Are they like demons?"

"No, Siggy," Glendil said through a giggle as she poured the tea. "Heaven and hell exist exclusively in our hearts. The beings who live in the earth are not supernatural but electrical, like the seraphs. There are great magnetic and electrical fields in the molten rock below our feet, you know."

I shook my head.

"They simply make up a different breed of electrical beings," Drusille clarified. "They occupy us not with ideas, like their sky cousins, but with visceral feelings. They are passionate entities."

"Somehow," Glendil spoke as she cleared away the mixing bowl and baking utensils, "the subterranean spirits are involved in the physical evolution of our planet's life. We don't understand exactly how. But they are the great form builders, and people have sensed them around us from the beginning. We call them the elven. Others call them the faeries. Or elementals. They're not much for sharing thought forms. But their vitality—their influence in the physical world—is astounding."

"Now, here's the thing, Siggy," Drusille said, drawing up a chair and sitting down near me. "The elven are furious. Mad as hell, in fact. The civilization that the Chaldeans conjured up has gone wild and is destroying all the forms they, the elven, built, wiping out whole species, threatening the entire life-net of the earth."

"Every day there seems to be some new tragedy with the ozone, the oceans, or the rain forests," Glendil said as she picked up and sat on a stool beside her companion. "Civilization is destroying the earth. And yet, if the Chaldean workers still extant in the world can call down sufficient sky spirits, perhaps there will be powerful new scientific breakthroughs that will save us."

"Like fusion," Daniel speculated. "Clean, cheap energy and an end to poverty and pollution. And gene splicing to create new foods and exterminate disease."

"Or a new, more terrible weapon that will hasten our extinction," Drusille countered. "The sky spirits are too concerned with the interplay of galactic energies to care one way or the other about our tiny fates."

"Not so much impersonal," Daniel ruminated, "as transpersonal, I take it."

"Exactly," Glendil said. "Siggy here has the gift to call down from the sky or to call up from the earth powerful and indifferent forces."

"Which is it?" I asked. "Seraphs or elven? Or is it both?"

"It's never both," Drusille answered flatly. "You will conduct into the world either new ideas or new vitality."

"Which do you conduct, ladies?" Daniel wondered.

Drusille laid a warped finger to the side of her thick nose.

"That is our secret. And we won't tell you or Siggy, not until you find out who *you* are."

"Why?" I asked anxiously.

"Because there are enemies around," Drusille said, fixing me with a lidless gaze of righteousness and rapping a knuckle on the tabletop. "Beware of them. Do not trust *anyone*—except the moon, of course." She tersely bowed her head to Daniel. "You are in grave jeopardy, Siggy, until you find out what powers you conduct and ally with them."

"Ashera Ferialle," Glendil said in a theatrical hush. "Remember that name, child. She is our opposite and our most dire enemy at this time. She brews her own poisons and is vehement enough to sneak or burst in here and ply them on Drusille and me. Beware of her."

"Where is she?" I asked.

"That's just it," Drusille bemoaned. "She lives under the city, in abandoned tunnels and sewers. She can emerge anywhere, anytime, bristling with her poison thorns and goofer dust."

"Watch out for the goofer dust particularly," Glendil warned. "It's a fine powder of hallucinogens. She squirts it in people's faces from bat bladders and knocks them out of their bodies."

"Turns them into zombies," Drusille moaned. "Without intercession, they'll wander mindlessly for days."

"How will we know her?" Daniel asked, perking up with interest.

"She looks like she escaped hell itself," Glendil answered.

"That merely sounds like half of New York," Daniel laughed.

"You won't sound so giddy when her poison scalds your blood," Drusille spoke sternly, then caught herself. "Forgive me, Your Highness. Ashera Ferialle is our most fierce and ruthless enemy. I fear for you."

The four of us stared in silence at one another. A sense of threat hovered in the redolent air of baking bread.

"Long the moon travels over ocean and mountain," Daniel spoke in a cadence, as if reciting. "Civilizations come and go. Species come and go. And long the moon travels under the carousel of the stars, overpeering the mutant earth." He frowned a smile of sad amazement. "I remember when the bivalve and the polyps reigned supreme. I lived much closer to the earth back then, and I watched them bloom in the shallow seas under my cool ether and the sun's hot drift. Nothing changed for a long time. A very long time." His hands flopped indifferently, and he sat up straighter and looked at each of us. "You know, ladies, I never got tired of watching their red and orange bodies bloom."

I gave him a baffled look, but the old ladies understood.

"The king is right," Drusille acceded, getting up from her chair to peek into the oven. "Let's not make too much of this naked, two-legged mutant that is ourselves."

"What will be—that will surely be," Glendil agreed with a reverential lowering of her eyes.

Drusille looked to me, her face flushed from the oven heat. "When you find out that you serve elven or seraphs, you will tell us."

"How will I find out?"

"You will lift the glamour higher in your body," Glendil replied. "When it flows freely into your brain, you will connect with the greater flow of the planet—and the worlds."

"Then you will receive a replenishment of your energy either from above or below," Drusille said, lifting her teacup. She paused for a sip. "There will be no doubt whom you serve."

"But—I thought I was the moon's wife."

Glendil nodded, tasting her hot brew. "You are his wife, but you do not serve him. Isn't that so, Your Highness?"

Daniel nodded readily. "You've got to first serve what makes you human."

"And so—like any of the wicce," Drusille quickly added, "you serve the Woman God."

"Is the Woman God in favor of the elven or the seraphs?" I wanted to know.

Glendil smiled, and Drusille cut in, "What you must understand about the Woman God, Siggy, is that She has two breasts—one that nourishes the spirit and the other that sustains the soul."

"I'm not following you."

"The spirit," Daniel expounded, "belongs to the sky and all things masculine, like the male Chaldean magicians, I imagine. The soul, traditionally, has feminine attributes and belongs to the earth. The Goddess encompasses both."

"She is big enough to encompass us all," said Glendil exuberantly. "She is not only the Lady of the Wild Things and the Queen of Horns but also Mother of Dreams and Star Goddess." The crone faced me with a gentle smile. "Whatever we call Her, She sustains our minds as well as our bodies. She will love you however you serve Her, Siggy."

"But how *do* I serve Her? How do I raise the glamour higher?"

"That is why you are here," Drusille said. "The Hause and its grounds enjoin sky and earth, and here you will have the chance, using techniques we will teach you, to lift yourself into the Flow while keeping yourself grounded in the body. And then we will see what we will see."

Astral light swirled in the sunstruck space like a rainbow smudge on a puddle. I looked into the old ladies and saw the violet hue of their body lights. It hid the truth of them, I realized. If I could see past that fluorescent haze, I knew I would see them for who they really were—faeries or magi.

I couldn't sleep that night. My mind was too crammed with everything I had learned about the spirit powers. I wanted to talk with Daniel, to touch each of these strange new thoughts again with him and see if together we could figure out what they meant to us. But he slept soundly.

Since first making love with him that radiant morning in the park days ago, the visceral energies of my glamour never seemed more stable. When the moon rose, there were no more demons slinking out of the dark at me, and I relaxed into the animal gladness that was the moon's gift. But just when I was getting used to my new-won clarity, the witches troubled me with thoughts of my role among the spirit warriors battling over the fate of the planet! Was any of this real—elven, faeries, and then that dread warning of the psychopathic Ashera Ferialle? My head spun.

I sat at the workbench in a net of moonlight let down through the mullioned windows, and I tried to find the serenity Daniel had given me. Watching him sleeping below me on the floor, his nakedness a pale mist, I could readily believe he was once a god and had become just a man. That thought made my glamour feel strong and sure in me, and I was once more possessed of an alertness as calm as a stone.

If I wanted, I could sit on that stone in my mind and see through the veneer of appearances, to the very will of things. Skeins of light underlay everything I gazed into. I could stare them into shapes, like the medieval cartoons I had seen before behind my lids, or I could just watch them shape-shift on their own. I came to understand that these psychic lights had a meaning, like the eternal bestiary one sees in clouds, a figment, a fancy, a waking dream, and yet a truth withal.

What I saw in Daniel was a troubled light, like looking into fire, with all its rendings and tearings. His life had peered pretty deeply into the maw where things are broken into their parts. I wanted to take him in my arms. Instead, I stepped outside so he could sleep in peace.

For a while I walked among the great trees under the whirlwind silence of the stars, mulling over my fate. The complexities that the two old witches had presented to Daniel and me were frightening. The world appeared suddenly crowded with vying powers I didn't understand. And, inadvertently caught between them, I felt afraid.

The soft light of the oil lamps shone from the windows of the Hause, and I drifted closer, hoping perhaps to glimpse the crones unaware and see something of their true nature. Were they all they claimed and seemed to be—or was it only madness we shared?

I wondered about the black light I had seen floating around the bodies of the witches. The pale purple fluorescence glowed identically in the two women. They had given no acknowledgment that they knew I had been seeing into their body lights, nor had their lights changed as did the lights in other things I fixed upon.

As I approached the drawing room window, where I could see the ladies sitting—Drusille reading a book, Glendil crocheting—I tried to peer through to the secret images I knew were hidden by the purple glow around their bodies. Glendil, as if sensing the weight of my stare, glanced up from her needlework and saw me on the lawn. She rose and cordially waved me into the Hause.

At the door, Drusille clucked at me for not dressing warmly enough and Glendil led me by my hand to the kitchen. Over a sedative cup of bergamot and chamomile tea, I found myself confiding my fears to them, despite my reservations. "I feel so caught in the middle, so helpless," I complained.

"We're all helpless," responded Drusille, and over her shoulder I saw Glendil rolling her eyes. "But those who accept that can make their way in the world nonetheless."

"Just don't be afraid to accept yourself for who you are," Glendil chimed in gently. "You did not choose this fate—but you can choose to love it. That alone will change the whole character of your life."

"*Amor fati.*" Drusille gave a jowly nod to her partner. "Love what happens. On that score, Glendil and I wholeheartedly agree."

I smiled at the affectionate way they looked at each other.

"Was it so with the both of you—I mean, *amor fati?*" I inquired.

"It's been a long unwinding to that point," Glendil nodded contemplatively. "We met way back in twenty-three, you realize. In Taos."

"She was a ranch hand's daughter," Drusille reminisced, casting a taunting sidelong glance at her mate. "I was there crystal hunting. Right off, we had a ferocious argument about the right way to saddle a horse. Two days later we were lovers."

"We were seventeen. Love is really just passion at that age."

"It was a conflagratory union," Drusille agreed. "It fused us in a naked blaze that's lasted a lifetime. I'd say there's something of love in that."

"Seventy years, and the embers are still warm."

"But embers nonetheless. Our passion now is our work. Shaping the glamour. It's all we can do to get it right."

I sipped my tea, its warmth dilating the spaces in my head. A thunderhead's purple light smudged the space around the old friends, and though I tried with all my might, I could see nothing of their interior selves. Finishing my tea, I thanked the witches for calming me down and then returned to the night.

I stood in the cold under the great trees and watched the moon drift. The wind, wounded by the trees, cried overhead, and laminar streaks of opal clouds shone against the immense emptiness of space.

"Do you see the glamour?" I heard the moon's voice ask, and Daniel stepped to my side, sleepy face lifted to the ruffling stars.

"I feel I could if I wanted," I said, linking arms with him. The air shimmered with crinkly planet heat, and the electric darkness around the quavering stars seemed ready to shape itself into illusions if I looked hard enough. But I didn't. "The night is beautiful enough without the glamour."

The pearly aura of the clouds brightened as the moon rose. I thought I saw neural flickers, but they were really shooting stars. It made me think back to that night alone on Tappan Down when I clearly saw the smallness of my life.

I fit myself closer to Daniel, and we stood in silent communion for a long while, watching the treetops toss against the moon and the running clouds. Wind eddies brushed through the hedges and walked across the lawn, carrying the heavy odor of mold and fallen leaves.

I still felt as small as ever. But that was okay now, because I wasn't alone anymore.

From somewhere across the thrashing darkness, the muffled call of an owl reached toward us.

Drusille and Glendil, sparkling with raindrops and the silver light of a drizzly November Thursday, barged into the gardener's bungalow, nipping angrily at each other.

"We may have to move you soon," Drusille declared in a huff. "Once the police realize we've been using a false address, they'll try and track us to here."

Daniel and I shared a look of alarm, facing each other across the clutter of paper and books on the workbench where we'd been writing.

Glendil cried out, "Drusille, hush! They're working on the hystery. We're disturbing them."

"We're *informing* them," Drusille stressed, doffing her glistening cloak and hanging it on a peg beside the hearth.

Glendil scowled at her. "There's nothing to tell. You're simply being an alarmist, Drusille." She looked benignly at us where we sat at the workbench in our paper mess. "You needn't be worried, dears. Nothing untoward has transpired."

Drusille waved her aside with annoyance and addressed us nervously, "The police questioned us today."

"And all the other volunteers as well," Glendil added.

"If they suspect we are involved in your disappearance—"

"The police suspect nothing," Glendil maintained. "This was a routine interview. Why would they suspect us over any of the others?"

"I've told you. When they see the home address we gave the clinic is false, they'll get suspicious."

"You're jumping ahead," Glendil charged and took Drusille's cloak off the peg. "Leave the future to the Goddess. She knows what to do with it. And you know what we have to do now. It's time to cook dinner. Come along. Put your cloak on."

A moment later they were out the door, their grouchy voices dwindling into the rain's small noise.

Daniel stared at me with a glazed urgency, weighing the chances of fleeing against those of staying. During the coming days, we would weigh that balance many times over; however, in the cold light of that wet afternoon, the uncertain life of a fugitive, without money or destination, seemed too drear. We chose to stay, to put our trust in the witches and in the Goddess who ruled them.

That was when I finally accepted that this particular moment on earth at the Hause with Daniel was going to be but a brief refuge. The fate the witches expected me to love hemmed us in on all sides—in the form of police, doctors, and Willa. As strange as the witches were, at least they allowed me to be with my Daniel. My feelings for him deepened each day. I memorized the geography of his graceful body, lost myself in his quirky mind, and ultimately forfeited my own lonely survival for a mutual destiny— wherever it would take us.

I was in love. Apart from my physical attraction to him and my desire to be like him, to live the wild freedom of my own secret identity, he was also the only man, apart from my father, who had ever actually treated me nicely, with real gentleness. Knowing the stormy and petty relationship he'd had with his wife, I grasped how very different he was now, how profoundly changed by the tragedy that had hollowed him out so that the moon could step in.

In my time with Daniel at the Hause—time stolen from the reality of having a job, shopping, cooking meals—I was making soul, as Keats would have understood. I was learning to live on my failures. My brain had failed to work properly. Fine. The witches would guide me away from the fixed paths where my heart was clocked by what I earned and the hours I spent earning it. Daniel and I had failed to obey the law, failed to stay where we had been placed, and now the police were looking for me. All right, then. We would disappear into each other and become invisible. Inside each other we found the absences that shaped our presence in the world—the death of his child, the loss of my father. Okay. Together we would bring back the dead inch by necrotic inch and learn how to love them for what they weren't anymore.

Late one night, huddled together under a blanket soaked in moonlight, I asked about his wounds, his hurts, his soul. After his frenzied account of Chloë's death, that suffering had sunken down to the bottom of his heart and he had spoken no more of that grief. I hoped to draw him out, to help heal him as he had helped me.

Instead, he shrugged. "You see my mooniness, Siggy, a moodiness like Pierrot Lunaire or some dreamy poet possessed by Hekate. Damn it! The rabid bitch poisoned me with her moonsickness." Groaning, he marveled at the details of his fate, his face pale and theatrical in the nightshine, his features casting bold shadows that the hollows of his skull held deeply. "Moon-sick with melancholy over Chloë, I sat in the middle of her emptiness for seven damned years—and that after the ultimate bitchery of a failed suicide! I know now, part of me died then, dead as any Aztec sacrifice or neolithic bog man offered to the Goddess. All along, unwittingly, I lived the fate of the moon-king, holding the fullness of light for a while—and then wasting away."

His words scared me. I hadn't expected him to talk of his own passing. The thought of losing him stirred a cold sorrow in me, an unkind hopelessness, like knowing you're dreaming while having a lovely dream, aware that you're inside a hopeless beauty.

During those luminous and soulful weeks at the Hause, I rarely thought of Willa. I called her only twice. The first time, she was so hysterical I told her I had to hang up until she got a grip. The second time, she seemed calmer but in a weird and brittle way.

"Willa, I just wanted to tell you I'm doing fine. I'm okay."

"Where are you?" she demanded.

"You know I can't say," I answered wearily.

"But the tumor—what about the tumor?" She called it that even though I told her it was an anomaly I had been born with. "I don't care what you call it. It's still in there, and I don't like it one bit or what it's doing to you."

"It's not doing anything bad to me, Willa. There's nothing wrong with me, I swear. That's what I'm calling to tell you."

"How can you say that and think that you're all right? You saw the X rays—the magnetic-wave whatever-they-are pictures of your brain. Are you still having fits?"

"No. And they weren't fits."

"Sigrid, for your information—do you know what Dr. Chen says? That thing in your brain is controlling you. It creates everything you're feeling. It's making you feel fine. But that's only a delusion! Baby, you need help."

I didn't want to hear anything about delusions. My palms were sweating, and I felt like hanging up without even saying good-bye. "Look, Willa. I'm *okay*, okay? I'll call again in a few days."

"Wait! What about the psychopath? Is he there with you?"

Her voice was rising and sinking about an octave in either direction. I spoke calmly, hoping she would hear the difference between us. "He's not a psychopath. He told me everything. It was an accident."

"Oh, baby, baby—how dumb can you get? That's what he's *got* to tell you!" Willa began to cry, and her voice sounded so pitiable that I held on like a stupid fool. "Siggy, you've got to get away from him. He's trouble, baby. The police say so!"

"Good-bye, Willa."

"Wait—don't hang up. Aren't you even going to ask about me? Don't you want to know what *I've* been going through since you . . . you ran off?"

"No, not really . . . " My voice trailed away.

"I'm ready for the clinic myself now, Sigrid. I'm going crazy with worry. I'm skin and bones. I've dropped fifteen pounds."

"So that's why I called you, Willa, to tell you to stop worrying. I'm having a wonderful time."

"Oh, that's rich. That's really super! *You're* having a wonderful time? And you don't care that I'm suffering, right? What the hell is going on?"

"I *do* care, Willa. I called to tell you to stop worrying about me. I've never been happier. I'm writing my hystery."

"Your history? Oh, brother, this is worse than I thought. You know you can't write to save your life. You couldn't even write your job resume, I had to do it for you, remember? Can't you hear yourself, baby? You're not yourself anymore. You need help."

"You're right, Willa. I'm not myself anymore. I've changed, but not in a bad way. Really, I'm not crazy. I'm just different now. Can't you accept that?"

There was a pause as my mother planned her next line of attack.

"Okay, so what are you going to do about Frank?" she started up again. "Do you know, he calls me every other day? And he's had his secretary send over so many groceries and take-outs for me I can't possibly eat it all. I'm actually *giving* them away."

"You're complaining?"

"Yes, I'm complaining, Sigrid! I'm the talk of all Arcadia, god-damn it. Everybody's laughing behind my back for what you went and did. Except Frank. Listen, that man is really in love with you. He tells me he wants to marry you and have children. He even has *detectives* out looking for you. He tells me he doesn't care how much money he spends, he's going to find you and save you."

That scared me. The word *detective* scared me. "Okay, I've got to go now. Take care of yourself, Willa," I said hurriedly and hung up. *Damn!* I'd forgotten about Frank. I should have foreseen him as a serious problem. But I wasn't thinking straight. It was all so sudden—Daniel, the witches, the hystery—I hadn't yet gotten used to the fact of my new life, let alone its consequences. I didn't even want to consider the possibility that Dr. Chen was right—that maybe my craziness was making me think I was sane. It felt too good, being in love with a man who loved me with tender passion. It felt too good being empowered by women of power, the old ones who knew how to use what the earned world rejected. I would not go back to the fixed paths and the clocked heart.

With news of Frank's detectives on the case, plus the ongoing police investigation at the clinic, the witches redoubled their efforts to prepare me for my initiation in the wicce. "Time is short," Drusille often muttered grumpily, "and the omens uncertain." The weather fluctuated between crisp, cold days and feverish, springlike interludes, as though the elements themselves partook of my uneasy mystical transition.

In front of Daniel, Drusille and Glendil still acted genially, but in his absence they treated me now with a kind of expediency bordering on impatience. *Is it possible,* I asked myself, *that the police are closer on their trail than they're willing to admit?* The recurrent thought that my days with Daniel were almost over was too awful to contemplate, and I buried it and concentrated on the work the witches expected of me.

For the next twenty-two days, I met with the old ladies in the treasure-packed library of the Hause. From late afternoon, when they came back from their hospice work, often till well past midnight, we sat at a massive table sliced from an ancient oak, presided over by totems and tribal masks standing against the book-lined walls. Daniel was usually not a participant in these sessions, occupying himself either by reading in the bungalow or sitting bundled on the lawn studying the autumn nights with a large bamboo telescope. Witchcraft seemed not to interest him very much, and he said he preferred his solitude to having to share me with our eccentric hostesses.

The witches taught me to spell in earnest. "The first letter is A," Glendil began, sketching it on a green slate with chalk. "We write it in the Roman style, adopted from the Greeks, who in turn learned it from the Chaldean magi. They wrote it like this." She drew an oblate circle with horns. "The ox. The bull of sacrifice. Remember—this was received from the seraphs at a time in history, nearly six thousand years ago, when spring and renewal began each year with the sun entering the sky-sign of the bull—Taurus."

"Now pay attention, Siggy," Drusille picked up. "The letter A is the prospect of heaven. The sacrifice to the larger will that returns life to the world each year. In the kingdom of trees, the letter A is the silver fir."

"Trees?" I asked through a baffled frown. "What do trees have to do with this?"

Glendil tittered behind her age-splotched hand. "It all seems a mishmash, doesn't it, dearie? I thought so too, once. Trees, stones, stars, animals, letters of the alphabet—so many separate things.

Yet all of them can be related to one another, connected in many different ways. Science is merely one of many ways."

"The Aristotelian system of categories by kind," Drusille sneered.

"Wicce is another way, our way, of transforming the many separate impressions of the outer world into a unity—a vision." Glendil drew a plus sign. "This is the ogham letter for *A*. It is the silver fir that grows on the highest slopes of the mountain, at the threshold of sky and earth—just as Taurus stood at the threshold of spring, the marriage of heaven and earth."

"The sound of the letter *A* has rejuvenative properties," Drusille added. "It is the sound of spring."

"And of the wind in the silver firs." Glendil's griffin face lifted, and her eyes slimmed. "The wind that touches the clear air above the far horizon—the air of long sight. The energy in the letter *A* is the wide vision of the mountaintop that sees across time and into the future. Just as spring carries the future alive in its seeds, so the letter *A* carries prophecy."

"Which leads to *B*," Drusille drilled. "*B* is the house, the sacred enclosure, the temple where the sacrifice takes place. In here, you will learn the mysteries of life and death."

Over the course of those twenty-two days, I did. Whether it was hypnosis, the visionary intensity of the glamour, or just sheer madness, I indeed began to see into the murky depths of the green slate and in the veils of hearthfire and in the lamplit air itself what the witches showed me. It was more vivid than any computer animation. It was more like dreaming but with my eyes open. Then I would return from my trances to the witches, and they would give me soothing herbs to drink, and they would inculcate me more in the ways of the glamour, the rapture that kept burnishing brighter each day.

The medieval cartoonery that had haunted me from my early, untamed spells began to make sense as I learned their parts, which were the letters of the alphabet—the twenty-two great powers of the world—in all their disguises. Combinations of these powers created different effects the way combining letters made words. The crazy, hallucinated spells that had assailed me earlier were nonsense words, jumbled-up energies. Once I began to sort them out, I started putting them together in the meaningful ways the witches called spellcraft, and my clarity grew stronger.

The spells the witches taught me sounded as nonsensical as abracadabra—a potent spell in its own right, good for entry from one world to the next. Yet the sounds worked! With one word, I could calm myself almost to sleep and with another, rouse myself to the ferocity of a linebacker. When I learned to read the trees as letters of the alphabet, I saw that the Hause itself was surrounded by a spell of invisibility.

One morning I practiced that spell on myself and Daniel in the park across the street, and we nearly got hit by a bicyclist, who swore he didn't see us standing in the middle of his path. Some of the spells seemed more frivolous, like when I learned to whistle three times to summon the wind. "Marvelous for helping fires along," Glendil instructed, "or for clearing the air after passing gas."

While the witches were away, I practiced the spellcraft, and I worked hard at my hystery. At its completion, the witches told me, Daniel and I would be wed in a simple but glorious ceremony of spellcraft and sorcery, the right and left hands of wicce brought together. Where spellcraft employed only knowledge and will and relied upon the magic of correspondence, sorcery involved natural potions and elixirs—powerful drugs the witches would not speak about until my allegiance was known and shown to be their own.

The spellcraft intrigued me, but I feared what I heard of sorcery—the poison thorns and goofer dust, the brain-blister snuff and night-flying potions. Were these the weapons the witches would use if some day Daniel and I were not to do their bidding?

Many a time at night when they were done with me, I stopped

in the yard on my way back to the bungalow and looked up at the black void with its ghost army of constellations. The city's glare wiped out most of the stars each night. But their light would keep coming for eternity. Was that what the city aspired to—eternity? Was that what the shining city signified, or was that the arrogance of the Chaldean magi and their modern descendants? The possibility that I might play some small role in the climb to the stars—or the fall of the tower—left me breathless. Only Daniel's love, the sound of his voice beckoning me to have faith in our shared madness, made me believe such a destiny was plausible.

Daniel, I learned, never used the verb *to be*.

"You're kidding." I laughed with disbelief when he told me. After all the thousands of words I'd heard Daniel say, I'd honestly never noticed this about him. "How can you avoid it? Everyone *has* to use it, don't they?"

"Nope. Never use it. Too phenomenologically sloppy. Let me tell you, that particular verb belongs to God. 'I am that I am.' It imputes permanence. But, hey, nothing stays the same in this changeable world—least of all, we mortals. Look at us. Can we dare think of ourselves the same as we did just days ago? Stop taking God's name in vain, Siggy, and drop the verb *to be*."

That was too hard for me. Learning spellcraft and writing my hystery for the witches were big enough tasks. The spellcraft, for all its strangeness, was actually easier for me than the hystery. I'd never written much of anything before and when I did, as I'd had to in school or for reports at work, I loathed it. I was so much more comfortable with numbers, which remained the same no matter how they were used. Words always seemed to mutate, meaning different things as they moved among sentences.

In my hands, words remained sloppy, their meanings runny and loose even when I knew what I wanted to say. That was what happened with the hystery. I knew every detail of what had transpired and what I had felt at each moment, but the words to say it kept eluding me. I was glad for Daniel's help, though even with his input, the labor was difficult.

It was Daniel's idea to call it "She of Days," because it was an account no longer of myself but of a former self, "an intermediary isomer," Daniel called her, someone who had existed with heightened powers for several incredible, magical days.

One night, after a particularly late session with Drusille and Glendil, I returned to the bungalow in a strange and vaguely evil mood. Daniel was asleep again, his book fallen across his chest. I crept past him to the bathroom and stood before the long mirror. My period was due in a day or two, and I felt bloated. Taking my clothes off, I studied myself for a long time, hoping to find something about me that would reveal my allegiance among the spirits.

What I saw was a hallucinated sun sinking into the planks at my feet, bleeding a dye behind it, moistening the space where I stood. I intoned a come-clear spell and scrutinized that red aura. Bloodsmoke dissolved in a slow vortex that drew my gaze inward toward its maelstrom core, its stillness, empty and fiery as all heartsink. I saw at the center the moon mated perfectly over the sun, an eclipse inside my own body, fumes of light spreading out in magnetic wings, a corona of blood.

In the grip of my vision, I fell into a sexual trance—but deeper than ever before, in the most flexible and frail hollow of myself— ending in a flutter-womb climax that ignited my interior and made me do a small, fierce dance before the mirror. A naked woman, in a flash of fish-silver skin and orange hair, leaped toward me, and I jumped back before her kabuki scream. Startlingly crimson, her bat-fang mouth raved in a glittery blur like a cutting tool.

I fell on my rump, and she was gone. A stiffening chill locked my spine, and my breath came in painful gasps.

I knew at once who that monster was: myself in dreamguise. The succubus that had reduced Frank to bones, that had killed Dr. Pop, lived inside *me!* And that knowing, that baffling horror of repressed, unrecollected malice, frightened the bejesus out of me. By what deception in my soul could I have forgotten the rageful truth that this devourer lived in me?

"The necrophagous sorceress dwells in every moon worshiper," Daniel said, his ink-dark eyes gleaming with interest. "She lives in the shadow of the moon and punishes sins of violence against the Mother. The old cultures feared her and thought her a deadly mistress of nightmares, phantoms, and madness. Her presence shouldn't surprise us, I guess. After all, the ancients knew Hekate as the goddess of child sacrifice and infanticide. Think of her coming to you, really, as my shadow."

The witches were not pleased when I told them about the succubus. "Ashera Ferialle" was all they could say to each other, nodding knowingly and looking deep into each other's eyes. I did not try to convince them that the succubus was myself.

That night, after the dinner dishes had been cleared away, Drusille came back to the table frowning. "The time has come—and perhaps it is already too late—to tell you something important, Siggy—one more vital, and terrible, point."

"The most terrible of all," Glendil acceded with a mopey look.

"This is a crucial time in the fate of our species and our planet," Drusille told me wistfully. "You know, of course, that soon your allegiance will be revealed. If you receive the seraphs, your broadcasts will affect all humanity, inspiring scientists, students, all people with their minds open to ideas. Your spells may foster revolutionary technological breakthroughs that will shape our future."

"Or," Glendil took over, "you may be fated to lift up from the earth the vitality that first shaped us and that eventually carried us out of the oceans. Your spells, then, empowered by the elven, will damn civilization for the threat to life that it is and will work to bring it down, to restore the earth to her pristine wholeness. And yes, the catastrophe of that will be terrible indeed—yet far, far less horrible than what civilization itself may do to the planet if it continues its cruelly cancerous growth."

I sat back and shook my head, uncomprehending.

"Of course you understand," Drusille said, her sketched eyebrows lifted, "that whatever polarity you are, you will have allies and you will have enemies."

"Our great hope," Glendil continued, "is that you will be as we are."

"But," Drusille said with a sinister cant to her large head, "if you are different than we, we will have no choice but to kill you."

I blinked, then let out a nervous giggle, assuming that she was joking. The light in the room seemed to char.

Daniel sighed. "Ladies, haven't you burdened Siggy enough with your . . . your tales?"

"Oh, Your Highness, we don't *want* to have to kill her, of course," Glendil spoke quickly and sympathetically. "But this is a war of vast, impersonal powers, you must know."

"In which the planet's fate will be decided," Drusille added direly. "No one life can stand against that."

I gaped as I saw that the crones were serious, then turned a hapless look to Daniel for his response.

"That appeals to the stone in my heart," Daniel replied with sardonic enthusiasm, sitting forward, his face carrying a harder look than I'd thought his boyish features could command. "Your honesty commends you and requires no less from me. You understand, I will defend my wife."

Drusille leaned closer, a small fist between her eyes. Before she could speak, Glendil said, "Surely, Daniel, you realize choice is an illusion." This was the first time I'd heard either of them call him by name. "We fulfill roles precut in the crystal of creation."

"Just remember," he said, "I came down to experience life, not death."

"They are the same," Drusille countered drolly.

"Others will find you," Glendil promised with great concern in her voice. "Ashera Ferialle already knows you are here. She has found Siggy in her dreams."

"And Ashera, I assure you, will be far less kindly and informative than we," Drusille said, facing squarely his defiant stare. "Forgive me for saying so, but you have much to learn from us about being human, Your Highness. You must pay heed."

Patting Drusille's hand to calm her down, Glendil addressed Daniel and me. "You may certainly walk away now or at any time. But Drusille is correct to warn you about the others, about Ashera in particular. Not all the workers know as much as we, and some have very peculiar notions about demons and angels. They can be so righteous."

"Like the Cult of the Dark Shrine," Drusille said, looking ill. "Go speak with Ashera Ferialle of the Cult—if you've a taste for poisons. She has no love for us, and yet she will confirm everything we've told you."

Glendil squeezed my hand. "It's simply a matter of knowing with whom your allegiance lies," she said sweetly.

Thus it became a pressing matter to write my hystery so that my allegiance would be revealed, and to that end I devoted my days. Apart from the sheer hard work of my task, it was a vivid and autumnally beautiful time of year, a time of columbine, vervain, and saxifrage. I was just learning the names and powers of those herbs. Their feathery seedpods, gleaming resins, and tiny bristly flowers painted our days in every shade of fire and water. They swarmed everywhere, in all the hedgerows and among the root mounds of the giant trees, a pointillist haze of thrashing colors and big scents.

The enchanted feeling of that enclosed garden helped me dedicate myself to writing my hystery, a labor that I was finally to accept as a way of molting my past so that the witches would tell me about my future. I asked Daniel to help me.

"Just don't lose heart," he advised after tearing up my first pages. "Nor feign passion."

Each day after forging my fitful paragraphs, inspired by the secrecy of the nooks and coves in the mazy hedges, Daniel and I made love outside in the garden. Though we were already in the throat of December, the weather was clement enough for sporting in the dry leaf duff and the milky grass.

Naked and buried to our chins in crimson leaves, we often lay together—I adrift in my rapturous simplicity and Daniel speaking his songs: "Under the spelling wall, the world appears dark. Of course! Writing creates walls, Siggy. It creates a substitute reality that separates us from what actually exists. It bisects the world into inner and outer. It gets dark behind the spelling wall, and no illumination reaches there except by the lamp of lightning."

Once again he tore up everything I wrote, because even with the spellcraft I was learning, he said, I didn't yet understand about the lamp of lightning, about seeing in glimpses.

"*Hystery*," I'd written. "It's not a word you'd know unless you were a witch. . . ." That was my next day's confetti.

"Most of us are asleep, even when we think we're awake, and in our sleep, our dreams exhaust us—the itch for money, the fear of love, the iron will—these use us up. But there is a deeper dream, one that does not take energy, but gives it. . . ." That confetti Daniel sprinkled on my head like wedding rice, saying, "I bless you with the simple mystery of words to go back and start all over again."

"There are dreams that must be unwoven from the ganglionic

gorgewall of the brain, dreams waxed with the sex-mucuses of the Woman God, the secret God. . . ."

"Jesus!" Daniel cried out, making more confetti. "You've begun to write the way *I* talk. I've ruined you!"

By the fourth day I had only enough energy and confidence to write: "It happened in the produce department, while I was picking through potatoes." Miraculously, this didn't become confetti.

I finished a draft in two days, and instantly Daniel began working with it, rewriting it and making me rewrite what he had done.

The witches were ecstatic that the work was becoming reality. In the morning, before they left, and in the afternoon, before my lessons, one or the other would appear at the bungalow with an elegant repast: salmon and red peppers in tangerine juice, or delicate turnip bisques, exotic salads of gingko flowers, borage and nasturtiums with cashew dressing. They began leaving us handmade garments—brown drawstring pants and flouncy blouses and shirts in earthen root colors—as part of my "dowry," they said.

Some days we didn't see our benefactors at all. We'd stay in the bungalow writing and leave only to make love in the hedges. On occasion we'd wander the neighborhood talking through what we had to write, though we were always wary of being seen and so used invisibility spells at all times. The best was when it rained. We'd get wet hurrying through the maze of hedge and shrubbery to the little blue gazebo at the center, and then we'd sit there listening to the drum of the downpour, reading aloud the pages we'd written.

We never talked about the future. The future seemed a tacitly forbidden subject. Toward the end of the hystery, Daniel began to slow down, not wanting our happy seclusion to end.

"We must act as our own Penelope," he would whisper cryptically to me, rewriting endlessly.

I became fearful he would overwork. Already I noticed his

sleep becoming more restless and haphazard. I watched him fretfully and wondered what it was like being the moon, grappling with a wife and a planet's orbit to tide his heart over. I saw that I had become the earth for him; it explained to me the way he made love, the way he'd break rhythm to probe for my deepest limit and just lie there, pressing hard against me, tapping my depths, hellbent on drawing me out. He would claim my shining insides for his own and lift me up into him, stroke by stroke, until I was the geyser pushing against him, lifting *him* up and away from the gravity of his earthly life to a lunar space where time did stop and finally reverse, all the way back. Then inside me he was inside every woman, even the very first, in the earliest silence, in that lubricious time when the wise yearning began in the old fish to flicker and grow, throwing off tail and fin for legs. With panting lungs and warm blood he would drive into me with his hardest strokes, under the strokes of his own human luck.

I could tell from the look in his face, just before he would climax, that forever meant something real to him. Instead of acting surprised or, worse, blasé, he always gazed into me quietly, a peculiar quivering transparency in his enlarged pupils, like the dark itself had begun to see.

Inevitably, the hystery was written. Daniel could have fiddled with it interminably, but I took it away from him, afraid that it would drive him to illness. The very day the writing was complete, I insisted that we run off a copy of the handwritten manuscript at the shop next to the grocery. On our way back to the Hause, we realized we were being followed. In my eagerness to see the hystery done and in the eager hands of the witches, I'd forgotten to use the invisibility spell.

Daniel noticed him first, a gaunt man with a face wizened like a monkey's. From the shop, we had seen him adrift on the street, a derelict, but in the residential neighborhood he had become a shadow lagging around corners.

While we were still some distance from the Hause, I hastily cast an invisibility spell over both of us, and we split up. I bolted along a side street until my breath burned in my chest. When I looked back and didn't see the whiskery man, I headed back toward the Hause, eventually darting down a neighbor's driveway and through a spidery gap in a thicket that delivered me to the leafless hedge maze. A few minutes later Daniel showed up, winded, his cheek scratched. He had eluded our shadow, but we had to assume from that point on that we had been found. Was it possible that my two phone calls to Willa had been traced, and Frank's detectives had been watching the pay phone near the grocery?

Upon their return, the witches agreed it was time for us to move on but assured us that their spellcraft would keep all intruders at bay. Flushed with excitement, they accepted my hystery graciously and, despite our anxieties, they quickly repaired to the Hause to read it. Daniel and I waited in the shed. I fed the fire in the hearth and made vervain tea to steady our nerves.

At twilight the witches emerged, Glendil smiling girlishly, Drusille, of course, all business.

"The modern mind is really the mind of the Word," Drusille began, in acknowledging our labor for them. "Spelling is a modern power, a mere five thousand years old. It stands apart from the rest of creation and names it and lives among the names. By writing your hystery, you have spelled out your destiny. And where the silence touches you, we can see your fate. This hystery is your psychic womb. In it, you know to whom you belong. Yet you do not know about the flow or the snake woman in you or even why the moon sponsors you. That is as far as the Word can go. That is the very bottom of the modern mind."

"This is a formal rite," Glendil confided in an exaggerated aside. "We heard the same thing when we were kids." She took Daniel by the arm, and he gave me a congratulatory thumbs-up and went with her. "Come, Your Highness, let's leave the prophetess and her initiate to the emblems and rites of their female mystery. Don't be jealous now. This is all being done for you. Come, I have some fruitcakes and Jamaican coffee I know you will enjoy."

Once Glendil had whisked Daniel away, Drusille motioned for me to follow her. She led me into the waxy daytime darkness of the coven house to a wood-storage room adjoining a small kitchen that smelled of walnuts. Despite her advanced age, the old woman appeared to suffer only mildly from a stiffening of the joints, for she nimbly slid aside a heavy shelfed panel that hid a descending flight of stone stairs.

A damp odor of ruin rose from the darkness. With one adroit hand, Drusille sparked fire from the wall and lit a taper, the feathery light illuminating a descent as steep as a ladder. The witch moved easily down the steps, but I had to touch the slick, cold stones to steady myself.

At the bottom, Drusille used the taper to ignite an oil lamp. The perfectly yellow glow filled the tiny chamber to the brim of its low, cobbled ceiling. "Here is the future," she whispered, and her voice sounded swollen in the tight space. "Here, inside the earth, time grows. When you're calm enough, you can feel it coming out of the earth." She urged me with a hand on my arm to sit with her on the wooden bench that was there. "What do you feel?"

I was, in fact, feeling a pliant sadness, sensing again a foreboding that a brief happy time of my life was ending. The sadness bent around all my thoughts and perceptions. The warty stones of the secret cellar reminded me of old faces, the packed crowd in the clinic, the imp faces that peered at me from the shadows before I learned spellcraft. I sensed that this was not what Drusille wanted from me, so I closed my eyes and let the cold breath of the stones hold me.

Almost at once, the silence of an understanding dispelled my sadness. I saw that I was part of a lineage. I had been chosen by accident—by the hidden anomaly of my birth—to be a link of that lineage. And because of it, I was becoming something larger than I had been, despite my disbelief, my pain, or my own lost ordinariness.

I didn't know how to express this knowledge. "I feel quiet, but I also feel something very loud inside this quiet," I yammered. My thought sounded silly out loud, and I wished Daniel was there to say something more profound and interesting.

The rasp of water in clay pipes came from above.

"Mysteries surround us on all sides," Drusille said. "And yet we know what we feel. We know it so exactly that words are too blurry to say it."

She reached up to a corner of the wall and removed a rock. It was round and flat, the size of a tea plate and with an off-center hole as big as a silver dollar. At first the stone appeared black. But as Drusille turned it and the light threaded through the hole, I saw that it was black and jellied with orange, like molasses.

"What I have here is a rubbing stone," Drusille said, holding it in the palm of one hand while her thumb caressed its smooth surface. "It is older than cities. Older than farms." With her free hand she pulled a bone pin from her hair, and her long silver locks spilled over her shoulders. She guided a braid through the hole in the stone and sawed it back and forth. "After three hundred centuries, this gentle movement has shaped rock. A thousand separate lives have carved this emblem. A thousand deaths have propelled it through time to us."

On the wooden bench between us was an iron-red stone flake the size of a thumbnail. At its center sat a pinch of dried leaf powder the consistency of sawdust. After Drusille had rubbed the pierced stone with her hair for a short while, she moved the stone close to the rusty flake, and a spark snapped between them. Drusille blew a sigh onto the flake, and the leaf dust wisped a string of white smoke and curled into a small flame.

"The pierced stone is an amber schist," the witch said as she lifted the ferrous chip and watched the duff curdle to ash. "It picks up the energy of our hair, and it makes fire. Think of the generations this stone has warmed."

Drusille presented the stone ceremoniously with both hands, and I took it the same way. It had the weight of an animal. It smelled like the tip of a stream. Where Drusille had held it, it felt feverish. In the gloss of its surface, the light sank deeply and came back mottled with grit and inclusions, as though the world were shining through it. It had obviously known darkness and smiting glaciers. Around the rim of the hole, years wrinkled and peeled away, and the marrow of the stone showed there, black as the path of a planet.

When I moved to return the stone, Drusille pushed it back with one skeletal finger. "You must make fire with it first," she said, "and then return it to its place with your own hands."

With my short hair, I had to bend my head close to the stone, as if I were listening to it. It was dense and hard in my hand, both smooth and, in places, gritty, the token of all geography, with a shape that could have been useful to Cain.

Drusille placed more dry leaf powder on the ferrous flake, and when I touched the charged stone to it, a tiny lightning set it ablaze. The tongue of fire spoke the first syllable of my name, and I pressed the rock to my breast, honored to know its millennial secret. My wakefulness felt tiny beside its deep sleep.

"This stone belongs as much to you now as to me," Drusille announced as I fitted the rock back into its niche. "You have entered the lineage of the pierced stone. You are a coven worker now, a maker of fire and warmth, a light worker. When you need its light, come and avail yourself."

A great upwelling of awe and privilege choked me, and I couldn't think of a thing to say.

Drusille, gratified by the wet brightness of my eyes, was moved to say more: "Always remember, my dear, when you hold the pierced stone, that you are the forgotten future of all the women who ever possessed it. But this stone is not those lives. It is a seed of the earth, filled with lives unborn. This is your touchstone with what comes after we have gone to earth."

Drusille stood abruptly, as if she wanted to say, "There. I have spoken the same words spoken to me so long ago." And her old life in her big body no longer seemed to me some obscure aphorism for a witch or a wizened worker servicing the Woman God. Her long years distilled to this dewdrop instant and the simple truth of what we had just done, a sharing of ignorance that with enough love had become wonder. The words she had spoken—and the words of my hystery—were human droppings, like the body at the end of a long life. All that really went forward through the centuries, the kingdoms, and the questions was wonder. Some called it awe. Some spirit. To me, at that moment, it was the open-lipped expression floating on Drusille's heavy face, a reflection of my own rapture floating within the empty space that held us and everything. Drusille had given me the privilege of the pierced stone, but she had kept her share of the emptiness from the hole.

Pulses of the Hunt

We are on our way to the wedding. Daniel sits in the front of the taxi, watching the witches fuss and pluck at me like great-aunts, primping my hair and removing lint from a great black cloak they have given me to wear. Sunlight spins in his large, quiet eyes as we cross the Brooklyn Bridge and the shadows thrash all around us. I wonder, as I often do, what he is thinking. But his eyes are dark mirrors. When I look deeper into him, I can see once again the tight, ripping flames tearing themselves apart. He catches me staring into him and cocks a lopsided smile at me, roughing up my hair so that my bangs flare before my eyes like fire.

He wears a cloak similar to mine. His is a handsome ruddy brown, of heavy wool and trimmed with a shade of purple befitting the oak-king. Mine is black. I am the darkness that carries his light. Our cloaks are warm and cowled and have many pockets with numerous drawstrings that dangle like beet roots. Tiny moonstones have been woven into the seams, to ward off bad influences, and they shiver the space around us like clear Jell-O. It's also warm under the thick panels of soft cotton, and the broad shoulders make me feel large, strong, and significant somehow. The witches call this garment "the mantle of presence."

After the high drama and intensity of our last days together at the Hause—the detective, the completion of the hystery, the pierced stone—it seems odd that all we can do now is chat airily about food. The witches won't be cooking for us any longer, so they talk endlessly about their favorite fish recipes, fish being the only flesh they will tolerate on our behalf. I taunt them with a description of one of Willa's favorites, her creamy beef goulash, which makes them roll their eyes in disgust. Daniel wants nothing more than to dine at expensive restaurants every night. He fancies himself something of a gourmet, scandalizing us with accounts of eating ortelans, tiny birds with crunchy heads.

The taxi deposits us on Riverside Drive, before an ornate, travertine white apartment building that aspires to cathedral heights. We follow the old ladies into an Art Deco lobby, where the doorman touches his gold-braided hat and greets us warmly, "Ms. Farrior, Ms. Braidwood."

"Siggy Lindo and Daniel Schel," Drusille introduces us with careful exactness, as if she expects him to write it down. "They'll be staying in the bower indefinitely. They will, naturally, have all the usual privileges."

The doorman's gingery face smiles so fervently he looks ready to weep. "Ms. Lindo, Mr. Schel—welcome to the Coven of the Shining Face," he says, actually dropping to his knees.

Daniel and I look at each other with mild disbelief and awkward amusement. As we ride the elevator to the top floor, Drusille remarks, "He's a coven worker, like all the doormen and staff. If he seems a bit ardent in his admiration, it's because he's a lunar votary. Like the rest of us, he never hoped to actually *meet* his deity in his lifetime."

"Drusille," Daniel complains, "you know I don't want worshipers."

"Bah," Drusille retorts drily. "These aren't worshipers. They're votaries. They want to study with you, hear about your empyrean life firsthand, bask in your reflections on matters philosophic and mundane, that sort of thing."

"They'll take up so much time."

"But you'll love it. What good are your reflections if no one receives them?"

"Since the world at large—apart from your votaries, of course—seems indifferent to my divinity, couldn't you maybe forget, you know, my godhead—just this once, to make room for my humanity?"

"You never objected to votaries before," Drusille says frostily. "Is our coven unworthy?"

"Of course not," Daniel replies. "I just thought that this time, maybe I'd go it alone—with my wife, I mean. A change of pace—laid back in an apostatic age—seeing what it feels like alone down here—you understand, don't you?"

Drusille's face looks disjointed, and I try to intervene by distraction. "Does the entire coven live in the building?"

"I own the building," Drusille says dully.

"Drusille's father contracted the architect for this building and had it designed to focus celestial and telluric energies together," Glendil confides.

"You will not only be safe here from the likes of Ashera Ferialle and most other agents of chaos," Drusille says, "you will also have the enhanced capacity to speak with spirits from both worlds. The building serves as an antenna."

"In a site this charged," Glendil continues, "if you use spellcraft properly, you will be able to raise the glamour from the base of your pelvis, where it has been lingering since the moon first filled your chalice"—she bats her eyes chastely—"to the pan of your brain, where you will connect with the planetary flow of your own polarity, be it elven or seraphic."

"Were it so simple," Drusille snorts grumpily, leading us out of the elevator, through a fire door, and up a flight of stone steps smelling incongruously of licorice. She opens a heavy metal-sheeted door on the silver sunlight of the rooftop, and we stride out under an enormous sky. Cloud reefs stretch overhead across the molten lead of the Hudson, past the cluttered houses of the Palisades, and disappear far into New Jersey. Their shadows carry the river wind, and for a moment its pungency reminds me of my job at the lading company in Arcadia, a dim, monotonous dream that seems estranged by great distance and a very long stretch of time.

The witches guide us through a small forest of aluminum ducts and pipes and past skylights and two metal towers painted a shiny enamel blue. "Here we are, dear hearts," Glendil says. "The bower is our home for the most virtuous. The unique architecture of this building nullifies the negative effect from all this steel and iron. In fact, our etheric fields are enhanced here. It is the best we have to offer the moon-king and his bride."

They gesture toward a large wooden water tank on concrete pilings that has been converted into a little house. Five red steps climb to a purple door with a glass doorknob, and big round windows with lavender curtains face away from the north in the radiant directions of the sun's transit. A fourth window, blinded by an open paper umbrella behind its glass, stares skyward from the conical roof.

The dim interior smells of dusk. Drusille pulls a cord, and the paper umbrella in the skylight shuts. A tree of white sunfire appears in the center of the waxed floor, motes spinning around it like pollen. To one side gleams a brick oven, a glazed sink of blue stone, butcher-block counters, and a puzzle of cabinets, bins, and drawers. A black toilet and wooden tub, like the ones at the Hause, occupy another third of the interior. The rest is given over to lacquered table, chairs, and a writing desk beneath one of the sunny mauve windows.

"It's beautiful!" I blurt.

Daniel runs his hands over the buffed walls and the nearly seamless fit of the door jamb and nods approvingly.

"Tea, anyone?" Drusille asks cheerily.

I offer to help, but she shoos me away and flicks a lit match into the oven's belly. "This bower is yours," she says, filling a glass kettle with chuckling water and adding a pinch of boiling stones. "Yours for so long as you are the moon's wife. Let us wed you here before the hearth, the world's navel, the doorway to past and future."

Drusille fusses over Daniel, helping him remove his cloak and draping it over his shoulders. He sits in a block-cut chair, as big as a throne and artfully carved with acorns and oak leaves. Behind him a ladder ascends to a loft where fragile birds of light hop about among dangling prisms.

I am to stand at his side. Glendil removes my cloak, and the hearth's first flush of heat in the chilled air penetrates the clinging silk of my red gown.

"Your Highness," Drusille bows to Daniel from the other side of the sunshaft. Behind her, Glendil removes her partner's mantle, revealing her pendulous and naked body.

Then Glendil takes off her outer garment and stands naked before us, spindle-shanked and sunken-chested. Daniel and I know enough to keep our faces impassive, but to make sure, I cast a be-calm spell over us.

"Naked we come forth shining from the Mother and naked we return," Glendil chants.

"In the presence of the Woman God," Drusille intercepts, "we are here to join your daughter Siggy Lindo to the moon-king in his guise as Daniel Schel."

She steps into the radiant pillar of sunshine, her voluminous nudity glaring so brightly it appears to dissolve in the light, leaving behind only her ghastly shadowed features. "Woman, you are the darkness—of what was never seen, of the womb, of the earth, of the enclosing and eternal sky of night. Will you carry this light in you?"

Glendil, her lean face expansive with her open-mouthed smile and wide eyes, jerks her head up and down, and I take her cue and say, "Yes. I will."

Then Drusille chants some spells, only a few of which I can identify—a love-and-lose-nothing spell, a fidelity-to-death spell, and a fidelity-far-from-home spell, from what I can gather—while around us, the glamour shivers like sunstruck water. I feel mentholated, as if a breeze inside me is brushing against the inside of my skin.

"Moon-king, Star-stepper, Red-champion who rises at the fall of the sun, will you walk this darkness that light may come into the night world, the world of the Woman God?"

"I will," Daniel says with conviction.

"Then, rise, Oak-king, Shadow-carrier, Moon-in-the-man, rise to the full height of your light."

Daniel stands. Glendil motions for me to sit, and I take his place in the chair.

"Now, before the eyes of the Woman God, you are the moon's wife." Drusille stares down at me with a solemnity that seems misplaced on her globular nakedness. I lift my chin so I don't have to face her large, withered breasts, with their black coins for nipples. "You are the darkness that receives his light. From here, you belong to the Woman God, for Her to use as She wills. No one owns tomorrow—but now, by Her will, today belongs to you."

A few more spells follow—wisdom-from-long-burdens, strength-between-journeys, know-nothing spells—and then Drusille bows out of the sunbeam.

"That's it, young hearts," she says, throwing her saggy-fleshed arms wide. "Your Highness, you may kiss your bride."

Before I can stand, Daniel bows and kisses me, softly, with a bright tenderness. It makes me tremble to think that our love has crested at this sacred moment. The ghostly slipperiness in the sun-shine, the rare feeling of utter accord with events, of joy, all seem entirely ephemeral, seen before and yet to be dreamt again. I don't want this harmony to pass, but there is, I think, no spell strong enough to hold it.

Daniel mistakes my shivering for a chill and drapes his cloak over my near-nakedness. I stand, and we embrace and drink each other's strength.

"Congratulations," Drusille offers heartily, wrapping her mantle about her flesh-folded girth. "Two are one."

"So now we must leave you alone," Glendil says gaily, donning her cloak. "Bride and groom in the bower and all that wonderful mystery. Who are you? That's what you must find out, and when you do, we will meet again."

After we have eaten a few tiny acorn-flour wedding cakes shaped like the phases of the moon, and drunk our thimblesful of rowan-berry wine, the ceremony is over. Drusille takes Daniel outside to show him the pipes and valves under the bower that admit heat and water from the building below, and Glendil guides me to a cabinet near the sink. Among numerous flasks and amber bottles of herbal extracts and tinctures, an emerald vial smaller than my thumb sits with a red cord tied about it.

"Drusille's wedding gift will be to show you a way to move the glamour higher in your body," she tells me. "But this is my gift." She removes the vial and hands it to me. It's heavier than it looks, as if the little bottle were made of glazed steel.

"If you're still confused about whether you're receptive to the seraphs or the elven," she tells me in a conspiratorial tone, close to my ear, "drink a tea with three drops, no more, of this in it. Such a small portion will take you directly to the spirit world of your ilk and return you wiser than you left."

I open the vial, and a chill vapor snakes out, numbing the rims of my nostrils.

"A drop too much," the small woman warns, "and you won't come back at all."

Outside under a cirrus-marbled sky, Drusille stands me at the roof's edge to present me with her initiation gift—the power of flight. Several white pigeons flare from their roosts, and Daniel, who holds his hands around my waist, tightens his grip.

"Shouldn't she have a broom when she does this?" Daniel asks warily.

"Just close your eyes," the witch commands, "and you are flying!"

The cold wind, flowing up the face of the building and lofting into the bleary blue, billows through my clothes and rips away all my body heat. Violent shivers shake me. I squeeze my eyes shut—and I *am* flying. I am thinning out in a sudden free-fall rush.

Daniel snatches me into his arms, and my eyes flash open, and the afternoon's golden dust stings me. Sunlight brightens, and small voices whisper to me from the surf's edge.

I shake my head, and the voices disappear, but colors continue gleaming, freshly painted.

Then Drusille begins whispering to me, her glabrous face pressed close enough for me to see the burst capillaries in her nose and cheeks, like tiny road maps. "The heat is gone from your body—from where does it come anew? Feel into yourself for that hearth in you, that living fire. Feel it!"

I listen past the static of my startled breathing, and I feel my way through my shivering to my feverish core. Underwater voices toll, and a radiance begins smoking out of the colors of things.

"Close your eyes if you have to," Drusille guides me, "but feel for the heat inside you. It is the same as your rapture. It is the same as your desire."

No sooner does she mention desire than that tingly, randy vexation appears, far down on the floor of my body. From the corner of my eye, I watch Daniel, close up, watching me with concern— and abruptly I want him and wish we were alone.

Gradually, with Drusille's coaxing, I find I can shape this desire, as I had haphazardly when I was pitching balls of blue fire in the asylum. Only now, I use imaginary hands inside my body to gather the erotic feelings in me and lift them up into my chest.

My womb throbs. The higher I lure the sticky itchiness, the more my sexual interior beats, engorged with impatient blood. I sense I'm going to climax, right here with Drusille's gray nose touching my ear.

But instead, as the chilled energy sluices up through my throat like a rippling growl, my lust quiets.

The starlight inside things shines softly. The sun rings like a harp. What I stare at, I feel. The harder I look, the more deeply I feel. The somnolent violet light around Drusille makes faces like smoke or thunderheads. Her great weariness penetrates me, and I have to look away, out over the damp alleys, the black streets, and the people below like moths.

"Don't look at me," Drusille whispers. "Don't look at anyone yet." She turns me to face the sun. Chords of light and jangling sitar music replace my muscles, and the golden ox in his blue yoke pulls me along, plowing the deep furrow of the street.

"Hold on there," Drusille calls me back to my body. "Watch out for the rapture. When you feel you're drifting from your body, flex your toes and tighten your buttocks. Keep your attention relaxed and moving."

Following her instructions, I discover I can regulate my awareness of the world. I can see into things or pull back and simply look. The translucence of the glamour carries me in and out of myself. It's going to take a lot of practice to get good at this.

Ingots of sunset glow overhead when the witches leave us alone in our new abode. Stunned, overwhelmed, Daniel and I walk among the anorexic shadows of vent pipes and aerials. "Let's get out of here," he says abruptly.

That stops me, and I stare at him quizzically, wondering what he's really trying to tell me. "But where will we go?"

"Anywhere. For once, I just want to live as a man. We don't have to buy into any of this craziness."

"But Daniel—" I feel as if I've misheard him, or perhaps the numbness just hasn't worn off yet. And anyway, Daniel, I've come to realize, is prey to many moods. "What the witches did for us wasn't craziness. Didn't you feel the power between us? You're the one who convinced me this was a life."

"Yes, yes, to have a life together—you and me." The impatient clarity in his face darkens. "Have you forgotten when they talked about killing us?"

"But only if we're enemies . . . and how could we be?" I protested. "The spellcraft really works for us."

"Do you hear how nuts that sounds?" He takes me by the shoulders. "Don't you realize that in the myth these old women want you to play out with them, the oak-king must die?"

The pit of my stomach winces tight. "Wait a minute, here. The witches are going to kill you? As a sacrifice? Oh, I can't believe that."

"You'd better, Siggy. The excarnation follows a ritual pattern of waxing, then waning, then waxing again, only to wane again. It happens every time."

"Daniel! Are you serious?"

"For chrissakes, I thought you knew. The moon does that, you know." His bafflement is big-eyed for a while, then he lets me go and stands back. "Forgive me. I forgot that you never really thought about the moon before. Except to know that a cow jumped over me once."

He smirks sarcastically, and I slump against a tar-papered ledge.

"Don't make fun, Daniel. I admit, I'm no great intellect. I've got none of your learning. But I am the one *you* chose. Remember that? I just don't want to lose you."

I fall to the ground in a miserable heap. Married not even a day and we're having our first argument.

Daniel, slightly chastened, comes over to apologize and sits beside me. "Well, we all have to wane eventually, Siggy, don't we? All of us. But I'm one of the lucky ones—you shouldn't feel sad for me. I get to come back."

"Oh, yeah, in my head, right?"

"Whatever." He jumps to his feet. "But right now I've still got some waxing left in me. So hey, now that the witches have really left us on our own, what say we live a little? Let's get out of here and truly make our own way in the world."

"But what about the witches?" I ask. "Do we have to leave them behind? They've been showing me so much—the spell-craft, the glamour—and they've been good to you, haven't they? They respect you. I don't understand why you would want to leave them now."

I know I'm clinging to a straw, but in this topsy-turvy world, there's little else to cling to. Riding through the streets of Manhattan, I have seen the homeless, the bag ladies with their parceled lives. It was not improbable that Daniel and I would end up like that one of these days if we had to live as fugitives.

Daniel stares into the green twilight for a long while. "It just pains me to think you might get hurt, Siggy. We have played out an extraordinary . . . mystery. I'd rather not—if I had a choice."

I look at his face, and his pain shines through his features with an effluvial glow. It has the color of raw meat. I place my hand on it in the dark air where it hangs between us. The dusky light makes my pale flesh look spooky as a minnow's, and when I touch the glisteny red wound and cast a healing spell, my glamour enters the scarlet pain and softens it to a pink froth.

Daniel faces me in the jaspery light with a dim smile. "But . . . I love you too much to ask you to leave here if you don't want to. Okay." He puts his arm around me. "We'll stay."

"You really think the witches are crazy?"

"Whatever we think will sound crazy, Siggy. Society doesn't believe in us. The moon can't exist in a man. A woman can't speak with spirits of sky and earth and cast spells. In Chaldean times, clever men learned on their own to measure time by the sky and carry thoughts with symbols. Spirits didn't teach us these things. If we believe otherwise, we find ourselves among the most helpless of outlaws—the mad."

I hear his words, but for once I don't, I can't, believe them.

The loft is dark except for a slant of gray dawn that falls from the skylight onto the futon where Daniel sleeps. His nakedness floats pale and serene on the blue sheets. I like to look at him like this, when he can't see me and I can see all of him. He's so beautiful in repose, like a museum marble. Or a corpse, I suppose.

I strip off my sleeping shirt and underwear and lie next to him. Now we look the same. If he is marble, we are carved of the same stone. We are two tomb effigies, together forever. Except that I can feel his heat. And if I look carefully, I can see it, or at least the astral light around him that wisps and buffets like heat.

I'm happy, almost feverish, belonging to this man. And I'm sad for him to belong to me. I have become a witch. I have no doubt of that now. My growing proficiency at shaping the glamour with my spells has replaced all doubt. I know I will only get better at using this power. But I know that's not what he wants. He has become totally impassioned with other desires, earthly desires, and wants all the fun I had as a teen. Not in the same way, of course. He's more urbane. But it amounts to the same thing, this carefree pursuit of sensual pleasure.

I want him to have that. But I would never have wanted this for myself, given the choice. I'm frightened sometimes when I cast a spell for strength, or energy, and the glamour moves around me, its windy colors blurring silently. It awes me to feel the viscid energy between my fingers and to smear it over my naked belly and Daniel's.

His eyes twitch when I touch his belly with the cool green fire, and he begins to dream. Closing my eyes, I watch the same silken dream—he and I playing tag among poplars and alders in Riverside Park, sunlight sparking flint in my tousled hair. He tags me and calls, "You're it!" But I'm gone, and a dew-lit hawthorn is in my place. I laugh at him from behind an elm, and he rushes at me. But every time he tags me, it's not me but a tree, and I am giggling at him from among the birch's claw-shaped leaves. And the magic we are spelling is the simple word *love*.

One night I have a nightmare that I am torn in half. My life bleeds out of me from below, a dark red squidsmoke. Drusille and Glendil hold my arms and drag me away over wet, kelpy ground, and another woman is holding my legs, big hacked pork shanks, and walking away from us into a chlorine-green distance. When she turns to look back at me screaming, I glimpse the genital-slick face of an eel. It is the succubus again, returned, but this time I question whether she is me. This time, somehow I know she is Ashera Ferialle.

• • •

"Willa, are you sitting down?"

"Baby, at last—you called!. Do you have any idea what you're—"

"Willa, don't say anything just yet. Let me talk first, okay? Willa—I got married."

"Oh, dear Jesus. Not the psychopath!"

"I'm just calling to say we're happy and well."

"What about me? Don't you care what you're doing to me?"

"We're calling from a phone booth, Willa, so don't bother tracing us this time. We're having a great time, and we really love each other. Wait. Here's Daniel. He wants to talk to you."

"Mrs. Lindo?" Daniel listens expectantly and then hands the phone back to me. "She hung up."

The air in Riverside Park has a satin weight and a smell of moss. I'm walking with Daniel through the hilly trails among the bare trees. Our cloaks ward off the damp cold, and with our cowls pulled up and our faces touching we can shut ourselves away from the gray day and enter our own slippery darkness, as soothing as the fetal darkness. We do this at intervals as we stroll.

For the first time since my childhood, my days have no structure. No school, no job, no needy Willa, no probing Dr. Chen, not even the witches to bring us meals. I have $60 in my purse and $3,686 in my checking account. That seems like a lot of money to me now, though before all this started, I ached with frustration over how little I'd been able to save.

Perhaps the intense effort of making each day so completely filled with pleasure is taking its toll, for Daniel needs more rest during the day, to recuperate for the night. That's when I walk through the city streets and practice spellcasting. Some days it seems as though I can touch animals with my energy. Birds and squirrels seem particularly receptive to my come-sing-come-dance spell, one of my own creations. I can sing aloud to a burnt-looking bird on an iron railing and I feel its dollop of life sparkling in my chest, as if my heart were growing wings. Soon a clutch of sparrows will be japing and twittering on the rail, and I'm stroking all of them with dream fingers. When kids slash by on skateboards, the birds blow away like ash.

Dogs, too, respond well to these spells. Once, a dance spell on an Irish wolfhound out for a walk in the park with its owner sent the animal prancing over to me. When its owner came to retrieve it, the dog snarled and snapped at her, which caused a small commotion. Even after I broke the spell, the dog kept returning to crouch at my feet and finally had to be led away, tail tucked between its legs.

I confess, I do these spells for the sheer sport of it, but afterward they usually make me feel bad. Most of the time, I concentrate on inanimate objects. I find a spell that lets me touch things and feel what they're feeling. I use it to reach with my glamour into the sidewalk and the curb, and I experience the huge weariness of the city—the stressed concrete, the cracked bricks and crumbly mortar, and the tired metal—all exhausted, deformed by fatigue, each day adding more embitterment to their mineral suffering. Staring too long at a manhole cover, experiencing its grimace of endurance, my courage for life at such times almost wavers.

Does this empathy with the weary paraphernalia of the manufactured world mean I belong to the elven? Daniel remains skeptical. "You must keep faith, as Goethe says, with the world of things *and* the world of spirits equally. Now that you've chosen to swallow the line those harridans gave you, you've no alternative but to let it work on you. But I'll tell you, Siggy, this idea still strikes me as dancing on thin ice. Talking to sidewalks! Don't get weird on me, kid."

"The pot calling the kettle black!" I retort. "Who sat in an asylum for seven years without talking, just for starters?"

"It feels just as weird," he allows. "And that scares me. I thought you and I had jumped out of the asylum."

"Hoping this would not be a bigger one, right?" I try to find a way to tell him how good it feels to touch birds and stones, but he won't hear of it.

"Siggy—I've come here as a human." He shrugs apologetically. "This crazy idea of ethereal, warring powers—with us as the battle-field—makes me just want to retreat from all this. It feels too complicated—I didn't foresee how incredibly complicated. And besides, it has an acrid aftertaste of nihilism. Can't you taste it? All of us as mere sparks in an eternal night, with no name. . . . "

I laugh. He makes me laugh. The moon criticizing an idea as crazy strikes me as funny. But then, of course, I remember he's earthstruck. And I laugh again at this idea, that the craziness of the moon is that he wants to be sane.

Today is the new moon, and Daniel and I wake up to find a half dozen people, all bearing mantles of presence, hunkering in the cold outside the bower. We agree to invite them in, but when Daniel opens the door, they prostrate themselves.

They claim to be his votaries, members of local covens who, upon learning of his presence from the Coven of the Shining Face, have decided to offer gifts.

Daniel huffs with exasperation, but I can tell he's really glad for the attention because he invites the people into the bower—two blue-lipped women and three bearded men—and I make them tea while Daniel receives their gifts: talismans crafted from the moon's metals, platinum and white gold, bowls of chilled lunar fruit—silver Japanese pears, lychee with their husked transparent flesh made of moonlight—and money, wads of it.

Daniel accepts the gifts graciously, dispensing his blessings on each of their bowed heads. In their eagerness to have an audience with him they ignore me, which doesn't bother me in the slightest. Daniel, for his part, seems in manic overdrive these days, constantly seeking out more stimulation, new experiences, unfamiliar sensations. His mood is subtle, imperceptible, but *I* can tell, having become attuned to his every rise and dip all these weeks long. Sometimes his changeability exhausts me.

The votaries pepper him with questions, and in his most didactic air, as if he were back in the seminar room, he delivers a speech about standing alone, daring to be oneself, which is only possible, he says, through detachment, returning to holy ground, like the moon detached from the earth, the first Zen Buddhist in the void of space, alternating regularly between self-reflection and the dark of self-imagination, where pain becomes suffering and what before was merely true becomes necessary.

Maybe, now that he's having a taste of a former excarnation, he'll be happier here and less restless. He certainly sounds happy, fielding the reverent attentions of the coveners, expounding on exactly what it means to him to stand alone: "Each of us persists as a solitary participant in a solitary event that remains exactly what we think of it as. If we get it right, we have a ritual, complete with blood sacrifice and everything, even redemption. If we blow it, however—well, then, *tant pis*—absolutely nothing happens. Life remains where it started—just another accident."

In the Egyptian section of the Metropolitan Museum of Art is a broken sculpture of a head, the top smashed down to the lips. Daniel has been standing here staring at it for an hour. I've gone off browsing several times and keep returning to find him there, mesmerized by its ruined shape. Maybe he's recalling a past excarnation. Or standing in awe that in this world even stone is hardly more than a dream.

*   *   *

We share a breakfast of apple, lychee, and out-of-season honey-dew, and I sit alone in the loft while Daniel occupies the writing desk, editing the pages I've been scribbling at night. Hystery is another way I've found to make love with him. This way doesn't use our bodies, yet I feel it in my flesh. By teaching me, he's touching me. When he takes a sentence I've written and shapes it to his voice, I fuse with him in a new way that's somehow as deep and important as our clasping bodies.

I once wrote about the strange cartoons I've seen in the glamour as "imaginary as animals in the clouds yet seeming to reveal something of myself, like a dream."

He rewrote it, "I knew from the first they had a meaning, like the eternal bestiary one sees in clouds, a figment, a fancy, a waking dream, and yet a truth withal."

Reading that sentence then—my thought in his voice—made me slick inside, and thinking of it now, knowing he's down there doing it yet, I feel slick again. I try fitting my attention to this ardor, and I use the spells I've learned to begin moving it up inside me, amuck with erotic fullness.

As it rises in my body, vision widens. The skylight's shine wrinkles with shadow-drifts, and phantoms file out of the void in thin streaks of rainbows. As the glamour encloses my heart in its enormous joy, I try with all my might not to lose myself in this pleasurable dilation. But the higher I lure the glamour, the lustier I feel, and the more vivid the illusions shine.

And suddenly I'm not alone anymore. Replete with hands and feet, childlike limbs stretch out of the shadows and fit themselves into tiny bodies. Nut-brown implings squat naked among the folds of the bed sheets, leering faces with mule-slanted eyes. Some have mighty erections and grapple with lascivious shakti girls. The sight of them cavorting clenches my antsy desire to an orgasm, and spine-jolts flop me to my back as the climax rides me into a centerless distance of pleasure.

At the crestfall I lie panting, seeing the loft railing, the hooped rafters, and the round skylight bigger, as if seen through water. But my body seems smaller. All the glamour is spent, and I feel lonely inside and want to call out to Daniel. I don't because I hear the rustling pages of my hystery, and I'd rather mate with him there, in the womb of my own making.

Daniel and I shop among the vegetable stalls on Broadway, and I give away half our groceries to the homeless on our way back to the bower. This is my way of paying them back for using them in my experiments. I paint them with glamour as I hand them the food, just to see what happens.

When I give tomatoes to a derelict on a street island, our fingers touch, and a blue spark jumps from me to him. His gray hands accept the tomatoes, feeling nothing, and he nods feebly. Then, as the glamour sinks in, the slack, toothless mouth gapes, and the jagged puzzle pieces of his face rearrange into a smile.

One scrawny, cat-eyed woman with a face of skull-shrunk weariness accepts her carrots from me sheathed in vaporous glamour and begins a bizarre dance on the street corner. She watches me intently, mute, wild-looking, with my proffered blue flames muting across her body to a violet smudge. I've only seen that energy around the witches, and this realization makes me jump.

I rush to Daniel's side, but he doesn't see the blue fire, and he questions whether it's the glamour or just my solicitous attentions that makes these exhausted souls exhibit flickers of life. But I *can* see the slow, sticky lightning pass from my hands into theirs. And I'm sure I recognize the witchy purple on that cat-eyed woman. But even though I no longer question the reality of what I'm seeing—only how much more remains to be seen—I dismiss this woman as a mere curiosity.

* * *

Daniel has discovered, or perhaps reclaimed, an affinity with jazz and modern art, so we spend our days touring Soho galleries and our nights at the clubs, whose habitués he finds pleasingly dim and lunar. I'm no longer afraid we'll be spotted by the police who are searching for Daniel, or the detectives Frank has hired to find me. It's been weeks now since our disappearance, and I've gotten good at my invisibility spell.

By chanting the right sounds and painting the astral fire around us like camouflage, the glamour somehow deflects the attention of others. In the beginning, back in Brooklyn, we nearly got struck by cars as we crossed the street. Now we've learned to fit ourselves into crowds at intersections, slipping ourselves into the negative spaces like figures in the Escher prints Daniel finds so fascinating. We've gotten used to getting no service in restaurants. But the peace of mind is worth the neglect and the occasional jostling we take on the sidewalks from hurrying passersby.

In a Village coffee shop, we sit with his espresso and my café con leche, which we've managed to get only because we've gone to the counter and poured them ourselves. There were times when we almost got sat on by oblivious customers, but even that seems to delight and amuse Daniel.

"You've made me happy, Siggy," he says idly, with his customary extravagance. He's been euphoric for days now, so much so that I wonder he hasn't burned out. His eyes shine like bioluminescent creatures and his mind spills over with observations and reactions to the feel of the world. "I've got to admit now, you had the right idea about going along with the old ladies and staying at the bower. I shouldn't have worried about it to begin with. But now that we've done all the things *I* want to do, it occurs to me that I haven't asked about you."

"What about me?"

"Well, do you feel happy?"

"You mean, has becoming royalty grown on me?" I kid him. "Yeah, I guess. Daniel, what are you getting at?"

"Nothing. Really. I never thought it would happen like this—all this leisure feels so fascinating, so wonderfully pointless. In the past, everything had a ceremonial purpose. Nothing just happened. I conducted ceremonies and obeyed calendars and tides. My wife would come to me at propitious times, you know, the fertility-of-the-fields routine. But this—well, I find this very different—very easygoing and . . . rather superficial. Everything I used to do carried significance, whole freights of meaning. If I changed my looks, combed my hair a different way or something, farmers scurried to rotate their crops or not plant them at all. My slightest gesture, a sneeze even, had portent. And during eclipses—oh, boy! But now, nobody sweats any of that anymore. Everything follows from inner direction, self-motivation. And the philosophers complain of meaninglessness. Yet what a glorious chance to invent our own! Yes, this feels like real living to me, real humanity, let me tell you."

I feel strong enough right now to be able to make a hundred lives possible for him. When it's time to go, I don't let him get up until I've rewoven the glamour's deflecting cocoon around us, just to be sure. Sometimes, before the spell kicks in, I get quizzical stares when people see me waving my arms around like a traffic cop, punching the air like a crazy woman. But soon the weave connects, and they invariably look away. As we leave, I hold my head high. Imagine that—I actually wanted to be a CPA once! I don't care what might have been anymore; I've never felt more important, never more powerful in my life.

From a pay phone on West End Avenue I call Marti. She sounds pretty chilly at first, and it takes me a while to thaw her. Finally, she blurts it all out—she never could keep a secret from me.

"Willa's falling apart without you," she wails. "She stopped going to work three weeks ago and the bills—you should see them, Siggy— she doesn't even open them anymore. I go by every few days to see if she needs anything. I'm so mad at you for letting this happen, I could wring your skinny neck. I mean, I don't begrudge you your happiness, Sig, but you can't just rip yourself out of people's lives. Willa's a mess. I told her I'd do her friggin' finances for her, if she'd just sign the checks."

"Marti, don't do anything for her."

"She's pathetic, Siggy. If she doesn't get it together soon, they'll be turning off the electricity, and the oil will stop coming."

The thought of Willa sitting in the cold dark surrounded by her satin coverlets and pillows and all her damned glazed figurines triggers a sharp spasm of guilt. "Forget her, Marti," I sigh resignedly. "If that's how she wants to live, what am I supposed to do? Am I *her* mother? I've got a life here. I can't just walk away from it."

"Okay, you don't have to recruit me. And, besides, it could be worse. Broughton's sending over groceries. The guy's still flipped on you—I mean, it's reached proportions of weirdness. Word around the office is he's canceled his business trip to Asia 'cause he wants to be around in case you're found."

I make a mental note to consult with the witches about undoing that inadvertent love spell, and I say, "Look, Marti, just tell Willa I'm okay—in fact, I'm more than okay. I've never been happier or stronger in my life."

"Really, Siggy?" She sounds supremely dubious.

"Really."

"Can I see you?"

"Marti, I'm all right. You'd be surprised how all right I am."

"Then surprise me. Tell me where you are. It's been weeks since I've seen you, and if you can take a little from the hip, you didn't look so good then."

I hesitate, but she keeps pleading. "Siggy—it's me, Marti. Come on. Meet me somewhere. I just want to see you and know you're all right. Then I won't bug you anymore. Big-time promise. Okay?"

I concede and agree to meet her near the tennis courts in Riverside Park in a few days. But as soon as I hang up, the anger begins to rise. Memories of my claustrophobic life back in Arcadia and Willa's doleful way of keeping me close at hand seize up inside my neck like a stranglehold.

In a husky whisper, I mumble a calming spell, and my throat relaxes.

Ah, well, I guess I can't entirely blame Willa. Dr. Chen once told me I had stayed in Arcadia with Willa because I was afraid to leave and my mother gave me plausible reasons to stay.

Yeah, but those reasons no longer apply. My anger is still there, heightened actually, but kept at bay by my spell. What the hell *is* going to happen to Daniel and me anyway? Whatever it is, I'm determined to accept it. I take my unhappy memories of Willa and Arcadia, mutter a be-gone spell, and poof, they become transparent. They're still there, but unseen and unfelt. The more control I have with my spellcasting, the more I feel I have a life.

Daniel is discoursing about gods and mortals with the coveners outside in the cold bright noon. I sit in the loft and try again to move the glamour into my head. This time I'm very careful not to induce a climax. Hovering at the delicious and tottery brink, I realize that the alchemical cartoonery I've been seeing behind my lids and sometimes even around me *is* the spirit world! I have been in the presence of the elven and the seraphs from the start.

I remember the hem of the Angel in the supermarket, that first time. Surely, it must have been a seraph. And the shadows it floated upon must have been the darkness of the inner world where the elven powers build our bodies and all the living forms.

I lie back on the pillows and watch the elven with their gnome shapes crouching in the shadows and the seraphs glinting among the fractured light of the prisms. Which are my tribe? The lusty heat in me insists I belong with the elven; their ticklish concupiscence shoves into me and withdraws and shoves again. At the same time, the sun shaft is gritty with hard points of silver fire whirling in rhythm to my mounting ecstasy. It is the slither-swirl feel of their floating energy that transports me, until it explodes in a glaring wallop that kicks me thrashing and mewling out of the spirit world.

With a soft smacking of chops, Daniel devours an amber-glazed duck in orange sauce. I pick distractedly at my food; somehow, I'm less interested in eating than in experiencing the energy of the handsome people eating here in this trendy restaurant, with its glass roof and carp pools. They have the sedate manner of the affluently bred, the kind that used to fascinate me back in Arcadia when I'd see them occasionally at the golf course near Tappan Down.

Daniel has readily taken to the high life, spending the coveners' gifts—the money wads and silver coins—on fine clothes and theater box seats and fancy restaurants. Today we had breakfast and lunch on a pleasure boat he rented that cruised the coast of Long Island. For fun we slipped down to the rest room and made love standing up, watching the pale villages and bleak December tracts spool past.

In the afternoon we went on a shopping spree for our evening wear, had our hair done, and took a sunset tour of the city by helicopter. It's weird, having this much . . . pleasure. Do I deserve it? I mean, is it right to indulge like this while the planet itself is dying?

PULSES OF THE HUNT

To assuage my guilt, I cast spells of go-in-peace and tenderness-feels-for-harmony wherever I find myself.

At the opera, Daniel wept over some dying consumptive girl and I vainly attempted to raise the glamour, hoping the crescendos of music and the palpable enthusiasm of the audience would help me connect with the planetary flow so I could discover my spirit allies. But I climaxed during the standing ovation. Blessedly, no one noticed.

Now, sitting in the cool, perfumed luxury of this super-refined restaurant, I feel calm, and the world around me is calm. Daniel is talking about opera. The word means "work" in Italian, and "pains" in Latin, he says. It is the painful work of all modern art to deliver the message that we can rely no longer on the gods. "And as a god, I can tell you what relief I feel not to have to carry all this raddled human consciousness around anymore, testing and teasing it. Let it sulk in its nihilism! When the human race finally traipses down the path of the dinosaurs, the gods will still go on in this world."

"Don't you miss being a god, even a little?" I ask.

"I will always exist as a god," he answers, with a smile that could be self-mocking or simply smug. He pours me more champagne and clicks the crystal of his glass against mine. "But only as a man can I live."

Daniel's napping. I go to Riverside Park, to the basketball courts on the lower level. I find a kid about my height swatting a blue handball against a concrete parapet, and I get into a game with him for the exercise. Back in Arcadia, in my high school days, I was a pretty good slammer. He takes it easy on me at first, because I'm a woman. But after dropping a game, he plays more avidly. Our breaths smoke, and some onlookers gather at the railing above us, but I ignore them, intent on baffling this spry kid with my butterfly shots that flutter drunkenly through space.

A trumpet peals from above. I glance up and see a rowdy-haired woman in leather-strapped leggings and a crazy-quilt shawl, brandishing a battered trumpet, waving to me. She looks like the cat-eyed woman who danced for me on the street corner and carried the violet witch light. But what I notice immediately is that she's dressed differently. The crazy quilt has the panels, pouches, drawstrings, cowl, and padded shoulders of a mantle of presence.

I thank the kid quickly and retrieve my black cloak from the railing where I draped it. Slowly, I climb the stone stairs to meet this witch, who I already know is Ashera Ferialle. Her purple body light has tangled threads of lightning in it.

Skeletal and begrimed, with hair like a tumbleweed, the witch opens her mantle and exposes her nakedness to the cold, gyrating a slow, lurid dance at my approach. She's unbelievably, almost sickeningly, thin: Her pelvis rocks, like antlers swaying, over a goat-beard of pubic hair, and her rib cage reaches out like a claw.

I stop, and she shimmies closer, eyes crossed, a lizardy tongue flicking at me. The precise mud-dot designs she's painted on her naked body with river grime dance in odd, contrary movements, her bones disjointed.

The smudged, wolfish face inside her extravagantly tangled gray hair floats closer—and I recognize her for sure now as one of the scrawny derelict women I've given food to and daubed with glamour.

A mephitic stink precedes her. That's the most precise word I've found to describe that stench. It isn't just foul-smelling, it has the same kind of rooty, rotting warmth that steams up from compost dumps. I nearly gag.

"My weakness sickens you?" she asks, cupping her dugs of shriveled leather in her hands. "This is the perfume of death I'm wearing, little sister. And you'll be wearing it yourself some day soon for sure."

"Who are you?"

"The one you seek."

"I'm not seeking anybody."

The shocking figure snaps her mantle closed and steps closer. "Who do you think I am?"

"Ashera Ferialle."

She shows gray teeth and black gaps in a smile that fits her shrunken flesh like a snarl. "Now *you* ask a question."

"What do you want?"

"The truth," she says instantly, thrusting her trumpet at me. "You serve the elven or the seraphs?"

A twitch starts in my upper lip to hear this living skeleton speak those names. "You *are* Ashera," I say, and this certitude breaks open a jangle of psychic impressions—a blood-beating ruby, then the feather-glow rays of the moon blotting the sun, and a young woman's dark face, devilishly beautiful—swift images, persuading me that what I'm seeing is not what it seems.

"Answer my question," she demands, solemn as an owl.

"I . . . I don't know."

"You don't know." She sneers and thrusts her face so close I can see the wens and chancre scars in her webbed flesh. "You better know, you want to stay alive."

I back away from her threat. "What do you mean?"

Her head snaps back as if she's just gotten a whiff of herself. "I'll show you what I mean. Don't you walk away from me." She crooks a bony finger and says in a voice so deep my whole life disappears into it, "Come here."

I start to move toward her and catch myself with a jerk.

"Come!" she insists, and the big muscles in my legs twitch like a frog's, throwing me toward her.

"No!" I force myself to stop, and my body stands rooted, popping with spastic twitches. In a fright, I thrust a go-away spell at her.

She waves her arms convulsively and backs off one step. "Hey!

Don't try that shit with me!" Then she shouts some spells of her own, in an accent I don't grasp.

Suddenly, I'm sitting on the damp cobbles, and my heavy head bobs dizzily. I think I'm passing out. Ashera's cave-squatter face looms before me, and my heart punches hard against my ribs.

"Relax, little sister, I won't hurt you. Just don't use that shit with me anymore. I don't like that."

She puts a dry, raspy hand to my brow, to steady my head, and the wooziness slims away.

"You ask what I mean," she says, helping me to my feet. "This is what I mean. When you know who you are, the spirits obey you."

I stagger a few steps away from her, but I'm less frightened now. I see that her feral features hold no malice for me. "How did you do that?" I ask, dazed. "How did you drop me so fast?"

"No." She wags her finger bone. "It's my turn to ask. You tell me. Why are you doing this shit if you don't know who you are? You tell me that."

"I'm just a beginner. I just started."

"Then start at the beginning, Red. Find out who you are. And do it quick."

"Why?"

"If you don't know that, the Shining Face hasn't taught you a damn thing." She walks over to an empty bench, puts down her trumpet, and motions for me to sit beside her. "What you're doing is dangerous. Don't you know that? Not everybody can do this shit. You need helpers. Without helpers, you're grass." She juts out her lower lip with certainty, then waves a rag-clotted arm at the towers of Riverside Drive. "You see all that? All that mightiness stands on a lot of grass. The whole world's a grave. You know that?"

I nod feebly.

"Your question. More lively now. I've got work to do, feeble as you might think it is, eating like you do every night in fine restaurants and going to the theater. The moon's wife. La-de-da. You're not so important as you might think, young thing. You look hot now. You're all the talk. But by spring, you mind me, by spring, you're grass."

This stirs defiant anger in me, but it falls away into a far place. And I blink at her, till I realize she's waiting for me to ask a question. "Uh, why—I mean, who do *you* serve—elven or seraphs?"

"That I don't have to tell. You know that." Abruptly, she leers. "But I'll tell you a thing. You see me? You see the way I look, gnawed to the bone? You see the stains of suffering in my face? You see the shadow on me? I will tell you this. The city put this on me. What I am, the city—and the seraphs who made the city— made me. They did."

I feel confused and say so: "That doesn't tell me anything."

"That don't matter, young thing. That don't matter at all. You're grass."

"Why am I grass? Who wants to kill me? What have I done?"

"No more questions." She sits up straighter and feels at the ripped and torn pockets of her haggard cloak. "It matters none. I came to give my gift to you. To honor the old ways. That's all that really matters in this whole damned dance. The old ways. But you'll see that for yourself. By the spring, you'll see that." She reaches under her cloak. "The Shining Face has given you the bower and its spoils. The Dark Shrine gives you this—a humble gift, something very small, nothing much, really—just the point between life and death."

Her charred spider's hand presents a splinter, like a sharpened matchstick dipped in tar. "Dreaming thorn," she says. "Prick your finger and you'll know who you are—*but that won't be you no longer.*"

Her last words carry a jarring voltage, and I jump up. The point of the poison thorn aims right at me, and with a dreamful fright I can actually see the death in it! It looks like warped air, like a force field spreading transparent wind-driven ripples toward me.

Panic tightens its coils, and I'm afraid to move, afraid I'll unspring wildly.

"If you don't take it," the skull-face says with a crooked smile, "I'll give it to you."

Ashera sidles closer, and I prance backward.

"Don't you run!" she shrieks, laughing horribly, and the joyous fury in her cry spins me about and whips me into a run. "Don't you run from me!"

Her trumpet wails like a thing being murdered, and I dash across a brick court and sprint to the trees before I look back. She's gone. I gaze up and down the asphalt path and into the trees but see no sign of her. Timidly, I return to where she had stood and look over the railing. The kid is still down there slamming the handball.

Nothing visible has changed, except that a clammy cold has penetrated the warmth of my mantle.

I arrive early at my rendezvous with Marti, nervously looking out for Ashera Ferialle. This is the first time I've been back in Riverside Park since my encounter here three days ago with the skeletal witch. I wait out of sight among the trees on the tier of the park above the tennis courts. My intent is to see my friend before she sees me, not because I doubt she will come alone—I know she will—but so that I can look deeply into her body light. She knows me too well not to notice me looking at her strangely—and I'm not sure I want to explain anything anymore.

She appears a little late, as usual. She's smoking a cigarette and wearing stiletto heels; her hair's cut short and moussed to bristles with black tips and blond roots. Despite the blustery river wind, she's got on a tight skirt cut above the knees and her red leather jacket is half unzipped. Her one concession to the cold is a yellow scarf demurely draped over her decolletage.

Around her body the light is sooty and fizzing with champagne glints. I don't know what this means any more than I understand the flame shapes around Daniel, or the obscuring purple mist swathing the witches. But I have this gut feeling that these luminosities do mean something. Part of my training, I guess, is to figure that out one of these days.

I stride down through the trees, and when she spots me, she flicks away her cigarette and stops walking, hands jammed in her pockets. Her body language tells me she disapproves, perhaps of my theatrical attire—I'm wearing a covener's gift of a bone and feather necklace and my black mantle of presence—or maybe she's unhappy with my lurking in the trees, or both.

"Siggy Lindo," she says in a peevish voice. "What is this getup you're wearing? Are you crazy? Are you really out-of-your-mind crazy, or are you just being weird?"

I open my arms for a hug, and she backs away.

"None of this friendly stuff until you tell me what's going on."

I pull my cowl up, miffed that she pleaded for this meeting and now is intent on razzing me. Slowly, I turn to walk along the asphalt path and wait until she's beside me. I hadn't intended on telling her so fast, but there seems no other way to explain myself. "I'm a witch."

She slips another cigarette between her lurid red lips. "Snakey," she approves with a slight nod. "So that's why the juju necklace and the robes."

"It's a mantle of presence. It protects me from evil emanations."

She huffs a vehement stream of smoke through her nostrils. "Like me, right? Like I've come here to put the evil eye on you or something."

"Come on, Marti. I'm serious. Why're you trying to break my face?"

"Right. I'll tell you what's serious. You *disappeared*—on purpose! You left me in the lurch with your crazy mother. What am I supposed to tell *her*? You're a witch now? That's swift. That's really swift."

"Don't tell her anything."

"Yeah, right. Like she's just going to go away. Maybe you could cast a spell that will get her to go back to the umbrella factory and earn herself a living wage."

"Marti, come on. If I could, you bet I would. But I'm just learning. This is all so new to me. I'm an apprentice."

"Oh, is that right? Who's teaching you? The maniac who killed his kid?"

Her anger is contagious, and what she's just said makes me want to grab her shoulders and shake the cigarette out of her wise-gal face. Instead, I subvocalize my calming spell and put my mind on the rapturous feeling turning softly in me. "He didn't kill any-body," I say, beginning to explain, but the hopelessness of making her understand stops me. "All right, Marti—maybe I am nuts. I'm not going to try and tell you otherwise. But what's important is I'm happy. Happier than I've ever been. And nobody's getting hurt."

"Yeah? What about Willa?"

I stop and turn so she can see the earnestness in my face. "Willa's forty-one years old, for God's sake. If she can't make it to work maybe *she* ought to check in for some therapy. But I'm sim-ply not going to shop for her anymore, or balance her checkbook, or listen to her stupid, shrill nagging—not anymore."

The anger disappears from Marti's face and the laid-back, wise-gal look returns. "Shit, Siggy, that's the first time you've made any sense since you went to business college."

"Which, you will remember, Marti Svoboda, I only did because you went and married that lummox Buster."

"Yeah, but school worked out for you—Buster didn't. You weren't the same after that. But now—Jesus, Siggy, I don't know who the hell you are."

"It's still me," I soothe her, touching her arm and trying to direct the languid reverie in me to her. I want her to like me now that I see there's a chance for that. If my oldest friend will accept me, maybe I can build a bridge to my old life. "Hell, I didn't want to change. This thing in my brain just turned itself on."

"You still having O's in supermarkets?" she asks with a mischievous twinkle in her languid eyes.

I playfully punch her arm like in the old days. She blows smoke in my face, and we laugh. Before I know it, I'm telling her everything after all about the bower and Daniel. But the spell of silence that the witches made me place on myself in the clinic is still somehow effective, and I can't actually talk about Drusille and Glendil, only in the most vague terms as old friends of Daniel, eccentrics who believe themselves to be witches. Nor do I want to tell her about Ashera.

Sketchy as it is, hearing my hystery spoken aloud as we mosey in a directionless way out of the park exults me. Everything I say really happened, yet I'm keenly aware of how it must sound to Marti, and I try not to come across as too enthusiastic or she'll think I'm ranting.

By the time we find ourselves in a coffee shop on Broadway, near the university, I've at least convinced her of my sincerity, if not my sanity, and that earns me the right to demand her silence.

"Yeah, like I'm gonna tell Willa any of this." She asks a dozen questions about Daniel, having a harder time imagining a man who can talk about philosophy and still be a great lover than she can believing I could help save or destroy civilization with my glamour.

"You and your lunatic lover better keep to your bower," she warns me. "Frank is as crazy as you are. I've already told you, the scut in the pool is that he has detectives prowling all over the city looking for you."

"I don't care," I tell her. "Even if somehow they get past my invisibility spell, I've got others that will turn them away and keep them away."

She pats me on the back. "Invisibility spells!" She laughs. "I always knew you were going somewhere, Lindo—I just didn't realize it was somewhere without a zip code."

"Hey!" I protest and unclasp the medallion of the Virgin. "*You* told me to pray, remember? You gave me this." I press it back into her hand. "Well, it really worked. She answered my prayer for help. Skeptical as I was, the Woman God loved me anyway."

Marti fits the medallion around her own neck and gives me a long, skeptical look. "I don't think the Virgin Mother made you a witch, Siggy."

"It wasn't what I had in mind, either, when I asked for help," I admit. "But I was desperate—and glad for any miracle at all."

I don't invite her up to the bower to meet Daniel and his devotees, because I know she really doesn't want to. Now that she knows I'm all right and not a drooling lunatic or a prisoner of a psychopath, she's content to let me go my way, like I did when I went to business college.

"I'll be in touch," I say in the subway as her train rumbles in. We hug, and I infuse her with enough glamour so that she parts from me with a blurred happiness in her eyes.

We are lying in a hot bath with the lights out, and the dark has the silica glint of stray ectoplasm from our earlier lovemaking. Daniel has been ill. Waves of lassitude have ebbed and flowed through him for four days now, and sporting with him in the tub earlier was supposed to confirm his triumphant return to health. But the weakness has come back. He watches me with that still, soft expression that makes him look as though he's daydreaming, but when I ask him what he's thinking about, he doesn't know. In these torpid moments, he is at great remove from his own mind—and that frightens me.

My healing spells are not strong enough to cure him, but they make him feel better. I've been using the glamour to paint his body when he sleeps and now to shine the water so he soaks in my vitality. The effort depletes my power and leaves me feeling calmer, more ordinary. The sexual urgency is gone and with it the star-winks, the comet streaks, and dandelion-fluff illusions of light, as well as the shadow shapes of bawdy trolls.

I miss the explosive leaps I've attempted that have fallen back into erotic paroxysms. Since my confrontation with Ashera, I haven't had the strength to budge my glamour. I've been too nervous. For days I looked at every derelict woman I passed, peering at each to see if she was Ashera Ferialle. At night, I listen for the sick cry of her trumpet. I know she's going to return. She wants to prick me with her dreaming thorn and force me to my destined allegiance.

Daniel didn't know about my talk with her for three days. I thought if he knew, he'd want us to leave. But I don't want to leave. I don't want this magical time ever to end. I feel this is where I belong, learning the craft and living with the moon. The rapture that has been my companion from the beginning of this hystery is still there most of the time. The only darkness is the shadow of the witches.

"We have too much happiness for fear to burden us," was all he said about it. "Forget the thorns and the potions. We won't play their game."

I keep thinking that if I can lift the glamour beyond my hungry heart and into my head, I won't have to face Ashera's dreaming thorn, or the witches' three-drop potion. But I can't. The moon waxes to full, and I feel time sifting away. I've had several more orgasmic disasters, with the gnomes leering and garish shooting stars freezing around me like ice rays. But that's it. The glamour won't budge higher than that.

Perhaps I'm more a mutant than the witches realize. Suppose I'm not tuned to the faery or the sky spirits but am instead an amalgam of the two, an elven seraph or a seraphic elf? What if I'm not good for anything more than what I'm doing, raising the sap of my glamour into bursting blossoms of sexual ecstasy and sharing the nectar like this, healing the sick?

I press my floating leg against Daniel's and wish more than anything that this is true.

Daniel has put a stop to seeing the coveners who seek him out with their gifts and their interminable questions. Which makes me glad, because I think we'll have more time together now. He doesn't spend it with me, however. He's moody, listless; he says he wants time to write, but all he can manage are some orphic lines about a pack of wolves. Something is wrong. He's constantly tired, takes a lot of naps, and our lovemaking doesn't have the passionate intensity it used to.

"Sickness," he tells me one bitter cold evening, candlelight undershadowing the angel breadth of his eyes, "exists like evil, separate and sovereign as the sun or any of the stars—a burning bitterness, astringent and caustic, corrupt, black, and evil-smelling with the stench of our bowels, the malodor of our mortality, the putrid digestion of all the mortal lives that have died sustaining us, the blackness of death and of moral darkness, the corruptible body of endless time and salty blood—" He looks down at my gelling mushroom spaghetti sauce. "Hey, don't let me stop you from eating."

I stab a mushroom with my fork and chew it without interest. "You sound like the shamans we've read about who can heal only the sicknesses they've endured themselves."

He muses over that briefly and pushes back from his full plate. "Amazing that healing works even in the dark, in the midst of the most putrid depths of physical existence, in the tar pit and the grave. Something other must exist, unreal, immortal, beautiful, fiery and yet cold, a strange wholeness latent in chaos, working toward unity. If the shaman finds that, you know, he calls it the poison cure."

"You've been taking that cure a lot lately. Daniel, I'm worried."

"Nah. The trumpet witch has spooked you. Now every headache we get looks like some blood-boiling voodoo curse."

I haven't felt sick or listless once, but I don't say this to him.

"The moon wanes," he says to fill my nervous silence. "Your glamour, too. You'll see, with the Christmas new moon, I'll have finished with this shamanic episode."

But Christmas comes, and Daniel is as sluggish as ever, too tired to celebrate. He spends most of each day napping or staring wearily into space. For my Christmas gift, I want him to have a complete physical, and he morosely submits. The next day, I take him to a doctor recommended by one of the coveners, and the following day, the doorman calls Daniel to the lobby phone for the coven doctor's results. I go down with him, and his tired face shows no emotion as he listens and then asks the doctor to repeat the results for me.

The doctor tells me that she can find nothing physically wrong with him. And then she levels a remark that blows coldly through me: "He may have moon-sickness—some weariness of the soul. For a moon-king, he has been with us a long time, you know. Perhaps now he is outbound."

In the auburn dusk, the moon is as slender as when I first met him. I stand at the south window watching him smile in the west. Darkness spools silently out of the day's murk. The fatigued light of stars winks on, illuminating the rungs of a reality that climb higher than this rooftop where we are all shrinking into disappearance, and I realize I must pay attention to what does not exist.

All day I troubled Daniel with my anger and my fears of losing him. "Why do you keep nodding off like some junkie? The doctor has found nothing wrong with you. Don't you see? You're going back to what you were in the clinic. It's all in your mind, Daniel. Why are you doing this to me?"

I should have remained silent. Nagging him did no good. He listened to me with half-lidded eyes and fell asleep anyway. I tried rousing him with strong tea and with the words he had preached to his disciples. I reminded him that only rebellion makes authenticity possible, and I challenged him to rebel against this dark thing that had come back to own him. He listened with glazed eyes.

Now as I turn and see him sitting before the west window, blindly watching the day's calamitous colors thin away into night, I remember that he came down here for me, to free me from those who thought me mad, who had battered me with drugs. He returned my life's instant and power to my own hands. I should have remained silent and let him have his rest. What did I expect him to say, anyway? That we would go on forever? That I didn't need him anymore?

I must pay attention to what does not exist—ghosts, like Chloë, like all the grief of his past before he became the moon-in-the-man. I think they have come back again to claim his existence—to fulfill their lack.

As if he feels me looking at him, he says, "It all looks so different from up there."

His voice makes me wince inside with more grief than I've felt since my father died.

"Sitting here at the edge," he says, "teetering at the fiery drop of the sky, I feel all the weathers that sweep up and carry the quick of this world. But up there—I feel only peace, unmindful of the loneliness deeper within the darkness. Here we've yet to part, and already I miss you."

I turn to look out the window again. I have this gloomy feeling that imminently I'm going to see my father's ghost wandering among the crimson sun shafts that flare briefly through the rooftop aerials and scaffoldings.

"It happens to me every time," the moon says sleepily. "I just didn't think it would happen again this soon. I guess my earth-struck spell has ended. The unpredictable vectors of free will have concluded, and the staid, processional, and fixed routines of my lunar life begin again."

His voice grows dull with weariness, and I don't have to look at him to know he's nodding off. I feel twelve years old again. The air is plush with summer heat, and my father lies on his stomach in the storm ditch. At first I think he's looking for something, because his head is turned on its side, and his eyes are open. But he doesn't blink. And before I can make myself breathe again, Willa is there, and her shearing cry reminds me I am here with Daniel.

The moon floats in its great remoteness, infinitely beautiful and solemn. Staring at it, I feel my smallness—a holy smallness, like that of a sacrificial thing. Enormous, invisible powers are at work. They carry the moon through the sky and pivot the earth's turning. But our eyes bear false witness and see the moon and the sun falling through reefs of scarlet clouds, when in fact it is we who are falling across the immense, star-littered emptiness.

I wait until I hear Daniel's breathing deepen to softly rasping snores before I take out the emerald vial and put three drops of night into a half cup of steaming comfrey and celandine. The potion has a sour reek, like rotted gingko berries, and I wait for the liquid to cool.

I can't express how heart-bruising it's been watching my spells to heal Daniel fail. I know now that I must break through the barrier that has kept me on the outside, tantalized but always looking in at the spirit worlds. I'm convinced that either of the powers have the ability to save Daniel: The elven, who build our bodies, can simply make more serotonin or dopamine or whatever brain chemicals it takes to keep Daniel alert and with me for years to come. Or the seraphs can transmit a scientific breakthrough that will cure his vapidity with one shot and at the same time perhaps help countless other chemically depressed people. They can transmit it through me! If I'm strong enough to receive it, I know it can happen.

I down the vile potion in one draught and have to grip the hard edge of the sink to keep from retching. A glass of water cuts the ghastly taste and leaves a bright, cold track down my throat. Nutshell faces peek through the black windows and green matchflares fizzle at the edge of my sight. But that's probably just my excitement roiling up my glamour. As if I'm caught in a powerful slipstream, I whirl outside to receive my first broadcast.

I step down the stairs and out of my body. Suddenly I see myself sprawled on the tar paper, one arm up, one down, still as a crime victim. A peach light sprouts on me like luminous fungus. Then a glacial wind lifts me off my feet, and I begin to rise. My body spins away into the dark mosaic of rooftops and disappears among the turning spokes of the lighted streets, and I soar.

Vision swings wide. Sun-thumbed colors dispel the night, and a chromatic panorama of the Indian Ocean rotates below me, its amethysts sparkling. I recognize the Horn of Africa and India's lingam before I rocket up and away and the eternal night opens its web of stars to receive me.

Clear light, a melodious flow of energy, enwombs me as if in a warm sea, amniotic, futureless, and free. Outward is the moon— vast and flawed—and inward lies the earth, vaster yet, marbled blue. Sere land masses drift by, the sea cobalt beneath fleecy clouds.

I look at my hands and see them, my arms, and then my whole body just like in the flesh, only brighter, clearer, almost transparent. The balmy expanse of daylight extends to the curved rim of the planet, where the edge of darkness appears as wavery curtains of auroras.

Beings of light, full of power and presence, seething with joy, swell closer. All the combined climaxes of my life can't compare to the teeming rapture I experience now in the company of these beings. Surely, these are the seraphs. This is the end of my life's journey, here among the creatures of light, the chromatic beings, whose dazzle is serene, imperishable euphoria. Below, the fallen world is an immensity of darkness, and above, tingling stars mass like majestic clouds. I am perched at the very point of love, where every other direction leads to less.

Radiant energy points spiral and whir about me, luminous as a night sea of mountainous lantern fish, and I am an illusion among these stupendous beings. Brushlike discharges of green light circle me, shaping the darkness. Fiery filaments fit together into blazing geometric wheels and spin off, looping a huge boomerang helix under the black span of stars. As they billow away above the blue feather of the earth's horizon into gusty boreal lights, I fade toward blackness. I am nothing.

Then the seraphs wheel close again, and I know—I *see* with my inmost mind—why I live this life. All my memories—past and future—the whole panorama of my life appears before me inside a congealed transparency that I know is time, stardust pixels of memories within a lucite egg. Looking at it, I start to slip, to glide toward the time-lost shape of my existence.

The seraphs close in, their luminous shadows covering me with drifting thoughts, untraceable strands of ghostly beautiful music, all the passion of life without any of the careworn begetting and losing. I think I am hearing the star songs that the seraphs sing. No. The spectral hues of brilliant light widen my mind, and I see that the seraphs are not singing, but are being sung!

Vast clouds of stars mingle their impalpable energies here in the electronic ocean, raveling songs out of the random patterns in the immaterial plasma that hovers over the earth. Those songs are the seraphs themselves—the song of the stardepths. The spark of my life resonates like a dew mote on the webwork of their linked power—free of time, free of death, free of care and longing and love.

If I want, I can go with them. I know this as well as I know my name. My dew mote will dissolve into the unbearable joy of their supernal freedom, and I can live with them forever at the crest of my sexual access. If I want, I will never have to die.

But I cry out, a desperate climax cry, remembering Daniel down below, my double-soul still trapped there in his animal heart—trapped with all the suffering that just one strand of this immortal pleasure could calm, if we could but bring it down.

Yet I know there is no end to the blood-need. I know I can't save everyone, perhaps not even anyone. It is all I can do to open my own being to the wraith-wind of the seraphs, and when I do, I feel I can drift away forever, alone, into a vastness of terrified love. If I will simply let go of Daniel—

The sorrowing star of my love pulls me back. I can't do it. I retreat from the anthem beauty of the auroras, and the diamond-dust vista of my life glitters before me again, glints of future memories already unlocking in thawed time, rays of glare bending toward darkness under the galaxies' eternal night.

Suddenly, I am standing in the dark beneath empty trees and a diamond-chip sky. The moon calls my name, and I look about for Daniel and see on the ground blond feathers of hair, a craggy face adamantly turned away, and the starlit satins and glowing white collar of a tuxedo. Good night! For several seconds my brain jams up, and I blink and squint and walk around the body, unwilling to believe what I'm seeing. Frank Broughton lies at my feet, mouth downturned like a temple demon, staring straight up past me with the night standing in his eyes. The moon calls my name again, and I kneel and feel the plastic chill of Frank's flesh.

"Siggy!" I hear Daniel crying to me. He drops weakly to his knees beside the fallen man. "Oh, my God," he moans. "What has happened?"

But I don't know. Where was I? I remember slowly, like retrieving a dream—something luminous among the aisles of stars and the seraphs. I look down and notice beneath Frank's grimacing face a poison thorn, like the one Ashera had pointed at me, impaling his Adam's apple.

The cold closes in as I try to comprehend. My scalp puckers, and I crouch under the weight of my fright, feeling into the dark for Ashera Ferialle's wolf stare.

Daniel lifts his head from Frank's chest and tells me what I already know, "Heaven help us, Siggy. He's died."

I'm so scared my heart thrashes like a caught fish. I stand outside the Hause with Daniel, not sure if I really want to go in. The big trees hiding the structures are bigger than I remember. I watch the impetuous wind surge through the green boughs of the giant yew and rattle the leafless, whiplash branches of the oaks.

"We have nothing to fear," Daniel says with gentle certainty. I didn't want him to come with me, but even though he's not well, he insisted. The fear I see in the dew beading his ghostly white face is for me. But I'm convinced the witches are seraphic. The way Drusille and Glendil talk and act, their civilized ways, even the Hause itself must testify to their orientation.

Yet in the heart of me, I don't know what to think anymore. My composure, my common sense, is as loose as this shaking world, and the wind sounds like night and its burden of souls. All I can think of is Frank dead, his horrible grimace ugly with fear. How did it happen? Could I actually have done it—killed him—while in a trance? When I think of my nightmares about him, I shiver with cold, though I feel simultaneously flushed and feverish warm in my thick cloak, with the cowl pulled over my head.

"We don't have to go in at all, Siggy, if you really think . . . I mean, if you don't want."

I chant a courage spell and call into myself from the sun exuberant sitar music, but I'm not comforted. Dragon breath hovers as clouds above the clattering treetops, and a pulpy moon witnesses my despair.

"I've got to go through with this," I say finally to Daniel and press my face against him. I breathe deeply his vigorous fragrance, like a wheat field on a summer night, and I know this is my one chance to keep him.

Now I'm ready to walk through the leafy shadows to the front door and take in my hand the wooden trunk of the elephant's head. *The lady or the tiger?* I know if I'm wrong, if the witches are elven, we may die here tonight.

I softly return the knocker to its rest and retreat into the green shadow of the cedar. For an instant, I panic to think Drusille and Glendil are elven, for their yard, luxurious even in the shabbiest pandemonium of winter, must attest to it. But the Hause—ah, now, that's not a thing elven would have, is it? Ashera, squatting in the tule grass, biting off curses against the city—she's the Destroyer. She must be elven, not these fussy old ladies, with their sturdy shoes and hoards of antiques and artworks.

"Whatever happens, Siggy—no regrets, okay?" Daniel says from close beside me, squeezing strength into my shoulders. He feels light and frail to me, and I wish again I had left him at the bower. "Remember what you told me about your journey into the sky?" he whispers. "The light walks in darkness. We walk in ignorance. Did I not lift Chloë in that ignorance? Our ignorance owns us—lock, stock, and barrel. Some may prefer to call it mystery, but it remains the same. Who can say that the mystery of death possesses less grandeur than the mystery of life? Leave prejudice aside, I say, and let our fates take us where they will."

The calm in Daniel's voice reassures me. I return to the door and knock loudly.

Glendil appears immediately. Have she and Drusille been waiting? She curtsies to the moon-king and beckons us in warmly, helping Daniel out of his cloak, clucking over his sickly looks. They haven't seen him since the wedding, and he has indeed lost some weight.

I won't take my cloak off, and she immediately recognizes my unease. I begin to tell her about the horror of Frank's death, but she shushes me and takes me into the grand living room where Drusille is stoking a rasping fire in the black marble hearth.

"Ashera has killed Frank Broughton," I begin in a breathless rush, and neither of them blinks. They are staring at me, not for a second taking their eyes off me. They mumble a few words, and I realize they are spelling me to tell them the truth.

"I know now that I have the power to receive the seraphs," I declare quietly, watching them both intently, seeing the violet shadow of their body lights shimmering over them. "I can bring down the ideas we need to save us."

Drusille nods, and Glendil smiles lavishly. My whole body unclenches with relief. They walk toward me in slow-motion happiness, and I open my arms to receive their embrace. The violet haze shreds away, and before me stand two pixie-faced children with long eyes and black seaweed hair.

"Watch out!" Daniel grunts with surprise, his arm tightening and pulling me back.

A sharp pain at my throat jerks me away from Glendil, and too late, I see the splinter between her fingers.

"I've killed you!" Glendil, a crone again, shouts jubilantly as she does a maniacal hopping dance. "I've killed you!"

"The wicked witch is dead!" Drusille, still a child, bawls.

Daniel claps his mouth to my neck like a vampire, but I know he can't draw the poison. My neck is already numb, and I shove him aside. He regards me with crazed eyes, the same mad look that must have witnessed Chloë's death. In a flare of panic, I stagger backward toward the door.

"Escape is futile," Drusille says, old but formidable, striding up behind Daniel. "Your death is already in you."

"Daniel!" I cry in a cracked voice, and a whirl of hysteria dizzies me and sends me careening backward into a scowling totem pole. From the ground, I see Drusille cast purple dust in his face, dropping him to his knees.

"Do not fight it, child," Glendil counsels with grandmotherly concern. "You only make it worse for yourself. Accept your fate, Siggy. Your time with the moon is over."

I swim forward and realize escape *is* impossible. My knees have become jellyfish, their stinging tentacles dangling down my calves. I don't feel my feet as I shuffle toward where Daniel lies writhing on the ground, clutching his face. My goal now is just to reach him and hold him once more before I die. Drusille grabs me by the scruff of my neck, stands me up taller, and regards me like something in formaldehyde. Her strength is astonishing. "You looked elven," she says with great disappointment. "A sadder surprise I can't imagine, Sigrid, for I carried a great wish for you. I'm sorry, indeed, it has come to this."

"Why?" I manage to croak, desperate to know why the crones have done this. Why have they hurt their moon-king? I try to ask, but nothing comes out.

Drusille thinks I question her great wish for me. "I can tell you now, Siggy Lindo, you might have been the strongest of the wicce. I have never felt the Flow as powerfully as I knew it in you. What a dreadful waste this is. Yet there is no other way." She shakes me like a rag doll and bows her head with remorse, toward where

Daniel lies still now. "Sleep, Sigrid Lindo of Arcadia. Every death is but a beginning. The moon dies and is reborn. And so with you as well."

She lets me go, and I collapse in a helpless heap, numb inside and out. I lie on my back gazing at a blue amphora with dead flowers in it beside a stuffed cobra sitting on its coils in a dark corner. Flitting spectra zip across my field of vision.

My face turns, and Glendil has my head in the grip of a gnarled hand. "Don't be afraid, child," she says, the crepe of her shriveled skin crinkling around a sad, kindly smile as she covers my eyes. "I'll kill you as little as possible."

Blood-webbed darkness encloses me. I feel nothing. Snippets of a dream unreel through the black of my brain. I am with my father on a baseball diamond, playing catch on some forgotten summer afternoon. White flames run on his thick arms and across the thick breadth of his shoulders, and when he throws the ball, it streaks a contrail of luminous vapors like a comet. Dr. Pop shouts encouragement from left field, his bald head tufted with green fire. And there is Frank out by second base, disconsolately kicking small clouds of silver dust, his body furry with blue fire. Daniel is nowhere to be seen.

The ball carries a rainbow over my shoulder, and my father shouts at me to look lively. I run past him, and he stands, hands on his hips, wavering into shapes of fire. When I get to Frank, I start slapping his chest and arms with my hands, snuffing the seethe of blue flames on his body. He is in a business suit as usual, but I make him lie down in the dust and roll around until the hellsparks are out.

He sits up shivering, staring at me frightened and confused, and I get him to his feet. Then we run across the open field, and a darkness like quicksilver, only black, is gushing after us, wobbling heavily, breaking into pulsing globules and inky pellets and splashing on all sides. A bucketful of shadow smacks me behind the legs, and I belly-slide forward. Frank stops to help me, and I wave him on, desperately I wave him on, and with a terrified look behind me, he dashes off. I see him fleeing in a downpour of liquid night. And that is the last I see before darkness closes on all that I have been.

For some reason I am awake. I don't remember waking up. I'm lying in bed in a yolk-yellow room with narrow windows. Above, a light bulb hangs in its wire cage. I can feel a bandage at my throat where Glendil stabbed me. All I can remember is blacking out and dreaming of the dead men in my life. Daniel wasn't in my dream, and my first coherent thought is that he may still be alive. My nose hurts, but otherwise I feel okay. I run my hands over my body and see that I'm intact. I'm just very tired.

Slowly I make out the shape of Dr. Chen in the doorway, watching me. When she sees that I've noticed her, she comes in. Her voice sounds remote and weird. "Sigrid, it's Dr. Chen. Do you remember me? The police found you unconscious in Ditmas Park. It's a good thing you had your wallet with you, or who knows where you'd be now."

Shock overcomes my grogginess, and I try to sit up. I didn't *have* my wallet with me, I try to tell her. I left it back in the bower.

Dr. Chen gently pushes me back to the pillow, and the shift causes my nose to ache and makes me wince.

"Now, there's something I have to tell you: We had to go in, Siggy. You were comatose, we almost lost you. If you'd been taken to any other hospital, you almost certainly would have been misdiagnosed and would in all likelihood be dead now. The defect in your brain was apparently affecting your heart and breathing." She paused. "It was also obviously affecting your mental processes."

Panic-stricken, I look around and realize it's true! The wattage in my body has dimmed. The rapture energy humming in my pelvis—gone! A furious scream seeps through my pores.

"I know you feel disoriented," Dr. Chen says in a gentle voice. "You've endured a lot. All I want for you to know now is that the procedure was a success. A great success. The defect has been removed. The seizures are over."

I gaze in furious despair at the perforated ceiling and the gray light bulb in its cage. "Damn you, my brain was fine," I croak, and my voice hurts the inside of my nose. "I was poisoned. I was stabbed in the neck with poison."

Dr. Chen reads my file and shakes her head. "The neck wound is the result of your collapse, Siggy. According to the police report, you passed out in some bramble in the park and cut yourself. You could have died there if the police hadn't found you. You're a very lucky girl."

"It was poison," I insist, but suddenly, Glendil's words come hauntingly back—"I'll kill you as little as possible," she had said. "My brain was fine," I repeat sullenly and look away.

Dr. Chen doesn't argue with me. She says that if I feel up to it, the police want to speak with me.

"Where's Daniel?"

"That, I think, is what the police want to know."

When the police question me, I feign amnesia. I'm afraid that if I tell them where Daniel is, the witches may kill him—if he's not already dead. The one thing I have on my mind is to get out of here and go to him, but that's not likely. A beefy detective has read me my rights and charged me with the death of Frank Broughton. Thorns—like the one that killed him—had been found on my mantle. The clothing fibers discovered at the scene will surely prove to be mine. And as for motive, Dr. Chen has offered evidence to show that I'm mentally unstable and capable of just about anything.

After the detectives are done with me, an officer is posted at the door, and I'm left alone at last, left to mull over all that has happened. What was Frank Broughton doing there in Riverside Park anyway? Could I possibly have done it? I play the events over and over again in my head but can't make sense of them. There are too many lapses, too many hallucinations. It does occur to me that Marti, damn her, tipped Frank off as to the whereabouts of the bower. Maybe he had gone there in the expectation of running into me.

I listen inwardly for the glamour and feel nothing, all right. I feel as lackluster, as normal, as I'd been before my first bandit climax in the supermarket. The rapturous hum in my body that I have been taking for granted these past weeks is gone.

I close my eyes and look for the alchemical cartoon of seraphs and elven and see only grainy darkness. The dark in me is simple and unoccupied.

I'm back to counting the ceiling panels, the wires of the light-bulb cage, the windows in the buildings I can see through my narrow window. The return of my old compulsion signals my normalcy, which I once so fiercely wanted. Now it sickens me. I lie on my stomach and gnaw a corner of pillow, feeling hopeless and powerless, knowing there is nothing I can do.

Marti has come to visit twice, and my mother once, but I have refused to see them. When I notice them looking at me furtively through the slim wire-glass window, I turn my head away. *Traitors!*

Everything has been taken from me. I wear only the hospital smock, not even underwear anymore. I sometimes think about the black medallion of the Virgin Mother that Marti had given me; if I still had that, maybe I would pray to the Lady for help. She's famous for miracles.

But what's the use? Can I really swallow that stuff anymore about appealing to the Woman God? You know what I think? I think She is responsible for my being here. After all, the witches are Her tool—they worship Her, and they were the ones who arranged for me to be taken here and effectively lobotomized. When I question the nurse who brings my lunch tray, she's surprised I even had to ask. She tells me that the surgeon went into my skull through my nose and used optic fibers to locate the anomaly in my brain. The bastards shriveled my one tiny piece of the moon with a laser! Damn it! That was *my* piece of the moon.

The bathroom mirror, a Mylar sheet that can't be broken into cutting shards, shows no indication that I've had surgery at all. My hair looks longer and unkempt. Bobby pins and elastic ties are not available in this place. Daniel wouldn't mind. He always preferred my hair loose.

I've come to the conclusion that Daniel must still be alive. The fact that the witches didn't kill me outright, but merely pithed me, shows some compassion, I guess. How much more care would they take with the moon-king? And given the witches' spellcraft and herbal lore, I have the additional hope that they will help him ward off the oppressive lethargy that is diminishing him. But that hope resounds hollowly.

I want to rail at the Woman God—what did I ever do to Her, anyway? I want to be furious at the witches for taking Daniel away, for taking away everything that was good and special in my life. But the sedatives I've been given won't let me. So loneliness steepens. Even though I never expected it to last forever, it hurts not to have it: his rambling talks, his earthstruck appetites, the way he smelled, most of all the silver sound of his voice. I wonder if I will begin to doubt that he ever existed, much less existed as the moon. Normalcy is already weighing my doubts, as compulsive as my need to count the bathroom tiles. But for now I hold on to the one thin thread of meaning I have left: that Daniel is what he says he is, a true excarnation, the moon come down to earth in mortal form, here where everything hides within itself.

The detectives question me again, threatening me with certain incarceration in an asylum—and one not as swank as this—unless I can somehow remember where Daniel Schel is, and if *he* is the murderer of Frank Broughton, having framed the whole thing on me. If they had any idea that I forsook a chance to live forever in the seraphic heights of heaven to come back to this snakepit *for* him, they wouldn't waste their time. I stare at them dumbly, abetted by the shots the nurse injects into my buttocks.

After a while they get fed up and depart, mumbling things like "airhead" and "ding-dong." Then Willa comes flying in. She looks no different, as pallid and startle-eyed as ever, but without the haggard emaciation I had expected from her frantic phone calls. Afraid for what she will find, she hovers timidly at my bedside and doesn't throw herself over me.

Whatever the nurse hit me with today makes me feel tired and passive enough to lie here and listen to my mother's ceaseless harangue. I try to be mad at her for letting them operate, like I should be mad at the witches and the Woman God for taking away my glamour. But I just don't have the energy.

"Talk to me, baby," she urges with that familiar edge of hysteria in her voice. "Tell me how you're feeling."

"Lonely, Willa. Lonely in my bones."

"How can you say that?" she gasps breathlessly. "Lonely for him, for that man who kidnapped you?"

"I wasn't kidnapped, Ma. I went on my own."

"Baby, baby—" Willa's eyes are glassy with tears. "The police say they're going to put you away unless you can tell them where that man is."

"I don't remember."

A mouse squeak twists out of Willa, and she sits heavily on the edge of the bed and puts her quavery, cold hands to the sides of my face. "Baby, you have to remember! I can't lose you again."

Willa looks so plainly herself, not a wisp of aura or glint of illusion light anywhere. She sees the regretful and alert stare in my eyes, and her face hardens.

"They *can't* put you away," she decides and sits up straighter. "That thing in your brain—it made you insane. But it's out now and you're okay again. They can't punish you for being ill. They just can't." She pulls away and dries her eyes, resolved to be strong for both of us. "I'm going to get us a good lawyer, baby. I don't care what it costs."

"Then I hope you're ready to go back to work."

"I'll take two jobs." She gives me a lopsided smile. "Maybe I'll even get used to doing my own shopping."

Her forlorn earnestness brings forth a semblance of my old caring for her—how it can be intact after all this, I don't know— and I take her hand and squeeze it gently. I ask her about her friends, and her expression turns to soft amusement as she begins to recount the latest gossip from the factory and the pool, the eternal passionate couplings and the betrayals, as if love, with its screwed-up misadventures, is all that people's lives revolve around.

I'm glad when the nurse comes in and insists Willa leave me alone. I get up out of bed and pace the room, dully amazed at the mechanical responsiveness of my body. The slick animality is gone. I stand at the window and stare at the concrete world, counting the cars at the stoplight and wondering why Frank had died. I can't help remembering all the lewd dreams of my succubus heat searing him to bones, and the accuracy of my nightmarish foreshadowings haunts me.

What power brought him there to be killed in the first place? Chance? Love? Or the witches? I still can't figure it out, though I'm pretty sure it was Ashera Ferialle who actually stabbed him. She loiters around up there in Riverside. His corpse was locked in a grimace of terror. I'm certain the last thing he saw must have been the wolf shadows of her evil, skull-tight visage.

Maybe she mistook him for the moon-king and sacrificed him to the Woman God's ancient claim. But then that, of course, means the witches in Brooklyn will have served Daniel the same.

The anxiety sluicing through me with these thoughts gradually mutes into a drugged haziness, and for several hours my mind skitters away across glossy surfaces.

I refuse my midafternoon shot. I get hysterical and chase the nurse away. But all the sobbing into my pillow for what I briefly held and lost, what good does that do?

Marti finds me stalking the room like a zoo animal. Her eyes are burnt red from crying. "Siggy, I'm sorry," she says, face quivering. "It was my fault." She plops onto the corner of the bed, arms hanging between the legs of her jeans. "It was me who told Frank where you were."

That stops me in my tracks, my rage chilling to something else. I knew it. "Marti, why?"

"'Cause he was so desperate, completely crazy for you. He wanted to give me money. I wouldn't take it, of course. But, my job . . . I couldn't *not* tell him." Her blood-smoked eyes stare hard at me. "I didn't think he was gonna die."

I look to the open door, where a short, scrappy-looking policewoman stands guard. "Did they send you in here, like they sent Willa?"

"No, I swear—they just let me come in," Marti answers meekly. "They say you killed him with a poisoned dart."

I feel disappointment at her betrayal, but deep down, I can't blame her—I would have done the same thing in her place.

"They asked me questions—about you, being a witch and all. I told them everything you told me—you know, about Daniel calling himself the moon-in-the-man. They say he's dangerous, Siggy."

"Marti, stop."

"But the good news is that the operation was a success and you're probably gonna be yourself again. Maybe you can put Daniel behind you and start all over again. I know it's hard. It was hard for me with Buster."

"Daniel's not like Buster."

"I know, I know. You've gotta be right. I wouldn't have gone through what you've been through for that scuzzball Buster."

"Marti," I say brusquely. "I really *don't* know where he is."

"And if you knew—" She gets up wearily. "I guess love is a kind of craziness no operation can cure."

The moon's silver rind hangs above the city, and I watch it from my seat by the window. The only voices I hear are the occasional cries and moans of the certified. The inflamed days I lived as a witch seem unreal to me now. What an enchantment it was, spellbound by the renegade chemistry of my brain. I can let all of it go—all the empowered glamour, the funhouse lights and illusions, the magical joy—all except Daniel. I want him. I'm half breathless with wanting him.

Out of a steel-gray sky, big snowflakes tumble. I stand at the window, gazing off down the street into the smoldering depths of the falling snow, getting dizzy thinking that each flake is different. I watch the drifts slowly erasing the world until a nurse calls me away.

The ox-shouldered detective and his weasely partner are back, but with softer faces and quieter voices. Dr. Chen has come with them. They have news, and they want me to sit down before they tell me. I oblige, bewildered, fully expecting this is it. I'm to be charged with other hideous murders.

"Frank Broughton is not dead," the large detective says right out. "The coroner found him alive on his slab in the morgue this morning."

I cock my head and slim my eyes to tell them I won't be taken in by any trickery.

"No kidding," the narrow one interjects. "Whatever was in that dart slowed his vital signs so much that he *looked* dead. His autopsy was scheduled for this morning. Instead, he's on IV at Saint Vincent's."

I look to Dr. Chen to affirm this, and she nods. "Not only is he recuperating, Siggy, he's communicative—and he's told the police it wasn't you who stabbed him with the poison."

My heart flip-flops, and I sink deeper into the chair as the implications weigh on me. I am innocent. Oh, my God, I have the right to go free now. I can go to my Daniel.

That thought stops me, and I suspect again that this is some police ploy—until the detectives read me Frank's vague description of the two old women he glimpsed in the dark—one stout, the other small and fleecy.

"Aren't those the hospice workers from Brooklyn who helped you escape?" the ox wants to know.

I gesture as though I have no idea.

"Dr. Chen and the staff at the clinic have already identified these descriptions as matching those of Farrior and Braidwood," the ox persists. "We want to question them, but the address they have on record is falsified. Can you help us find them?"

"The operation must have impaired my memory," I say. "I don't remember a thing."

"You should know," the weasel adds, "that all charges against you have been dropped. But if you're withholding information and further crimes are committed by these women or Daniel Schel, you'll be charged as an accessory.

I give them the wise look Marti taught me in seventh grade.

The short detective smirks, and the big one hands me his card with a vexed grin. "Call me when you remember something."

I stop the doctor at the door. "I'll be signing out at once."

Dr. Chen presses her lips together regretfully. "I'm afraid not, Siggy. Until you're declared once more mentally competent, only your mother can sign you out."

I bite back a curse. "Then send Willa in."

Willa has been waiting impatiently while the police finish their business, and when she rushes in, she's startled and flushed with the news. She hugs and strokes me and tells me how wonderful this is and how I can come home now—"Well, not right now," she says looking regretful, "but in a few days."

"What?"

"Dr. Chen and the other doctors think you should stay here and be observed for a couple of days. Then they can free you without the risk of liability. It's better that way, baby."

"No, it's not. I want out of here now."

"Sorry, baby. After all you've put me through, the least you can do now is sit still for a while. Just for me?" I stare at her, and her voice turns hard. "It's only for a couple days. And it's for your own damned good. Stop being such a selfish brat."

Her weakness scalds me. "Willa, if you don't sign me out of here right away, we're through. I mean it. I'm not a child anymore. You'll lose me."

Willa's young eyes suddenly crinkle old, and her whining implodes to knuckle-biting despair. "Then I'll have to lose you!" she sobs noisily. "I'm your mother. I'm not going to let anything bad happen to you. Trust me, baby."

She backs away, wrought with tears. Jesus, she's such a baby! Sobbing real tears, she jerks out of the room.

Dr. Chen holds my angry stare as compassionately as she can and closes the door. The lock clicks like a laugh.

Now I understand what Glendil meant by killing me as little as possible. All that is left of my glamour is memory. My every attempt at spellcraft has no apparent effect. I might as well be praying to Marti's Virgin to stand in for me, because I am dead in the spirit worlds.

Of course, it's entirely my fault. It was my eagerness, my greediness to drink the three-drop potion that put me in the witches' power. Once I accepted their potion, I gave up my freedom to the drug; its sorcery owned me. It was an ambling sorcery, sending my mind into the sky and my body on a jaunt across the earth.

Glendil and Drusille must have reasoned long ago what to do if I were not of their allegiance. The night that I drank their three-drop potion, they were ready, probably even in our building at the time. They owned it, after all.

That would explain the voice that woke Daniel after I left. One of them went back for him, to bring him to the ritual. The witches knew what the potion would do to me. They knew it would walk me out of the confines of the building and away from the blare and glare of the city into the steep darkness of the park.

What kind of ritual they had in mind for Daniel and me I can well imagine, but I know poor Frank had no part in it. If Marti hadn't blabbed, he wouldn't have been there for the old biddies to jab.

With an emotional swerve, I move from amazement at his survival to pondering yet again Daniel's chances. Hopelessness creases through me. Without the ideas of the seraphs and my spellcraft to transmit them, I have nothing to offer him. My giddiest hope is just to hold him in my arms again.

I have to choose my escape carefully, for I know I'll have only one chance. At my insistence, my street clothes have been returned to me, and I wear them now.

The nurse enters and takes my tray, and as she's leaving she nearly bumps into Frank Broughton. He's in a wheelchair and backs up to let her pass. Whiskery and scoop-cheeked, his chrome-blue eyes haunted, his temple hairs scorched gray, he has the plangent weariness of a shell-shocked survivor.

He stops in the middle of the room and squints at me. "You look different," he mutters in a raspy voice.

Through my surprise, I don't know what to say.

His mouth works, but no sound comes out. For a long while he just stares, weepy and yet reserved, amazed, and probably relieved, at finding me so ordinary, sitting there cross-legged in bed, in my street clothes, not at all a dreamy enchantress with a mysterious aura of glamour.

"What I mean is—" he mumbles and touches his forehead with quavery fingers. "You don't look as I remember. There've been so many dreams—so many—I forgot how you actually look."

"Are you okay?" I ask, because his eyes have become hooded and his head dodders like he's about to fall asleep in front of me.

He pinches the flesh between his eyes and faces me alertly. "I'm sorry you were falsely accused."

"Forget it. That wasn't your fault."

He shakes his head once. "It was entirely my fault." The wings of his nostrils whiten as he draws the energy to speak. "Of course, I shouldn't have been in the park at all that night. I shouldn't have even been in Manhattan. I was supposed to be in Singapore." He smiles tiredly. "Instead I—well, to be blunt, I seem to have been obsessed about you. I'm sorry. I had these dreams—I wanted to talk to you about them. But I didn't know where you were. I made your friend tell me. I drove to where she said you lived, and I sat in my car all day working up the resolve to approach you. I can't tell you how foolish I feel admitting this. I've never behaved this way before, not even as a teen, when my hormones were raging and it was okay to be smitten. I can only assume I've been overcome by some . . . by some weird midlife crisis."

I'm glad that the spell is broken between us and relieved he believes it's his fault and requires no explanation from me. But I need to know, "Can you say what happened to you in the park that night?"

The crease between his eyes deepens. "It was late, and I was about to leave to go to my hotel when you came out. I was elated. I called your name, but you didn't hear me, and I followed you into the park. When I caught up with you, you didn't recognize me. It was dark. You looked very different yourself, very pale and angular. Your eyes wouldn't focus on me. I thought maybe you were sleepwalking. I tried to turn you around and walk you out of the park. That's when I was grabbed from behind, and I broke free. I expected to face a mugger. Instead I saw two old ladies. You can imagine my surprise. I dropped my guard, and one of them grabbed my hands while the other stabbed me in the throat with a dart. I threw them off, but it took all my strength. After that I couldn't even reach my throat to take out the dart. My arms suddenly wouldn't work. For a moment I saw you staring at me, aghast. Then my legs stopped working too, and I fell down. Dead, for all appearances."

"You passed out."

"No." His jaw tightens with conviction. "I believe I died, quite literally, I'm sure. My life went out of my body and took me with it, and we lay in a cold wind together on a flat, featureless plain, shivering for what seemed like forever. And then you were there. Only you looked like my mother. She's been dead since I was seven. But there she was, vivid in every detail—except that she looked like you. And she told me it wasn't time yet. And she got me up and we ran away from a black wave of night that was ready to crash over us. And it did crash. But you pushed me away from it. The last thing I saw out there was you looking like my mother, birthing me again, out of the darkness, pushing me into the light. And the next thing I knew, I was awake in the dark—in a body bag."

He chews his lower lip, biting back tears. Then he calms down and adds, "I came to say I'm sorry." He peers closely at me again, as if to be sure he's talking to the right woman. "Also, I wanted to ask you—strictly between you and me, I have no desire to press charges: Do you know who those old ladies were who killed me?"

"No," I lie. Or am I lying? Is the spell of silence still working? "I wasn't myself. I was in a kind of a dream. There were people who took advantage of me whom I really didn't know anything about. I never knew those old women." That part is true, and it seems to satisfy him.

He lifts his chin, accepting that what has happened to him has simply happened and cannot be explained. "The doctors tell me you're going to be okay now," he says in the louder voice he uses for business. "I hope—" he hesitates, then continues again, "I hope you'll come back to Broughton Lading when you're ready."

He nods cordially and pushes on one wheel to turn around.

"Frank, wait." I hop out of bed. "Take me with you."

Puzzlement plays over his craggy face.

"It's important for me to get out of here," I tell him, kneeling at the side of his chair and clutching his arm. "You were dead for a while—you know. The same thing happened to me. I was dead, too. Now Willa and the doctors are keeping me locked up like I'm still crazy. They've already cut out a piece of my brain. Won't you help me?"

Frank frowns sympathetically. "Where will you go?"

"You don't have to know. Just leave the door unlocked when you go."

He pats my arm, hands over his trench coat, and with his other hand stuffs some money in my sweater pocket. "Be careful," he whispers.

As he leaves, he has a coughing fit, and when the distracted nurse who let him out is getting him water, he releases the door lock. I wait until I hear his coughing fit diminish with distance, then I open the door a crack.

Frank has succeeded in occupying both of the nurses at the care station down the corridor, and I slip out of the room, dash across the hall and through the fire door without being seen. The route through the kitchen still works, and soon I'm standing in a strange bright landscape of muted coral shapes of snow. The storm is gone, and the vein of sky above the alley is pure blue, sparkling with wings and tails of wind-cast powder.

The pristine snow between the giant, frosted trees crunches under my sneakers. No one answers the elephant-trunk knocker. I'm so scared that my jaw hurts from chattering. I try the door, and it opens a little, then jams. All my strength budges it another inch, barely enough for me to squeeze through.

"Hello?" I call. "Drusille! Glendil!"

My feet slide. Ice sheets the floor, and I realize it's blocking the door. Inside, glittery ice covers everything. With widening amazement, I take in the frozen devastation. Stalactites hang like fangs from the ceiling and in lacy macramé along the walls; a small, clear glacier, pleated at the bottom like a giant trousseau, cascades thinly over the stairs.

I steady myself on the glazed and kiltered banister and call out nervously, "Hello! Anyone here?"

Sliding my feet, I enter the front room's clutter of amphoras, idols, drums, and lacquered furniture, all gleaming coldly. In the seep of blue morning light through the brittle draperies, the packed room shimmers with diamondstars, like a magical grotto.

A rubble of hoarfrost has replaced the flames in the massive fireplace of the grand living room, where under a plank of hard sunlight, a nest of pythons lies frozen and clotted with ice. Grimacing faces appear in the twisted mess, and my brain tries to catch up with the terrible thing filling my eyes. The pythons are actually limbs, blue-fleshed arms and legs mottled black with blood.

Naked and grotesquely tangled, the three witches lie in a wrathful heap, locked in a furious grappling. They look as though they have fallen from a great height and smashed together. Glendil's sheep face is locked in a death-rictus between the scissor-like thighs of Ashera, whose own head scowls vehemently in the strangling vise of Drusille's arm. Ashera's clawed hands still clutch the poison thorns embedded in her enemy's throat, and Drusille's big face stares at me upside down with a crooked, cloudy gaze, a gray tongue protruding from her gaping mouth.

Ice that spilled from the broken ceiling has welded the corpses into a hideous configuration, a grisly contortion of flesh and violence, a hex-wheel of death. I back away drunkenly. I'm afraid to look in the other rooms, scared I'll find Daniel frozen in some grotesque death pose. But I search anyway, wading through my fear like a sluggish dreamwalker, because I must find him. I cannot go on living another day until I find him.

I enter all the downstairs rooms and discover every one shellacked with ice, some with collapsed walls and fallen rafters, where I despair of searching for limbs. The greenhouse looks verdantly intact, but it's frozen too, every frond and blossom glassed in ice.

The coven house remains intact, untouched by the ice. Its brown, sparse rooms look as though they've been vacant for a long time. I pause in the kitchen before the open cupboard. One shelf sits ajar, revealing the secret stairwell that leads into the dark earth. I retrieve an oil lamp from the cupboard shelf, and by its gelatinous glow descend into the cold crypt.

The cellar is empty. But I notice someone has taken the pierced stone out of its socket in the cobbled wall.

Back upstairs, I'm struck with the hope that maybe Daniel is in the gardener's cottage where we once lived. But he's not. I stand staring out over the snowbound yard, verging on the ghastly thought that he could be out there, covered in the drifts, when a movement from the Hause catches my eye. A viper of smoke wisps from the peak of the cupola, snaking away from the weather-vane wyvern and disappearing into the frost-glittering blue. Daniel, his image blurred by glass, holds high a teacup, toasting me through the window, and I rush back into the Hause.

Skidding on the iced steps, I nearly topple over the tilted banister and have to crawl up the crippled stairs on my numbed hands and bruised knees. I slide over the buckled floorboards of the hallway and bang through a closed door into a room with no floor. My feet fly out from under me, and I just catch the jamb of the door in my rubber fingers and squirm back into the hall.

Gingerly, I creep to the next door, this one already open on some kind of ritual chamber. A black-shrouded altar squats below an ebony sculpture, a downturned pentagram with a mirror eye at the center that reflects my startled face.

The entry to the cupola pours a dazzling shaft of light down the hall. It's a corkscrew stairwell, like submarines have, only carved from mahogany into a spiral of interlocking dragons. At the top, Daniel is grinning, his hair wild, the sun shining through it in a golden crown.

"Siggy! Come! I didn't know how long it would take you to get here, but I knew you'd come."

I climb up the stairs into the warm and luminous cupola,

where the snowglare in my hurting eyes makes everything look translucent. "Daniel! Are you okay?"

"Yes! Seeing you again, I've never felt better." He takes me in his arms and I press myself to him, glad for his warmth, giddy with relief. He looks thinner but otherwise okay.

"I was so worried." I sound like Willa, and that stops me. I pull away and look into his smiling face. "The witches didn't hurt you?"

He blinks unhappily. "A little at first. Because I wanted to get away, to find you. But they promised you would come back." His face brightens. "And you have."

He sweeps me close to him, and we touch each other's faces. "Work your magic, Siggy," he urges. "Make me feel the glamour."

I pull away, stricken. "I don't have it, Daniel. They took it away from me."

"You don't feel the rapture anymore?" A pained look seeps into his face.

I tell him no, and he sits down on a cushioned bench, head bowed under the weight of his disappointment. I sit beside him and tell him what happened at the clinic, and he presses his palms over his eyes and doesn't move.

When I'm done, he speaks slowly, trying not to weep, "You lost the only gift I could give you." He clasps my hands, and his eyes are wet. "I don't know what to say. I have nothing more to give."

"It's okay," I tell him sincerely. "Everything's okay now that I've found you."

He smiles sadly, and we hug and settle our bodies comfortably together, our backs to the indigo north. Winter light shining through the beveled margins of the windows scratches prisms on the red clay stove and narrow flue that warm the cupola. From the bamboo coffee table beside the stove, he lifts a blue porcelain teapot and pours me a cup of hot water. The pierced stone lies beside it.

"The witches are dead downstairs," I say. "Ashera, too."

"I know. It happened last night. Ashera came for them during the storm. I think she had gotten so enraged at losing you—your connection with the seraphs—she came here actually willing, finally, to sacrifice her own life to take out those crones. I didn't see the battle, but believe me, it sounded like Judgment Day. The witches had already locked me in for the night, in that black penta-gram room with the altar. I crouched in the dark and listened to their fighting—like wild dogs and ripping metal, all over the Hause and for the longest time. At one point they banged against the door to the altar room, splintered its damn wooden hinges, and pierced the darkness with sharp blades of light. God, I thought they intended to break in and devour me! But then—silence. The weak-ened door opened, and I found them as you did, dead by the hearth.

"The Woman God had a bitchy day, I'd say. You know what I did then? When I found them like that, all tied together in their ugly death knot? I killed the fire in the central hearth and turned on all the upstairs spigots! It took some doing—it seems my fatigue and the sleeping trances have gotten the better of me, Siggy—but I managed to use a stone dagger from the ritual room to gouge a hole in the floor above the witches. That way the water flowed over them."

I shake my head, confounded. "Why did you do that?"

"To make sure they stay dead." He smiles cryptically and slaps my thigh, but I still don't understand. "Spirits can't cross water, Siggy. I did it to break their hold, not only on their physical bodies but their psychic hold on this place where we loved each other. Burning and hanging extends their power into other forms, but water locks them out of this world. An age-old truth. I think it has to do with water's electrical properties."

I can't tell if he's kidding me or not, but even so, I rest my head on his shoulder and listen to his music. So long as he's with me, I don't need the glamour. But I want to get him away from this hideous place. "Let's go," I urge.

"No use, Siggy," he tells me with a tristful smile. "I can't go anywhere. I made a deal with them."

"The witches? But they're dead. We can get away from them now."

"No, you don't understand. The crones worked a spell for me—to call you here—so I could see you again. But in return, I have to go back where I came from."

"Not right away, Daniel," I implore.

"Far sooner than I'd like, I hate to say." He buries his face against my throat and blows his hot breath under my sweater. When he looks at me, his eyes are wet again. He points to a cup empty except for a black zero of liqueur at the bottom.

"Daniel, no!"

"If I didn't drink it, if I'd cheated, the spell they cast to bring you here would have wound up killing you."

"No, Daniel." I grab his shoulders and shake him. He seems crazier than I remember, and I want to snap him out of it. "That's stupid! They're dead. Their spells can't touch me."

"You know better," he says with a cockeyed smile. "You've touched the glamour."

"Screw the glamour. I don't even know if it was real. All I know is, I don't want to lose you."

"You haven't lost me, Siggy. But you know I can't stay in this world any longer. You saw how the torpor got worse for me each day. You saw that. I wouldn't have the strength to talk to you even now except for the side effect of the witches' poison. It makes me feel stronger—for now. But if I hadn't taken it, my illness would continue making me less. Eventually, I'd completely return to the emptiness that owned this body before I came down to help you. Then I'd grow old without ever waking up again. The witches knew that. After they took you out, they expected me to live here until I faded away. I didn't want that. But I did want to see you again, one more time. I want to make sure it all makes sense to you."

"This doesn't make any sense at all," I complain.

"The truth remains the same. I sought you out for a while. Now you must look for me. You'll find me up there almost every day if you look."

"It's not the same," I gasp through my tears.

"We must expect something better from the future," he says. "I'll go on living inside you—as I always have. Only this time you will know it."

"But I want to hold you," I whisper. "I want to make love with you."

"Siggy—you'll find another to hold and love. Your glamour will lead you to him."

"I've lost the glamour," I say with stinging regret.

"No," he says kindly and kisses my forehead. "You haven't lost it. You just can't see it with your outer eyes anymore. But the inner eye still sees. Look, and you'll see you have it."

He puts his hands over my eyes, and with alarm I feel the cold in his fingers. I grab them and stare wide at him. "Daniel—"

"Relax. The witches said it would take some time. Let's talk." He holds my hand. In broken cadences, he tells me how he remembered from my hystery where the pierced stone was hidden, and he used it to start the fire in the small stove. It seemed poetically just, using the oldest human tool in the Hause for his last fire.

Only when I listen to him talk about ritual, about the necessity of the blood sacrifice for the renewal of the world, only then my grief evaporates. As always, it's the sound of his voice that calms me. What he's saying about the poison cure and finding a hidden order in chaos—all that I lose track of quickly.

"The witches told me the coven watched us the whole time we lived at the bower," he says. "When you drank the three-drop potion, they knew. They used their sorcery to rouse me, though I don't remember that or them bringing me along with them when they followed you into the park. If you had received the elven that night, they planned some celebration; otherwise, you'd have gotten the thorn, as you did, finally. But before they could find out anything, Broughton intruded. Everything fell apart. They fled."

I don't care what he's saying. I only concentrate on watching his mouth, memorizing his soft eyes, and listening to the sound of his voice. It reminds me of the fright I felt the night the moon first spoke to me and how much love came out of that fear. That love is not dying here now. He woke it in me—and I refuse to let it die.

Seeing my distracted look, he rubs the pierced stone on his head and brushes it near my face. A blue volt snaps from the tip of my nose, and I jump out of my reverie with a surprised yelp that makes us both smile.

"And you thought you lost the glamour," he chides me and pants, trying to catch his breath.

"Daniel—" I press closer.

"Sooner than I thought." He leans back with a small smile and closes his eyes. "The witches promised no pain." He gulps for air. "They didn't lie. They never lied, did they?"

He's whispering, and I can't hear him, because my heart is thundering too loudly. His hands feel rubbery, and I let them go and take his face between my palms. I press my ear close and catch, very softly, in the hot, sharp rush of his last breath, the words "I am."

I sit with Daniel until the moon appears in the lilac sky. The fire in the stove has gone out, and my breath floats like a blue soul, coming and going in front of my face.

He's gone, yet I trust in what he did. He is whole and beautiful forever now, and his body will not shrivel around him, because he's not in his body anymore. He's left it and gone back to the moon.

The Woman God who shaped us, the secret God, has no temple. And so She lives among the pearly larvae and thriving maggots in the landfills, the waste yards, the industrial swamps and dumps, incandescent and ignored in the bacterial murk, alone in a slick night of rotted and growing things. Her wrath no longer confines itself to banewort, nightshade, and hemlock. These days, She pools toxins, pesticides, all the manufactured venoms in Her poison sac. Her solitude has driven Her mad, and She has gone weeping back to the womb, wanting to die if She cannot live. She births new sorrows. Fish kills litter Her beaches. Blights wither Her forests. The Woman God is mad.

I am her daughter. My name is Enchantress, for I weave dreams and raptures. I live by spells, a witch with red hair and fish-silver skin, sister of phantoms, clove-queen vixen in tight jeans, necrophagous sorceress of the renowned lamp-skin complexion, naked worshiper of the night. I am the moon's wife.

On a clear full-moon night, look at the blotched shadow in his face, the shadow that, in time, will eat him. That is the shadow of death. And the light that shines through it is the same light that shines inside our darkness, in the night with our eyes closed and our brains bright with dreams.

All this comes to mind under the cold stars as I walk away from the Hause. The snow-soft trees glow blue in the night spaces between the street lights. I am cold. But that is what makes this dream so real.

It's spring. I stand before the same bin of potatoes, in the same supermarket where my rapture began six months ago. I promised myself that when I finished writing my hystery, I'd come back to this exact spot. I'm ready for it to end here, ready to become ordinary again.

For a while I missed the glamour, the sexy energy that softened every woe. My world went flat, as flat as the cutout rabbits and cardboard egg-baskets dangling in purple and yellow streamers over the aisles. It took me a while to get used to the quieter feelings in my body, the dimmer colors, the skullbound tightness of perception that still sometimes makes me feel claustrophobic.

Writing helped, and I tried to finish my hystery as I imagined Daniel would have wanted. At lunch today, on my computer at work, I wrote down what I remembered of my walk through the snowy Brooklyn streets after Daniel died—about the Woman God being mad. Clearly now, it was me who was mad that night, mad at Daniel for taking his own life, and for depriving me of time, which is all we ever have of each other. Maybe I was mad at myself, for loving someone that crazy.

But being mad like that is normal and so belongs outside this hystery, which is about less ponderable madness. The story of my double-soul ended that night, when I walked away from the Hause, muttering about the Woman God, still believing I was an orphaned enchantress wandering the muted night land. It was my last act of madness.

A long walk later, at a busy intersection, I caught a cab and a cold. I returned to the clinic shivering and sneezing, and the staff took good care of me, though they doubled security around me on the chance that I might try to run away again. Their anger was well justified. Willa, at Frank's instigation, had hired a lawyer weeks before to sue the clinic for their negligence in letting me escape, a suit which the doctors contested, claiming I'd been kidnapped by a known criminal. But after the second incident, they settled out of court, and now Willa can forget about her job at the umbrella factory if she wants.

Willa keeps going to work anyway, so as to be with her gossipy friends and enjoy her new celebrity as the wronged mother who helped save her daughter from a brain tumor *and* made the doctors pay for it. The boost in her self-esteem has worked wonders for her. She not only shops on her own, she's also learning how to drive a car. Her teacher is a curly haired manager at the factory who takes her golfing on weekends.

I've taken a studio apartment in downtown Arcadia, close enough to the river to walk to my job at Broughton Lading, and I've sold my car. That's my one big concession to the Woman God. I personally will not blow smoke in Her face again, but that's all I can hope to contribute in the holy war between seraphs and elven. The fate of civilization and the planet is out of my hands.

I've tried using the spellcraft that the witches taught me, but only carefully and for insignificant things, like when I'm bowling with Marti or playing bridge with the girls in the pool. But it doesn't work. Which is good, because it means I can't touch the spirit worlds anymore, and that leaves me free to concentrate on what I *can* do in this world.

I've got my old job back, with more responsibility than I had before. But not because Frank is favoring me. I haven't seen him since he helped me escape the clinic. In fact, he has nothing to do with the business these days and spends all his time hiking and backpacking while his managers run everything. He's gotten on some kind of survival kick.

I'm determined to have my own accounting firm in the next two years, and I've been working hard. I need the money and the experience to prepare myself. What happened to my brain last winter makes me appreciate all the more being alive and clearheaded. And learning to move the glamour around my body has made my own internalized awareness familiar, so that concentrating seems much easier than before. I get a lot more done in less time, and what used to be my dreams are now my plans. All in all, it's white magic.

Because my life is so busy, I don't think much about last autumn, other than to miss Daniel, which I know I always will. Sometimes I didn't think I'd finish the hystery because I miss him so much. It was too painful to find the words for his death, much less make sense of what I had witnessed. But the same drive that makes me count slats in a vent or windows on a bus insisted I complete it. So I did, even though I'm not sure how much is true remembrance and how much the smoke of extinguished dreams.

I've read a lot about the nervous system since the clinic released me, and I know now that everything that happened to me in this and the spirit worlds can be explained by the chemicals that kindle the auroras of the brain. I'm glad the anomaly was removed. Its dire and wondrous visions were wider than my heart could hold.

Daniel, too, I've come to believe, was hurt more in his heart than in his head. His unspeakable tragedy forced him to invent himself anew. At least, that's what I think now. How else could he live when the doctors wouldn't let him die?

Yet at the same time, I believe the moon really *did* excarnate through him. For that one radiant autumn, when I could actually see the psychic fires that shape the world, he was mine—the moon-in-the-man.

Now, without Daniel around to tear my writing apart and put it back together for me—to re-member it—these words have become a very different act of memory. Not of carrying images from the past forward, as he and I had done, but of going back into the memory, of bearing the present back to the past, to be there again.

And so here I am, standing in front of a khaki heap of spuds, Muzak unfurling in the air and some bratty toddler in a shopping cart making faces at me while his weary mother picks among the fruits of the nightshade.

I listen for the onrush of the glamour's sexual riot. Dense energy pools in the cup of the pelvis and holds us upright, different from other animals. I don't feel anything, and if I did, it would probably be cramps. Nor is there an electric tingling in my sacrum just yet. I suppose for that, my lonely body will have to find a man someday.

I'm grateful to be my old, familiar self again, and yet I'm tempted to play the witch one more time and chant a spell over these treasures carried up from underground, torn from the belly of the Mother. It should be more than a spell of thanksgiving. It should be a fearful propitiation, a begging of forgiveness from the God who has given us no other commandment than to live, the Woman God who doesn't hide in heaven but dwells right here with us in the matter of the material world, in the mutterings of our stories and explanations and in our blind, physical gropings to understand—Mother Earth, poisoned by our industries, debased by the filth of our voracious lives, et cetera, et cetera.

I smile and turn and walk out of the supermarket. I have no spells to cast, other than this one, which is over now.

The silver ax of the quarter-moon hangs above the parking lot, and the cars huddle together in the light, afraid of the dark.

The moon says nothing. He knows I'm just an ordinary woman.